The Boathouse by Stepping Stone Bay

Helen Rolfe writes contemporary women's fiction and enjoys weaving stories about family, friendship, secrets, and community. Characters often face challenges and must fight to overcome them, but above all, Helen's stories always have a happy ending.

The Boathouse by Stepping Stone Bay

HELEN ROLFE

ORION

An Orion paperback

First published in Great Britain in 2023 by Orion Fiction,
an imprint of The Orion Publishing Group Ltd
Carmelite House, 50 Victoria Embankment,
London EC4Y ODZ

An Hachette UK company

1 3 5 7 9 10 8 6 4 2

A CIP catalogue record for this book is
available from the British Library.

ISBN (Mass Market Paperback) 978 1 3987 0621 7
ISBN (eBook) 978 1 3987 0622 4

Typeset by Input Data Services Ltd, Somerset

Printed in Great Britain by Clays Ltd, Elcograf S.p.A.

www.orionbooks.co.uk

Chapter One

Nina

Agentle mid-September breeze blew Nina's blonde collarbone-length hair as she walked down the track from the main road where she'd parked towards the cabin that had been in the O'Brien family ever since she could remember. She'd taken this walk countless times before and yet doing it now after staying away for more than a decade made her insides churn. Because not only did this track lead to the family cabin, it also led to the boathouse that still stood in the former boatyard in Stepping Stone Bay. And it was the owner of the boathouse who Nina had walked away from all those years ago and not spoken to since.

The boathouse came into view, although now that the sun had begun to set she couldn't see it very clearly. Nina had spent the afternoon with her grandad, Walt, before coming here this evening. She could've waited until the morning, but she knew she wouldn't sleep if she did that. She wanted to get this first visit over with and then the rest she'd tackle as it came.

Walt had given Nina the big torch he kept beneath the sink in case of a power cut and she was glad she had it now to stop her from stumbling on any uneven ground as she turned left past the boathouse to go to the cabin. She could've driven all the way down here and parked right outside but she hadn't wanted to bump into anyone coming the other way, preferring to discreetly take the short route on foot, at least this first time. For the last twelve years she had successfully avoided a trip down memory lane by sticking to brief visits on the south coast with her grandad who lived a couple of miles on from the centre of the seaside town of Salthaven and the bay around the corner. The distance had allowed her to hide out at his bungalow whenever she came to visit and avoid any interaction with the locals in the town or the bay.

As Nina's focus changed to the cabin, her pace slowed, as memories, a blast of feelings, good and bad came back to her. She shivered despite the long cardigan she wore over a summer top she'd teamed with faded jeans. The cabin with its warm honey-brown window frames and small veranda looked exactly as she remembered. She could recall treading the steps up to the front door time and time again as a toddler, a kid, a teenager and an adult. And as she reached the steps now her hand trembled so much she clutched the front door key tighter to make sure she didn't drop it between the wooden sections and have to get on her hands and knees to retrieve it. She daren't shine her torch beyond the cabin either because it wasn't the only one down here. There were just two cabins in such close proximity to Stepping Stone Bay – the O'Brien's and the one belonging to the Magowans. Or in particular, Leo Magowan, the love of Nina's life once upon a time. Leo not only owned the boathouse nowadays, he owned and resided in the second cabin that was separated from the O'Brien family's by a mere thirteen stepping stones.

Up the steps and the sound of the key going into the lock on the cabin door felt unique although Nina knew it wasn't. But the significance of her opening this place up after so long wasn't lost on her. After so many years, she wasn't here for a holiday, but to do up the old cabin, bring it into modern times, and once she'd done that she had been tasked with selling it for her grandad. Something she'd never seen coming. The sale of the cabin would mark the end of an era. And it felt like the final stamp on her leaving Stepping Stone Bay well and truly behind.

Nina stepped into the cabin. The inside smelt exactly the same as it always had – a little bit damp but not in a bad way, just in a way that suggested a few windows needed to be opened. Along with that came the salty tang of the sea that had seeped into the walls over time and could never be escaped, given the sandy stretch of beach and the gentle waves were less than a couple of hundred metres away. She shivered because there was a certain chill that came with an empty place, no matter the warmth of memories that came with it. There wouldn't be many personal items littered around any more; even in the dark she knew it was in need of some tender loving care, and more than that, she noted how bereft the inside of the cabin was of chatter, laughter and togetherness, the sounds and feelings she'd always associated with coming through the front door.

She closed the door behind her and reached for the light switch, smiling to herself that she'd remembered where it was, but the bulb must have gone and so, careful not to bump into anything, she used the torch and made for the table in the corner of the lounge area straight in front and hoped the lamp worked. It did, but she'd only just flicked it on when her phone rang and nearly made her jump out of her skin.

'William, you scared me.' But she was happy to hear from him, to get the update on his wife and children and their relocation to Geneva a few weeks ago. Hearing her brother William's voice as he chatted excitedly about his new home made Nina think of the children she'd seen on their way to Salthaven. She'd stopped for petrol shortly before she reached the sign to the town and they'd been there buying sweets and crisps as well as a huge set of brightly coloured plastic beach accessories which looked to have everything they needed to build the best sand-castles, from moulds with turrets and rakes for the sand, to little shovels to dig a moat, and flags to put on top of the structure once it was finished. Nina and William had once been as carefree as those two children, they'd loved their days spent going from cabin to beach and back again. But they'd grown up and had both left the bay, William for love and his job and his family, Nina for very different reasons.

'You're there now?' William asked, after her niece and nephew had both come on the phone to say a hello.

'I sure am. I couldn't wait until morning.' She screwed her nose up at the sight of a cobweb in the far corner illuminated in the lamp light and turned her back when her eyes fell on the window that looked over to Leo's cabin. The only positive was that there were no lights on at his place; nobody was home, she wouldn't have to face him yet.

'Does it look exactly the same?' William asked.

'Pretty much. Smells the same too.'

'Of wet feet?'

She began to laugh. 'It never smelt like wet feet. It smells like the sea, but a bit musty.' She knelt on one of the sofas covered in a sheet and opened the small window, staying in her position to inhale the air and listen to the distant sound of waves rolling in. She only opened it a fraction, she'd air the place more once she was here properly.

'Are you sleeping there tonight?'

'No chance,' she laughed, looking around her. The place was bare; no shoes cast aside, no colouring set littering the coffee table, no beach towels draped across the backs of chairs or over a plastic airer and no smell of dinner cooking or glasses of wine out on the benchtops. 'I'll sleep at Grandad's; just wanted to have a check around and see what I need to bring with me tomorrow to make it semi-habitable. I'll probably stay here on and off while I'm doing it up, seems the easiest thing and I can get more done rather than annoy Grandad.' She loved her grandad to pieces but she knew both of them would need their breathing space, her particularly when it came to processing emotions of being back in the bay.

'I don't think he minds.'

'Probably not,' she admitted. But she knew she'd be better off if she wasn't hiding away at his the whole time. She had to face her fears, it was high time. And then she had to get on, get the cabin looking impressive enough to sell for a good price.

In the main room where she now stood she looked over at the small yet perfectly adequate kitchen space with the benchtop along one wall that jutted out a bit to separate it from the lounge area. In the dim light she noted the appliances were all there, but none of the little touches – a mug tree, a utensils pot, maybe a pan stand or a pair of oven gloves waiting to be used. She'd sat at the bench on a high stool as a kid, feet dangling as her gran or grandad made her toast and jam, always cutting it into four triangles, the way she liked it.

Nina and William turned to reminiscing the way only a brother and sister could, with all the joint memories they'd have forever. 'Remember baking cookies with Gran?' William chuckled. 'The first time I mean.'

'How could I forget?' She ran a hand along a rather dusty workspace next to the cooktop. She'd loved making cookies with Gran – it never mattered what sort, in fact the more variety the better, and she'd wrap them up into little parcels and leap over the thirteen stepping stones to the Magowan cabin and leave a parcel at their door, hoping it would be Leo who found them first. The first time they'd made cookies Nina had begged to use a recipe for chocolate chip and once they'd shaped the mixture Nina had been in charge of watching them in the oven while her gran hung out the beach towels and swimming costumes. Nina had burnt the lot, she'd thought she had time to duck out to find Leo and have at least a single game of conkers with the shiny beauties they'd found that morning, freshly dropped from the big horse chestnut tree near their school, but one game had turned into many and the next thing she knew Gran was yelling and flinging open all the windows, smoke billowing out of the oven. Nina ran back inside and rather than mouth-watering cookies found black morsels stuck to the baking tray.

'Gran said she'd never get the smell out of the oven,' said William. 'She didn't leave you in charge for a while after that from what I remember. Too easily distracted she said.' After a sigh William admitted, 'I thought Grandad might change his mind about selling up. I never expected it to come to this, you there and ready to get to work.'

'Me neither. But he's set on the idea, so here I am.'

'Maybe he just wants it to look nicer and have a good clean and then he'll fall in love with it all over again,' he suggested hopefully.

'Nice thought, William.' In truth Nina had hoped for the same. She'd thought her grandad would back out at the last minute and tell her to come for an extended visit with him instead. But he hadn't. And looking around, this place wasn't just wonderful because she had so much nostalgia tied up in it, its proximity to the bay and the sands made it a winner and with a bit of work it could be a luxury escape.

Thinking of it that way made her even sadder that it wouldn't be in the O'Brien family for any of them to enjoy at their leisure. And not only that, it made her thoughts flit to the owner of the other cabin who really had made it his home by the sea and never left.

Walt had told them of his decision to sell the cabin over a farewell roast dinner for William and his family as the gravy was poured, the vegetables spooned out of the bowls, and the lunch Nina and William's wife Anna had cooked together was served. When he'd made the announcement he'd added a diplomatic, 'It's time,' when both William and Nina failed to disguise their shock and utter disappointment. 'Our family is grown up, it's time for a new family to make their memories at the cabin.'

William seemed put out as he tilted his head towards Fliss and Perry who were six and eight respectively. 'Not all of us are grown up. The kids haven't had much time down there at Stepping Stone Bay at all.'

It was a desperate plea even to Nina's ears. Her brother was rarely in this part of the country and now he was about to move even further away.

'It needs a lot of work,' Walt went on. 'It's tired, neglected. And let's face it, you haven't been to stay there in the last twelve months.'

William reluctantly agreed. 'Work takes up too much time and we went to France and Italy for our holiday this year, then we tried to go to the cabin but the weather was having none of it.'

Talk turned to the rain that had hit the last time Fliss and Perry were here at Grandad's and rather than use their buckets and spades at the beach or the inflatable ring Fliss had found that looked like a giant doughnut with sprinkles, they'd played monopoly and left without seeing even a glimpse of the golden sands.

'I suppose it's a lot to do with nostalgia,' William confessed as he looked to Nina. 'We had some good times there, didn't we, sis?'

'We sure did.' But she'd also had some bad times in Stepping Stone Bay, times she wasn't going to bring up here and now. Perhaps selling the cabin would draw a line under all of that at last, because there'd be no reason to return to the bay itself ever again.

After she declined the offer of more roast parsnips from Anna, Nina pushed some more. 'Why are you really selling up, Grandad?' His reasons sounded far too simplistic and practical for a man who adored his family and had a lifetime of memories at that cabin as well. He and Grandma Elsie had been the ones to paint the walls, they'd embraced being grandparents by spending every day in summer there with their grandkids, they'd loved the cosiness of it come winter and its proximity to the most beautiful stretch of beach on the south coast as far as he was concerned.

'I'm getting older by the second.' Walt winked at Fliss who was obsessed by what happened to people as they aged. That morning she'd asked why old people's skin looked like the dates she'd had at Christmas, and right before lunch she'd wanted to check her great-grandad's mouth to see whether he had any jewellery on his teeth. Turns out she meant gold fillings or crowns. 'I need things doing around this place to make it safer for me,' he added matter-of-factly.

'Any changes here would be inexpensive, Grandad,' William put in. 'And I'm happy to fund them if needed.'

'You shouldn't have to.' Walt had never wanted hand-outs, it was next to impossible to give him anything in the way of financial help. 'And I can afford a few minor changes.' He looked at William and then Nina and explained, 'I also want to be prepared. I was able to look after my Elsie in her last days and have her here in our home, the home she adored. And the end was quick for her. But I've seen what can happen when it's not. It's a fact of life, but I would like to live out my days in this house too and without anyone close by to help, I might need to have someone come in on a daily basis. And that doesn't come cheap. I'd like to be prepared financially, it'll stop me worrying.'

Hearing him talk that way, planning for an end, might be part of life, but Nina didn't like talking about it one bit. She would however always be on Walt's side and do whatever he needed, whatever made him happy. And that day at their grandad's house might have been for William and his family's farewell but it also marked the point where it was time for Nina to step up and be the one to take the reins, with her brother so far away. Nina and her brother had talked about it prior to that day already. With William working in Switzerland for at least the next two years, Nina was more than ready to take responsibility here, especially after she'd left the bay behind and only graced her grandparents with the odd phone call in a whole year while William, despite the demands of his job and being married, had come back to see Walt and Elsie every weekend. He'd done jobs around the house – he'd overhauled their veggie patch, fixed up the fence around the back garden, installed a new shed. Nina hadn't helped much at all back then, she'd not even visited for that whole chunk of time for fear of bumping into anyone she knew and having to answer questions about why she'd left, why she didn't want to come back. Questions she couldn't even answer herself. But slowly, as she got herself together, she'd braved coming more and more to see her grandparents and then just Walt since her Grandma Elsie died eighteen months ago.

Now, at the cabin, Nina finished the call with her brother. 'I'd better get on, see what I need to bring back with me tomorrow,' she explained, already thinking of checking other lightbulbs; the one in the bathroom, those in the two compact bedrooms.

'Make sure there's toilet roll, nobody likes to be caught out in that situation.'

'Thanks for the warning,' she laughed. 'Give my love to Anna and the kids.'

She ended the call and was about to carry on walking around to see what else she needed when she heard the sound of whistling coming from outside the cabin.

She reached quickly for the lamp and switched it off, crouching down in the corner of the room so she couldn't be seen through the small window above the table with the lamp. She held her breath as the whistling continued, carried inside through the other window which was open ever so slightly.

Her heart raced at a million miles an hour at her first sight, or rather sound, of Leo Magowan, the man who made her heart skip a beat for years until she'd left Stepping Stone Bay behind. He might only have been whistling, but she'd know that sound anywhere.

Nina waited where she was until she couldn't hear anything else apart from the swishing of the sea.

She sneezed with all the dust and she jumped when her fingertips met something that the torch, when she switched it back on, revealed to be an eight-legged creature on its back, legs curled up, a casualty of this old cabin. And when she realised she couldn't stay there huddled in the corner forever she got up without turning on the lamp again. She closed the window she'd opened, not ready to announce her presence tonight, and if Leo was the only person who lived down here, too much activity would be sure to alert him to the cabin being occupied. And that could wait for another day.

Nina did her best to scurry around the cabin and make notes in her phone of everything she needed, unscrewing lightbulbs and taking photos of their specifications, looking in cupboards for what might have been left behind. She nipped in to use the toilet – thankfully there was enough toilet roll and some soap for her convenience although she made a note to bring back more supplies tomorrow – it wasn't as if she could call on a friendly neighbour to ask for some, was it? That might be a little cheeky under the circumstances.

Before she left she braved looking through the smaller window on the far wall of the lounge area again and sure enough all of the window coverings in the other cabin were down now, a dim light coming from behind.

She'd be back tomorrow.

And she had no doubt she'd be seeing Leo Magowan again, very soon.

Chapter Two

Leo

Leo waved the delivery driver off from the parking area at the front of the boathouse and took the last of the boxes inside. As he did so he regarded the O'Brien cabin. He'd returned home to his own cabin late last night after going to see his brother Adrian, who had finally settled back in the Stepping Stone Bay area in a flat not far from here. They'd had a few beers together and Leo, happy to have his brother back in town, had whistled his way home down the track, past his boathouse and the O'Brien cabin and across the thirteen stepping stones to his own place. But when he'd gone to let himself in through the front door he'd had the feeling of being watched and had stopped whistling and turned round, thinking he'd seen something in the corner of his eye. He'd told himself he must've been mistaken and with his desperation to use the bathroom, ignored the niggling feeling until he was unable to let it go and fall asleep. He'd taken a torch and gone outside, across the stepping stones, and over to check up on the other cabin. He had a good look around the outside and nothing seemed untoward, no sign of forced entry. He'd even got a chair from his veranda to enable him to look in through the windows which had curtains which weren't drawn completely and it had been enough for him to determine that the cabin was indeed empty, the way it had sadly been for a long time. Not even Walt O'Brien, the cabin's official owner, came down here much any more apart from to do the odd once-over of the place.

Now, as Leo unpacked the first of the many boxes, he still couldn't shake the feeling that something was different. He just had no idea what.

'Jonah, you're back.' The young boy with an accent he'd initially mistaken as American but was in fact Canadian had been here twice before. He hadn't bought anything the first time, and on the second occasion, only a key-ring with a navy and white sailboat ornament fixed to a silver ring. And on both times he'd hung around for ages, talking to Leo, asking questions about boats, the sea, anything he could think of. Now, here he was again, still in school uniform, still with the same smile that made it hard to say no. 'Do your parents know you're here?'

'I'm eleven,' said Jonah and then shrugged the way he'd done before when Leo tried to do the right thing and make sure his family knew where he was. Leo put down the box he'd been about to unpack and went over to the boy who had gone straight to the window at the end to look out over the bay, the sand and the kayakers beyond.

'You ever tried a paddle board?' Leo asked when Jonah's attentions moved to a teenager taking one out and wobbling a good amount before he got going.

Jonah shook his head, dark hair moving at the same time. 'It looks fun. But not as much fun as kayaking.'

He put a hand on the boy's shoulder. 'It's great having you here and I don't mind at all, you can even help out like you seem to want to, but I do need to have your parents' permission first.'

The boy nodded. 'I know,' he sighed reluctantly. 'I need to get Mum to come down here.'

'Or Dad,' Leo suggested.

The boy looked away. 'My dad isn't around.'

Leo didn't want to pry any further. 'Tell you what. If you were a customer you'd be rooting through the racks to find what you wanted, so I don't see there's much difference if you take the contents of that box over there and put them in their rightful places in the shop?'

Jonah's smile broke out. 'Thank you!' And he charged over to the box filled with roof rack straps in packets, surf leashes in similar packaging and a couple of SUP leashes.

Leo wondered what the boy's story was, what really brought him here to the boathouse. Was it that he didn't have a dad around and wanted male company? Was it a love of the water perhaps or simple loneliness or problems at school? But he wasn't the parent, he couldn't be the one to worry, and his main concern had to be that the boy let his mum know he was coming here, and so he'd remind him again before he left today.

When Jonah finished dashing around the boathouse, which was a shop area above the shed that housed water craft and equipment, to put everything away he wanted to sweep up.

'Seriously?' Leo laughed and gestured to the broom propped up in the corner behind the till. 'Go for it, mate.' He got the impression he could've asked Jonah to pick up a piece of litter a customer had dropped and Jonah would've happily done it. 'But your mum really does need to come and see me, soon. I mean it.'

'She will, I promise.' He was already sweeping up the area around the counter. 'Can I help clean the kayaks next time?' When Leo opened his mouth to reply he rolled his eyes. 'I know, ask my mum.'

'You guessed it.' Leo was mostly alone in the shop unless customers came in to hire or he was giving lessons, and he was quite enjoying having his young sidekick. Young boys could be annoying, mess about too much and get rowdy – he should know, he'd been one once – but Jonah had a serious edge and seemed to know how to behave. Whoever his parents were, he'd obviously been brought up right. And he had an enthusiasm too, something not all casual staff had. They were there for the money and nothing else whereas Jonah seemed to slot in with his willingness to help and sunny smile. Of course what Leo really wanted was for his brother Adrian to eventually come back into the business, the way they'd always planned it. But Adrian, like so many others, had turned his back on the bay after a summer tragedy and Leo wasn't sure his dream would ever happen. It certainly hadn't happened with Nina, the girl he'd given his whole heart to and thought she'd done the same.

The Stepping Stone Bay Boathouse had retained its name and its position in the bay. Once a far bigger operation for building and fixing boats, it might no longer be used for the same functions but it had kept plenty of its character, with the long concrete slope leading from the double doors below down to the golden sands and the sea beyond, and the big window at the back of the boathouse at the far end of what was now a shop afforded the same spectacular view it always had no matter the season.

Now the boathouse was Leo's business and a successful one at that. He sold water craft – kayaks, SUPs, paddleboards, surfboards and bodyboards, plus all the paraphernalia that went with them. The boathouse also operated as a hire place for the same equipment and Leo sold buoyancy aids for all ages; they had a range of clothing – wetsuits, fleeces, ocean shoes – and accessories with everything from repair kits and dry bags to waterproof phone cases and insulated water bottles. He ran instruction courses too, popular with tourists who managed to find it. It wasn't that the bay was hidden – anyone out on the water could see it, the buoys marking out the safe and calm waters where lessons took place or novices could use the kayaks, SUPS and everything else in relative safety – but it was more of an effort to find than the bigger beach in Salthaven which served as the main drag for beach lovers, with its pier, eateries and the cute little café, as well as the nearby town to cater for all your needs. Stepping Stone Bay was like the calmer younger brother to Salthaven and it suited Leo down to the ground, always had. It was a place he never wanted to leave and couldn't really understand why anyone would.

Leo gave Jonah the go-ahead to open up the packets containing new t-shirts and he began to hang them out for display as Leo saw to his next customers, a couple of newlyweds who had hired a SUP each for two hours. He knew they were newlyweds because they'd told him how they'd just returned from honeymooning in Spain where they'd tried stand-up paddleboarding for the first time. Given it wasn't as warm as usual today they'd both come in in wetsuits that reached down to the knees even though a lot of stand-up paddleboarders didn't bother with the warmth of an additional layer, although some of them regretted it and cut short their two-hour slot, coming back to the boathouse covered in goose pimples, teeth chattering, and running on about paying for wetsuit hire next time.

The couple asked about waterproof covers for their phones and when Jonah overheard he ran over with a selection of colours for their perusal and even explained to them, not that it wasn't obvious, that they could be worn around the neck so you'd have your device ready for photos. He even added that having the phone in one of those cases and therefore handy was a good idea in case of emergencies – it was something Leo usually suggested, especially if individuals came in to hire equipment. He knew from experience, having had to call out the lifeguard more than once when someone hadn't returned at the expected time and the weather had taken a sudden turn. Luckily nobody had ever come to harm; the majority of them had simply lost track of the time, but having a phone would've cut down on a lot of worry, an extra charge for them – he gave a bit of leeway because it was the polite thing to do if they were in dire straits – and using up valuable resources at the seaside where things could go from fun to disaster in the blink of an eye. Something he knew only too well.

'So you've got some experience of stand-up paddle-boarding already,' Leo confirmed after he'd perused the couple's booking form.

'A good number of hours' lessons as well as practice when we were in Spain,' the man smiled, his tan still lingering as well as what Leo presumed must be the honeymoon glow that both of them seemed to have. 'Wouldn't mind a run-down of the basics though,' he admitted.

'We'll do that out by the water once we've selected your boards and your paddles.' Maybe their minds had been more on each other than the lessons over there – understandable, Leo suspected, although he was surprised he could remember, given how long it had been since he'd been all loved up and besotted with someone.

He hadn't really felt that way since Nina if he was totally honest. There'd been flings along the way, he was only human after all, but no woman had ever really captivated him in the way she had. And no woman had ever left him feeling quite so bereft either. His business had become his one true love, the reason he got up in the morning, the reason he could carry on when he was in so much pain. And over time he'd adjusted and these days he sensed it might be easier that way.

Leo pushed away the memories and instead ran through the safety information with his customers. 'There is a lifeguard here in the bay right up until the evening and as long as you don't go beyond the buoys as I already explained, you'll be in sight,' he tacked on the end. More experienced paddlers or kayakers often went beyond the markers for the calm bay, but only with prior discussion with Leo when they were hiring his equipment.

Leo selected buoyancy vests, returning to the rack for an alternative for the lady who was more petite than he'd realised and needed a smaller version so the shoulder straps fitted the vest against her in the correct way. Both of them had come with ocean shoes, something SUP users either liked or they didn't, and so once they'd signed the relevant paperwork Leo motioned to Jonah that he had to go downstairs. Jonah knew the deal. And what Jonah loved was that Leo let him go and position the wooden sign out front that said: 'Back in 5 – wait here or follow the path and find me on the beach', with an arrow pointing in the direction that descended a grassy slope at the side of the boathouse and emerged next to the doors beneath as well as the concrete ramp leading down to the sand and the sea. He had a different sign if he was running a lesson and on that one he could use chalk to let the customers know what time he'd return to the shop, but this sign Jonah was positioning now was enough when he'd be back shortly.

Once Jonah had sorted the sign Leo slid the bolt across the shop door, and using the internal stairs with direct access to the shed below he led the way.

The bottom of the boathouse was a type of shed-cum-garage with lockable doors at one end to keep all the equipment safe. Leo opened up those doors allowing access to the ramp at the far side, the sandy beach and the bay beyond. The doors were nice and wide, unchanged from back in the days when much bigger craft had been stored here and they made it ideal for hauling hire items in and out as needed before checking them, cleaning them and seeing to any repairs so the craft were ready for the next time.

On the sand-sprinkled concrete beneath his feet Leo walked to the correct row of equipment and pulled out two paddleboards, handing the larger to the man and the second smaller one to the lady, who was a good foot shorter than her husband. He indicated for them to head down onto the sand while he and Jonah followed with the paddles they'd need, which he'd selected according to size from the next row of equipment along.

On the beach Leo ran through the basics, and once the happy couple had their ankle leashes fixed on and they were launched into the waters of Stepping Stone Bay Leo and Jonah returned to the shed, did up the doors and raced up into the shop area. The customers would return the equipment at the allotted time and usually Leo would be there to take it, and if not his customers usually came upstairs to let him know they'd left everything by the doors so he could bring it in as soon as he could if he was with someone else. Lucky for him, so far nothing had ever gone missing; he supposed that was the benefit of not being on the main tourist drag.

'You're way faster than me, kid.' Laughing as he got to the top of the stairs after Jonah beat him to the back of the shed, Leo put a hand against his chest.

But Jonah had already clocked the time and grabbed his backpack from beneath the desk in the corner with the till. 'Gotta go! Bye Leo!'

'Shoelaces.' Leo urged before Jonah unbolted the door. 'Not safe to run with those undone, you know that.'

Reluctantly Jonah did up both laces that had come undone, the left worse than the right as Leo unbolted the door. 'I'll be back tomorrow!' Jonah enthused.

'With your mum.'

'Yes, Leo!' he yelled as, backpack wobbling on his back, he took off at a rate of knots towards the track that led to the main road.

'Watch out for cars!' Leo called after the boy. The Stepping Stone Bay Boathouse was accessed from the single-lane road, or more like a track, given its surface, with little pockets for passing vehicles to pull in along its length, some of which might have trailers with water-craft, given he sold accessories for private equipment and people came here if they needed to mend their own craft.

There was enough parking in front of the boathouse for four or five cars including Leo's truck with its thick tyres that made getting up and down the reasonably steep track easy enough.

Leo waited until Jonah was out of sight and then picked up the sign his little assistant had placed outside for him when they went downstairs. Leo had one more sign which was a permanent one and positioned down at the double doors of the shed below pointing people up here should they wish to hire water craft or shop for their sailing needs.

Back inside the boathouse Leo picked up his binoculars that were stationed at the side of the window at the far end. From here he could watch anyone who had hired equipment from him, and he took a moment to check up on the happy couple he'd just sent out. He smiled; they weren't bad, their balance was quite good and he felt as though he was intruding when he saw them share a kiss across paddleboards. Talk about romantic and still in the honeymoon phase. He watched them head towards the buoys, careful of the young lad in his own kayak who was trying to keep up with his dad who had just reached the buoys and was skirting their perimeter now.

Satisfied that all was well and knowing that as well as an on-duty lifeguard there was a lifeguard station on one side of the bay if anyone ever drifted and looked like they were in trouble, Leo set down the binoculars. At least today's couple were relatively sensible. Only last week a trio of teenage girls had hired paddleboards and gone beyond the buoys without so much as glancing back. Leo had called out to them using his megaphone and they'd reluctantly come back to where he'd explained they needed to be, given their lack of experience. It wasn't a hard and fast rule of course but he was a pretty good judge of whether some-one would be able to cope beyond the area he could keep a good eye on. They'd at least stayed closer to the shore after that, not going beyond the buoys, but water savvy they were not. Leo had spotted one of them attempting to do a headstand on her board – she'd fallen off quite spec-tacularly, and he'd seen her mate attempt a cartwheel from one board to the other – a stunt which did not work out. He'd seen the other girl remove her buoyancy vest and put the bright pink item on her board at the end ready to do who knew what and he'd been about to call out over the megaphone again when her own, more sensible, friend must have told her to put it on. As he'd watched them, every time they went out of sight for longer than they should have done, he had a feeling of dread pool in his stomach. The three of them had come to shore laughing away but Leo had wasted no time giving them a warning not to repeat that kind of behaviour. He'd tried to sound serious but not a total ogre but it was difficult, and most of his focus had been on avoiding the attention of the girl who kept adjusting her bikini in a way that suggested she was doing it for his benefit every time she moved the ma-terial. He hoped they'd got the message about water safety but he was more than thankful they weren't locals but holidaymakers who would hopefully move on to another beach and someone else's watch next time.

Leo ran a one-on-one kayak lesson at five o'clock for someone who'd been gifted with a voucher for her birth-day and was thankfully water savvy and ready to listen, and just before he closed he sold keen surfer and local man, Steve, wax for his board as well as a new wetsuit, so he was ready for his usual surf session in the morning.

Leo locked up the downstairs, turned off all the lights there and back in the shop and after making sure the front door was locked as well as his truck parked in the parking area, he made his way home from the boathouse to the cabin that some would assume was a holiday rental given its size – not very big at all – and proximity to the beach. It was one of only two down here, hidden from the main road, secret to anyone else unless they came to his place of business. The cabin was where he now called home and he loved everything about it, from its proximity to the beach and the water to the short commute he had, and the fact he could see his home from work and vice versa. The commute still made him smile every so often and if he went to the pub and overheard people bemoaning their bi-weekly trips into London for their job or daily drives up the motorway to the office, he'd be reminded of how lucky he was to stroll from A to B the way he was doing now.

Leo lived and breathed Stepping Stone Bay, just the way he liked it. He couldn't imagine giving all of this up, not for anyone or anything, even when the weather was wild and the sea air clung to his hair and he took it home with him, he wouldn't have it any other way.

Some days Leo gave very little thought to the other cabin down here. It was just there, separated from his by the stepping stones. But since he'd inspected the place last night he was thinking about it again, conjuring up old memories, good times. He hated it when that happened, it made it hard for him to move forwards, and after Nina had left it had taken him a long while to do that. In years gone by the Magowans and the O'Briens had fully utilised these cabins as their holiday escapes. The kids – Leo

24

and his brother Adrian, Walt's grandchildren Nina and William – had spent hours and hours down here every summer and indeed in the off-seasons. But those hazy days of summer hadn't lasted and neither had Leo's relationship with Nina. One wild and windy evening everything had changed, a tragedy had left its mark.

As he walked past the O'Brien cabin Leo thought of Walt. He always seemed well, jolly even, and he was usually talkative when they crossed paths, as long as Leo wasn't busy. Walt always wanted to know about the boathouse and how business was going, and his friendship with Leo's Granny Camille saw to it that even though Nina had left Leo's life, their families remained entwined.

Past the O'Brien cabin Leo strode easily between stepping stones to reach his own cabin. When he was a kid he'd bounded from one stepping stone to the next, turning to do it again back the other way, then repeating the game over and over again until he was puffing and out of breath. When they became friends Nina had joined in, the game keeping them amused for hours. Nowadays it didn't hold quite the same allure.

With the absence of street lamps, an automatic light came on to welcome him up the steps that led to the front door of the cabin set back on a modest-sized veranda that wrapped partially around the back of his home. The veranda was big enough to invite a few people over for drinks, it was wide enough for the bistro-style table and three chairs as well as a barbecue. He'd strung festoon lights from the grand tree on a patch of grass beyond to the tip of the roof of the cabin and he spent many an evening out here listening to the waves crash against the shore, feeling the salty breeze on his face. You'd think he'd have enough of it in his line of work, but he never did. It was a cosy place in the winter too – constructed to withstand proximity to the beach and the sea and the ups and downs of the weather throughout an average year.

Inside, after a long day at work, Leo wasted no time getting in the shower, the steam soon filling the room and taking any stresses away.

Over the years Leo had taken his cabin from a basic beachside residence to a real home, adding in better-quality everything. The bathroom had gone from having a questionable floor and useless extractor fan to having a walk-in rainfall shower and a window to properly get the air in and circulating when you left the room. As a kid he'd had to endure the drippy effort of a shower head hanging over the bathtub, but not any more. Now he stood beneath jets of water that had a bit of oomph to wash his day away down the plug hole, the water swirling and gurgling to its finale.

With a towel wrapped around his lower half Leo went into the main bedroom, which was just big enough to fit a double bed, a wardrobe and two bedside tables comfortably. He pulled out a fresh pair of shorts from the drawers hidden behind the wardrobe door and after another once-over his body with the towel, pulled them on before heading to the kitchen where he took out a beer from the pale-yellow retro fridge. The original fridge in the cabin had been yellow and as a little boy he'd always thought it was like the sunshine, that it had a place in a home by the sea, and so when it went kaput and he saw a photograph in a magazine of this model in the same colour he knew he wanted it and that it would fit perfectly. He'd sympathetically remodelled the kitchen, which was more of a kitchenette given its size and the way it was at the back and to one side of the lounge area, giving it oak wood benchtops atop glossy white cabinetry with a sleek oven and smooth induction cooktop. The lounge area had been repainted a fresh white with the merest hint of blue and he'd added in comfy dark blue soft furnishings along with a walnut coffee table with a super-soft-beneath-the-feet shaggy seafoam aqua rug in front of the log burner he'd installed. These days the Magowan cabin, or Leo's place as it was now referred to by the family, was a beachside paradise no matter the weather.

Leo headed outside with his beer. It was a Friday night and although he was working tomorrow, Friday was Friday, time to kick back. He switched on the festoon lights and happily sank into the comfiest of the three chairs and put his feet up on the bistro table. He wouldn't get away with it anywhere else, but could get away with it when he lived on his own. He wouldn't do it if he had company, but these days he rarely had anyone here to reprimand him, although he was working on getting Adrian to come down and visit, to sit with him and soak up the joys of the bay he'd once loved. His brother would get there, he had to, the sea and Stepping Stone Bay were in his blood, and deep down Leo had always known he wouldn't have turned his back on it permanently. Seeing Adrian so lost was difficult, but being back in this part of the country seemed like a significant first step in the right direction. Not that he'd say that to Adrian, at least not yet. His brother tended to deal with things in his own time and in his own way. They both did.

The wall on Leo's veranda was low enough that he could see the sea from here, the bit of beach he'd been on with water craft today, and if he had a set of binoculars he'd be better able to see the very end of the pier that sat round the other side of the bay and past Salthaven's main beach. He could just about make out the lights from the café at the end of the pier now and as he tipped his head back to get a swig of beer, he wished he'd had the foresight to go there to grab something to bring back here for dinner. He hadn't been for a few weeks, he was always so busy, but they did such good food, with a specials board that changed according to the seasons.

It was only after he'd finished his beer that Leo couldn't ignore his growling stomach any longer and without much more than a tin of beans in the cupboard and not even any bread, armed with a torch, he trekked from his cabin, followed the thirteen stepping stones past the O'Brien's cabin, and went on up the track towards the main road and the pizzeria he frequented so often they didn't need to ask his order – thick-crust with onion, three types of cheese, tomato, herbs and anchovies, along with a sprinkle of chillies that left his mouth tingling. As his pizza bubbled in the special oven he chatted with the owner Nico and his wife who seemed to have a baby permanently glued to her hip.

Before too long he was setting off back to his cabin, pillowy-doughed pizza encased in its box and the aroma teasing him as he whistled a random Italian tune he'd heard in the pizzeria. The festoon lights from his own cabin welcomed him back but as he drew closer to the O'Brien cabin ready to pass on by, he froze. Last night he may have doubted his sanity, thought he'd seen something when he hadn't, but tonight there was no mistaking it. The front door was propped open and inside someone was milling about.

And not just anyone.

Nina.

Chapter Three

Maeve

Outside beneath the sunshine Maeve took two glasses of freshly squeezed apple juice over to Molly and Arthur, the original owners of the little café at the end of the pier in Salthaven. Now of course the café was owned and run by Jo, their granddaughter, who was pregnant with twins and, lucky for Maeve, looking for extra help in the café for twelve months minimum.

Molly had her eyes closed to feel the warmth of the sun on her skin as she tilted her head back while Arthur sat next to her reading the newspaper with one hand holding the pages, his other hand pushing the stroller with Jo's one-year-old daughter Ava inside, back and forth, keeping the toddler asleep.

'Thank you dear,' Arthur spoke softly, closing his newspaper and putting a hand-painted paperweight on top of it as Maeve set his glass down in front of him and Molly's in front of her.

'She's sound asleep,' Maeve smiled, braving a peek at Ava who looked so peaceful it gave Maeve a little pang of nostalgia for the days when Jonah had been like that, all chubby cheeks and innocence. It wouldn't be long before he was taller than her, the rate he was growing.

'We've had a whole ten minutes so far,' Molly put in, 'she usually dozes for forty-five minutes if we're lucky.'

'She's a ball of energy when she's awake,' Maeve grinned. Jo's husband Matt had brought Ava in yesterday to say hello to her mummy while she was at work and when it wasn't too busy, but Ava had only lasted a few minutes before Matt took her outside where she could toddle along the pier holding his hand.

'She most certainly is,' said Molly. 'She keeps us young as great-grandparents.'

Maeve suspected it wasn't only Ava's arrival that did that. According to Jo, ever since Molly and Arthur had retired from the café full time it was as though they'd shed ten years. They might both have deep silver hair and lines on their faces that showed lives well-lived, but neither of them lacked joie de vivre, in fact Maeve felt sure they had more energy than she did if they weren't concerned that Ava would soon be awake again.

Molly sipped her apple juice and delivered compliments on its freshness to Maeve. 'You seem to be settling back in just fine around here.'

'I am, thank you.' Because this wasn't a new town for Maeve, it was a long-awaited return to the place she'd once called home. 'Although it's a big change from Toronto, that's for sure.' Maeve set the tray on the edge of the table next to them and tightened up her ponytail which kept her dark wavy hair well out of the way of her customers and their food and beverages. It was warm today although the breeze she felt while standing here on the pier was welcome.

'I'll bet it's beautiful over there,' said Arthur. 'Although you haven't lost your British accent. Maybe the odd twang here and there,' he chuckled.

'I seemed to fall in with a lot of expats over there,' she smiled. 'That helped keep my accent from changing too much, and it's funny how I've only been back in the UK for a month or so but it feels like I never left in some ways.' And in others it felt a lifetime ago.

Maeve had emigrated with her parents more than eleven years ago, but when Maeve's aunt fell ill and Maeve's mum had toyed with the idea of moving back to help her, both of Maeve's parents had realised that deep down they had a real yearning for Salthaven that they didn't seem to be able to move past. It was the right time. And Maeve knew it was time she came back too, she'd left it long enough already.

'The question is, are you here to stay?' Molly continued to probe.

Maeve beamed a smile their way. As difficult as it was in many ways to be back here, she desperately wanted this move to work out for the best. 'You know I think I might be. Mum and Dad certainly are, they're even back in their old house.'

'Funny how things work out,' Arthur mused.

Maeve's parents had sold up before they emigrated to Toronto and had only been thinking of returning for six months when they saw their old house came up for sale. 'It's a sign,' Maeve's mum had declared and that was it. They started the wheels in motion and Maeve jumped on board.

Maeve plucked her tray from the next table as another couple took the seats, nodded to Molly and Arthur who knew she had to get back to work and pulled her notepad from her front apron pocket to take her customers' orders as they'd just come up from the beach and declared they were famished.

'Mind if I sit with my grandparents and Ava?' Jo asked when Maeve went back inside the café. Jo was positively glowing, her cheeks rosy as she put a hand to her hair to check the dark waves were indeed still in the bun she'd styled. Big flowers graced her maternity top that covered an undoubtably pregnant belly. In her second trimester after falling pregnant only nine months after Ava was born, Jo was refusing to admit she might be getting a little tired, especially when Matt liked to pop in and make sure she wasn't overdoing it. Jo had told him off last time for checking up on her but Maeve knew she'd meant it in jest, that she was enjoying his attentions. Maeve wondered what it was like to be so in love, to have someone who cared so deeply they almost made a nuisance of themselves by making sure you were all right.

'Of course,' Maeve replied to Jo who already felt more of a friend than a boss. 'I can handle things here. You go spend time with your family.' Maeve had only been working at the café for a few weeks but Jo was so welcoming that she'd slotted right in and wasn't tense about having a new job, being judged on her performance. She'd even go so far as to say she was enjoying herself. Maeve had never forgotten the café of course, despite being thousands of miles away. The café was known far and wide for its prowess for changing a menu along with the seasons and they had continuous steady local as well as not-so-local custom. It was iconic to Salthaven, which also drew visitors, with its impressive beach, and Stepping Stone Bay beyond. And at least it wasn't quite as busy now as it had been over the summer holidays that had just passed. Maeve had been thrown right in at the deep end when she secured a job here and wondered how Jo ever managed,

33

even with Molly and Arthur's help when they emerged from their retirement and came back from Spain to spend time with family and do the odd shift at the café to help out if they were around.

The couple outside each wanted a latte and a raspberry-swirl roll and so Maeve got to her task, made the coffees and used the tongs to pull out the sweets from the covered unit beside the till. There weren't too many customers now, given they were approaching five o'clock when most people finished up for the day at the beach and wanted to be home in time for dinner.

As she took the loaded tray outside Maeve glanced at the clock once again, bang on five o'clock now. Jonah had been back at school for three weeks and had texted her as per the agreement they'd struck at the start of term, an arrangement that granted her eleven-year-old a little independence to cushion the disruption of a move. She'd originally wanted him to come to the café at home time and wait with her before heading back to their rented flat, but no sooner had she told him the idea he'd asked her to let him go home alone and have an hour to play on his Wii before he had to come to the café. She'd relented, given in to his demands that he wasn't a baby, because she'd already ripped him away from the only country he knew, and his friends and his school to settle back here. Everyone told her kids his age were resilient, that it would be a smooth transition, and she hoped they were right, because they weren't only returning to England's south coast, they were coming back to the truth she'd always known she'd have to share with him eventually.

With no sign of Jonah yet, Maeve saw to her other customer at the corner table near the specials board. She'd call her son if he wasn't here in the next couple of minutes; he knew he had to be on time and usually was.

Her customer seemed to be in for a lengthy chat and Maeve didn't have it in her not to reply to conversations about the tide, the weather, the specials board that drew such attention here in the café. But as she did her mind drifted to Toronto and the early days in another country. She'd emigrated without a whole lot of warning but it felt like the best solution following a traumatic summer, the tragic drowning of a girl her age – Rhianne, a friend of sorts. Maeve had settled with her parents in a suburb far enough from Toronto that they had a bit of space but not so far that Maeve couldn't get to and from the city easily enough. And she'd relished the change of pace, leaving her hometown behind for a fresh start.

The fresh start hadn't been quite what Maeve thought however when only a few months after arriving, just when she thought she was going full-steam ahead with a new job as a catering assistant to start her career path after obtaining a hospitality management qualification, she discovered she was pregnant. She fell apart. She'd just begun to build a social life, she was making friends and was loving life away from everything she knew. She'd been seeing someone she met on her first day at work, a guy who was kind and made her laugh, but she'd never thought of him as in it for the long haul and he left before she even found out about the baby. He'd moved to Vancouver, the other side of the country, for a job opportunity.

Maeve suddenly felt as though she'd made a mess of everything. None of it had been a part of her starting-over plan. She'd had a clean slate, she knew people, she had friends, but nobody was close enough to help her cope with this big change in her life and to navigate her next step. And she was hesitant to tell anyone back in Salthaven what was going on because she'd drawn a line under that part of her life. She'd left that town and what had happened with Rhianne behind. It was too painful to think about, let alone discuss, and with the onset of morning sickness that left her exhausted, she couldn't cope with anything else.

And so once Maeve knew she was expecting, she did what every good mother did. She put her baby first. She made sure she ate properly despite the nausea and vomiting, she went to all her prenatal checkups, and she told her parents.

Maeve had thought when her parents first discovered she was pregnant that they'd be angry or upset, but they were neither. They were practical. They asked her once who the father was and apart from her dad trying to persuade her to contact him when the baby was born they left the subject alone. She'd suspected they would, it was part of what had made it almost easy to confide in them. Maeve's mum Jocelyn had been pregnant once before, twelve years prior to when Maeve was born, and her own mother had badgered her about the father and refused to help her if she wasn't going to marry the man. Maeve's mum ended up giving her baby up for adoption and that was something Maeve knew had haunted her mum ever since. And so Jocelyn had never wanted to do anything to drive a wedge between her and her own daughter. Jocelyn had never fully repaired her relationship with her own mother who'd died only a few years after Jocelyn gave her baby away. Maeve had never met her.

When Jonah was six months Maeve's parents urged her to pick up her career, and she knew for sure that she couldn't have done so without their support. They looked after Jonah, they loved every minute of it, and Maeve studied hard. She found a hospitality and catering apprenticeship and worked her way through that before becoming a catering manager at a hotel. And for a while life ran smoothly for all of them. It was a new life and a good one.

Maeve hadn't completely forgotten about the father, how could she? She'd tried to pick up the phone and call him more than once but she never seemed to get that final push. And then she'd heard talk that the man wasn't in a good head space at all. 'He's a mess,' was how those who were close to him had described him and Maeve couldn't bear to throw anything else into the mix for him. And so she'd put it off again and again until it got even harder. That was the thing about secrets, the longer they were kept, the more complicated it became to admit the truth.

When her parents announced they were returning to Salthaven it didn't matter that Maeve and Jonah were living their lives and settled in their own place in Canada, Maeve had suddenly felt the same urge. And along the way she'd learnt to take life's cues. She couldn't explain it, but she knew it wasn't just that she'd lose her parents support, it was more than that; it was time.

Toronto had been a total change from life here in Salthaven. There'd been the buzz of the city, the vibe and liveliness and sense of adventure a contrast to the sedate town and bay on the south coast. But when Maeve's parents began to make plans for their return to the UK,

Maeve fizzed with the possibilities of giving Jonah the same upbringing she'd had, by the sea without the brutal winters Toronto gave them. He could wander from school to the pier or one of the parks in close proximity, even sail a toy boat on the boating lake before the entrance to the boards along the pier. Her little boy complete with Canadian accent became as excited as they all were and Maeve hoped she was doing the move at just the right time, not just because of his age, but because he deserved to know everything. She wasn't sure how she was going to tell him; all she knew was that she had to. She owed him the truth.

Just like the house being a sign, Maeve's dad had been investigating catering establishments in Salthaven online and Maeve applied for a handful of jobs, knowing that now she and Jonah had had their own place she didn't want to regress and move back in with her parents unless she really had to. Most of the applications came to nothing and it was only the day after they all arrived back in Salthaven when Jocelyn bumped into Arthur, Jo's grandad, that they pointed Maeve in the direction of the café at the end of the pier. Maeve had called Jo immediately and she'd been honest that this was a stop-gap for her until she was settled enough to pursue catering manager opportunities. Jo hadn't minded one bit and had readily taken her on, telling her the arrangement suited her perfectly because she wasn't sure what hours she'd be able to offer long term when she came back to work after her babies were born. Maeve had wondered whether she might want to stay at home with them more but Jo had an incredible love for the café that had been the hub of the community for years and still was since she'd taken it on.

The job at the café wasn't the catering manager position Maeve knew she wanted eventually but it was a start. Along with her savings her wages gave her enough money to rent the small flat she'd found, with her parents acting as guarantors, and eventually she'd look for something else. And for now, Maeve couldn't be happier at how she was settling in.

But Jonah, he was another matter. Not only was he asking questions more and more lately, but now as she glanced at the clock again, he was pushing the boundaries. He was late.

Maeve pulled out her phone from her apron pocket about to call Jonah when he came flying through the door out of breath. And he leapt in with his apology so quickly that she didn't have the heart to moan at him when already he was getting out his school books to do his homework at one of the tables.

'Is that oil on your shorts?' She put her fingers to the leg of his blue shorts, definitely oil, not easy to get out in the wash.

He looked down. 'Don't know,' he tried. But then added on, 'might have been Billy's bike, his chain came off and I helped him put it on.'

It felt nice to know he was talking about other boys at school, it meant he was making friends. 'Well that was kind of you.' She ruffled the deep dark curls he'd inherited from her along with her brown eyes that ran in the family. She'd leave the nagging about the shorts for later on when she was trying to scrub at them with some stain remover. 'Did you see Mr Tumbles outside the flat?'

He shook his head, already rooting through his pencil case for the right pen. Mr Tumbles was her parents' cat.

Her parents lived on the same side of the street as the flat Maeve was renting and it seemed Mr Tumbles was on to them and liked to curl up in the communal doorway hoping for a fuss. Jonah was rather fond of him and the feeling was mutual, but Maeve didn't want the cat, who had been alive longer than Jonah, to get lost by wandering into the wrong flat so she tried to encourage him back to her parents' house whenever she saw him.

As Jonah beavered away at his homework Maeve collected an empty cup from the next table, a cloth in her other hand reaching out to wipe the surface clean ready for the next person. She wiped down the counter again, made a couple of takeaway coffees for customers who drifted in, and when she got a moment, watched her son. It was a mother's luxury, observing your child when they didn't realise. When he was a baby she'd watch him for a long while as he slept; when he was a toddler she'd done the same, but it was difficult to do now he was getting older. He often asked what she was doing if he caught her staring, but really she was just appreciating the boy he'd become, the man he would be one day.

The café had a burst of customers as they came to the end of their working days and Jo, after wrapping Ava in a big hug, came back inside to rescue Maeve. They'd laughed about this, the busyness that seemed to happen at the time of day you assumed most would've gone home. Maeve had wondered why anyone would walk down the end of a pier after work or college or working in the town just to get a coffee or a slice of cake and Jo had shrugged as if it was obvious. Since then Maeve had realised exactly why it was; she'd remembered how much she'd enjoyed coming here and had done the same. This wasn't just any café, it was a place for locals to come and hang out even if only for half an hour, a place to meet others, somewhere to talk away your worries or pick up some cake to take home to a loved one. It had already started to become that way for Maeve too.

Jonah had moved on to reading his book, his brow furrowed in concentration now as Maeve handed two cans of cola to the teenagers who'd come in and were mid-conversation about an annoying aunt. Jonah had always been a keen reader and Maeve wondered how much of that had come from the lack of outside space at their last and now current home. He'd always had access to green spaces but with his age he didn't have much freedom to enjoy them at will. It was part of the reason she'd wanted to come home here to Salthaven, so her son could have the same upbringing as she'd once enjoyed. And the independence would come, he just had to be patient, and she had to learn how to give it to him. At least she'd made him happy by agreeing that he could go home after school and then meet her at work after some time on his own. That little bit of trust had buoyed him along and it was good for Maeve too. She hadn't had to cut her hours to get home for her son or have him bored in the café for too long and so for now the arrangement worked.

As well as loving books Jonah seemed obsessed by the sea, something Maeve didn't embrace but knew she had to accept. She'd been wary of the sea for a long time since Rhianne had drowned. She'd been part of the gathering that night, on the same boat Rhianne had fallen from and she'd seen her lifeless body dragged from the water. And hearing Jonah talk about the sea, how he wanted to go into the waves, how he longed to try out different water sports, filled Maeve with a dread she knew she had to move on from not only for her sake but for her son's too. She couldn't let her fears become his. But that was easier said than done. And now, he was asking to go along the beach again. But she wasn't ready. It was part of what she'd loved about going over to Canada. For a long time Jonah had had swimming lessons and apart from those he didn't talk much about the water. Here, he saw it every day, he woke up to the smell of the sea, the sound of the waves.

Maeve deflected from the subject of the water by telling Jonah to get on with his homework. 'I won't be too much longer, promise,' she smiled at her son.

'But Muuuum . . . I only want to walk along the sand.'

'Don't "but mum" me. And you'll get me in trouble with Jo if you make a fuss.'

But Jo passed by and winked at Jonah and Jonah knew full well the café's owner wouldn't do anything of the sort. The first day he'd come in here he'd been shy, but Jo had put him at ease straight away and now they talked all the time.

'Your mum's right though, Jonah,' said Jo, two empty plates save a bacon rasher someone couldn't finish lined up on one arm to take to the kitchen at the back. 'And the light is fading. Those waters out there get very dangerous.'

Jo knew the details of the tragedy. Jo knew about Rhianne. Everyone here did. But Maeve had never wanted to tell Jonah; it was a story she wasn't ready to share, not yet.

But he was still watching the magnificence of those waves, mesmerised by the scene out of the window as he went over and knelt on one of the scatter cushions. It was as though he couldn't help himself, it didn't matter that he had homework to do. 'I love the water,' he said almost to himself and every time he got this way it tore Maeve's heart in two.

Jo smiled at Jonah and called over to him, 'Steve told me you were asking all about his surfboard when he was in here last.'

As Jonah talked with Jo about Steve and his colourful surfboards Maeve's insides did a loop-the-loop at the thought of her son asking anyone he could about the water. It was as though the universe was grabbing at every opportunity to remind her of her fear and that she didn't want to let it affect Jonah. Her dad had even wondered whether she'd agreed to come back here partly because subconsciously, it meant she'd have to deal with her demons and perhaps he was right. Although it wasn't only water that was her demon, it ran so much deeper than that.

Maeve hadn't kept Jonah from the water or the beach completely. Of course there'd been the swimming lessons which she'd never once shied away from, their importance only too significant. She'd taken Jonah for a couple of beach holidays when they were living in Canada and like any other kid, he'd loved it – sand play, water fun. They'd taken towels, buckets and spades and the last time Maeve had even let Jonah buy a gaudy inflatable octopus he'd had hours of fun with. But from behind her sunglasses she hadn't taken her eyes away from her boy and it had been she who'd ensured they were closest to the lifeguards on duty, she who'd cut their time short in the water when she thought her nerves might fry at any moment.

When Jo gave Maeve a nod that she could finish up for the day, Jonah saw his freedom and packed up the school books he'd left scattered over the table.

'Home time,' she smiled and got a beam of delight from Jonah in return as they left behind the little café at the end of the pier.

Maeve had rented a place in Salthaven and Jonah's school was only a short walk away. Luckily his walk meant he didn't have to go all the way up the hill that headed away from the town and also gave access to one of this area's drawcards, Stepping Stone Bay. It was a beautiful spot and offered water-lovers a plethora of craft to choose from at the business that operated from the classic boathouse which still stood in place. Once he discovered that place, she knew holding him back would be even harder; he was born for it.

As they walked the short way home Maeve wondered how much longer before her son discovered Stepping Stone Bay and everything it came with. For Maeve the water and her nervousness around it was one of the biggest challenges of being back in Salthaven. There were plenty of others – settling into school, making new friends, finding his way around and for her, finding work and renting her own place. And for both of them she knew that sooner or later she had to answer the questions Jonah had about who his father was. Because his father lived in this same town and she couldn't avoid him forever.

Chapter Four

Nina

Nina was back at the cabin today armed with buckets, cloths, sprays of all sorts and a heap of towels as well as Marigolds. She hadn't done much at all yesterday because she and Walt had spent the morning together, enjoyed lunch at a tea room in a little village not far from Salthaven, and then gone to visit the cemetery where Elsie was buried. Nina and Walt had talked to Elsie – it hadn't felt at all strange for either of them, but Nina hadn't wanted to leave Walt after that and so all she'd done yesterday evening was pop to the cabin and change a few of the lightbulbs as well as prop open the front door to get some air fully circulating.

Today the O'Brien cabin smelt much better. And so far so good, no sign of Leo. She wanted a bit more time to gear herself up to face him. Pathetic really, given what he'd meant to her for so many years before she broke his heart.

What Nina had done yesterday was stand in the cabin and think about the finished job she wanted for the place. Given its proximity to the sea, a nautical feel was perfect and she already had a few ideas on that score. She could add finishing touches to each room with the same theme. The bathroom suite was close to new – she remembered

Elsie talking about it a year or so before she died, how they'd had to bring it into this century. Looking around, Nina decided some of those wooden-framed seaside pictures that had shells inside and hung by rope on the walls would go perfectly in here. She'd keep the walls white to match the fittings and add lots of blue touches – perhaps a dolphin ornament, a sea-scene bathmat for young kids, some novelty soaps in the shapes of sea creatures could be arranged in the corner of the bathtub. Her grandparents had insisted the cabin needed the bath even though it was a squeeze and the bathroom small, and Nina knew her brother had appreciated it with his children, bundling them into the tub after a long day at the beach. The times he'd told her about it she'd kept her cool, she'd let him talk, because he had managed to find a sense of being happy and she was glad for him. He hadn't let their parents' behaviour dictate his future and she only wished she had been strong enough to do the same. She had no intention of ever making him feel guilty for the happiness he'd found.

As she filled a bucket with hot water and added some soap, bubbles formed and Nina thought about Leo making his permanent home down here in what had once been only a holiday cabin, not a full-time place to live. She'd known he'd done that because Walt had always seen it as his duty to keep his granddaughter more or less up to date about the locals, including Leo, in the briefest most bearable way possible and she hadn't really minded. He meant well.

Nina picked up one of the cloths she'd brought with her and as the water got to a satisfactory level in the bucket, she dropped it in. According to Walt, Maeve was back in

46

the bay too. She had a son and that was one local update
that really had piqued Nina's interest. Like Nina, Maeve
had turned her back on the bay and on Salthaven, but
she'd ventured even further, to Canada. Nina had heard
from Walt that the entire family had returned and that
Maeve was working in the café at the end of the pier, but
so far Nina hadn't braved going anywhere local, let alone
the café that was so busy all year round and hugely popular. Nina didn't know Maeve all that well, but she could
remember the summer before she left the bay behind
when Maeve had started to hang around with their group
a bit more. She'd sat with Nina on the beach a few times
as Nina watched the Magowan brothers surfing, express-
ing her admiration at Leo's love and adoration for Nina
when he came running out of the sea, beads of water drip-
ping off his jaw and running down his chest, just to give
Nina a kiss.

Nina wondered whether the town and the bay were
in their blood – Maeve's, her family's, her own, because
something seemed to have pulled them both back and
maybe it was more than the cabin for Nina, more than a
family's relocation for Maeve. It felt strangely settling to
know someone else was in the same situation though, because it wasn't easy coming back after all this time.

'Come on Nina, get a grip,' she said to herself, starting
work in the kitchen. If she didn't get on and stop daydreaming she'd never get this place ready. There was a lot
to do and she was only at the basic cleaning stage right
now. The vision, the transformation, the fun part would
have to wait. And so would the memories.

For now it was old-fashioned hard work. She sloshed the
cloth with plenty of water onto the benchtop and began

to scrub at any stubborn marks. She'd shivered when she first arrived and opened the window but it wasn't long before she'd worked up a bit of a sweat as she scrubbed and wiped each and every surface, the window sill, the top of the extractor fan above the cooktop, around the kitchen window. She braved opening the oven door and pulled a face at the distinct pong of grease and neglect. It saddened her that this cabin hadn't been a part of the family's life, at least not properly, in such a long time. And she blamed herself partly for that because she'd run away from here, the place that was once her escape, her hideaway from her mum and dad who had behaved like part-time parents who had eventually been unable to even tolerate one another. Both of them were self-absorbed, but Walt and Elsie had more than made up for their shortcomings. And it was those memories of being here with her grandparents that Nina would always hold close to her heart even though she'd never ever felt good enough, especially not good enough to find a happy ever after of her own.

Nina had a rest from wiping down and took out a pad of paper and pen from her bag to make some notes as thoughts popped into her head. The first note she made was that the veranda was too dark and it needed lighting as well as a seating area. It wasn't all that spacious but she could find something small to make it inviting and welcoming, perhaps a bistro table and a couple of chairs, somewhere the new owners might be able to enjoy a glass of wine in the evening.

In the kitchen she made a note of the repairs required. Three of the cupboard doors needed new handles as the current ones were chipped, and in one case not there at all. The hinges were off on the end cupboard too and one of the doors had dropped. She had a quick search online using her phone and found that new cookers weren't all that expensive, so added that in as a requirement. It wasn't just that she didn't want to clean the oven, it was more that it was old and it needed bringing up to date so it would go with the revamped cabin once she'd finished. She didn't want anything to put buyers off, and if she was going to do this place up she might as well make sure everything was done properly. The alternative was to sell the cabin as it was, but she and Grandad had immediately decided against that. They'd be wasting money doing it that way and Walt deserved to get a good price if he was going to part with something so meaningful to the O'Brien family. Nina had just about got her head around someone else calling it theirs but she wouldn't accept giving it away for less than it was really worth.

Nina looked up at the wall where the old clock had once been between two mounted cabinets, all that remained now a faded circle.

With their father Graham in the forces, he and Christy, Walt and Elsie's daughter, had made the decision early on that they wanted their children Nina and William to have a stable home. It could easily be mistaken as a sound parenting attitude, but unfortunately they'd taken it literally by having Nina and her brother remain in Salthaven with Stepping Stone Bay at their doorstep, stable in the physical sense. And with that they'd lost an emotional connection with their children that they'd never really got back. Nina wished Graham and Christy had been able to see that home wasn't only a place, but a feeling, and as parents, it was their job to try to give their children both. Sometimes she'd felt as though she was asking too much.

But Walt and Elsie had stepped in and become the parents both Nina and William needed. Christy would never admit she had several failures as a mother and Walt and Elsie never would've accused her of it either. And nowadays Nina looked back, and despite her sadness, knew she wouldn't trade having Walt and Elsie in her life for anything, not even the two people who should've been there for her and William the most. Perhaps all along it had been the best thing, although Nina had always wondered why their parents hadn't loved them enough to put them first, and it had made her doubt whether she was worthy of anyone's love for a long time.

Nina blew out her cheeks. She'd known that being back here would bring all kinds of thoughts and self-doubts to the surface. She just hadn't expected it to happen quite the way it was now, stopping her in her tracks every time her mind wandered at will.

Time to get on again. Nina had been a nurse for more than a decade, and if she kept stopping in her job the way she was doing today she'd be fired quicker than she could say Stepping Stone Bay. Her days at work were usually filled with rushing here and there, always busy, regularly moving from one task to another, and it had been good for her. Coming here, she had time to think and reflect and she wasn't sure it was helping her at all.

Her next task was to clean the window sills in the lounge area and all the surfaces, but first she pulled back the old sheets that covered the fabric furniture to inspect what she had to work with. With the sheets balled up and out of the way she felt a bit more warmth come to the cabin, a touch of homeliness as she put a hand to the same old sofas she remembered, except now they were covered in navy blue rather than the pale blue they'd once been. On closer inspection however, the replacements had already succumbed to the sunshine, with faded patches on the arm of one sofa, the seat of the other slightly worn. She'd search for some more covers, sure she'd find something suitable, and they were still good sofas, no one side sagging more than the other. She'd also get a rug, this room needed it to give warmth. Right now it was too echoey despite its small proportions and she envisaged something like the original blue and white rectangular nautical shaggy rug covering the bare floorboards.

Nina pulled on her Marigolds again and with the bucket of water at her feet, wiped the shelf on the farthest wall in the lounge. She'd keep this shelf. Made of reclaimed driftwood, it stretched all the way along and was now dusty and empty. Once upon a time it had displayed the hand-painted seven dwarfs Nina and William had made from a kit their grandparents must've grabbed to alleviate their boredom one freezing February half-term when their dad Graham was away with work and their mother Christy was away in Spain for a wedding. Nina thought fondly of the memory of making the dwarfs using the specially provided moulds, waiting impatiently for them to dry, painting them in bright colours when they were finally done. The Magowan brothers had come over as they'd finished up and William had leapt up from the table denying he'd had anything to do with the activity, that it was all Nina, wanting to be as mature as Adrian who was the eldest out of all of them. But Leo had sat down and asked Nina if he could paint Grumpy's hat, a nod in Adrian's direction that had made Nina giggle at the implication his brother could be moody.

The dwarfs that had once sat on the shelf Nina had a hand against now had gone with William and his kids who, last time they were here, had made up a game using the figures, despite their fragility. William had cleared it with Nina first of course, but given the way she'd already detached herself from this place she'd had no qualms agreeing. Even now she was glad they'd gone to a good home, although she wondered how long they'd survive with Fliss and Perry.

Nina caught a waft of the sea flowing in from the open window and she went to stand next to the glass. She'd opened the curtains up fully, the green and cream material good enough to block out the light but in need of updating. From here she could see the boathouse she scurried past every time she came down here, and on a deep sigh she wondered, was he inside there now? Or was he out on the water?

Nina scrubbed the rest of the surfaces to within an inch of their lives and by the end her arms were aching more than she thought possible. Bucket of dirty water in hand she looked around the cabin at all her hard work. It was cleaner than it had probably been in years. It was ready for her to make the changes necessary to make this into a seaside treasure, one someone else could fall in love with. Satisfied with her progress and done for the day, she emptied out the filthy water and rinsed the bucket and cloths, leaving everything in the corner of the kitchen for the next stint.

Nina left the cabin and locked up behind her before trotting down the steps ready to scurry past the boathouse again. Except this time she didn't get very far at all.

A voice boomed over at her from by the bin store. 'What are you doing here, Nina?'

'Leo.' His name came out on a breath so soft her voice was barely audible.

He dropped what sounded like a couple of bottles into the recycling bin and closed the lid and then the top of the bin store he'd made back when he was a teenager. Both families had hated the look of their bins, and being good at turning his hand to DIY he'd offered to make something, and this was what he'd come up with, a wooden structure with a lid that hid all the bins inside and was easily accessible for taking the bins up to the main road on bin day.

'I'm cleaning up the cabin,' she said to him, this man she'd hurt so terribly when she left the bay behind and by default, him too, without so much as a phone call, never mind a better explanation. It was terrible leaving the way she did, she'd beaten herself up about it, but she'd also known that if she'd tried to explain how lost she was, how much she needed to get away, even if she'd called after the fact, he'd have done his utmost to talk her into staying. And it might well have worked, she was so in love with him and the promise of a future.

'You're back to stay?' he asked gruffly.

She grappled with the right words and couldn't find them. Instead she said, 'We probably need to talk.'

He looked as though he was going to agree but instead he said, 'Nothing to say.' He looked across at the cabins as though he wanted to look anywhere but at her. 'I didn't think we were good enough for you any more, that's why you left isn't it? Why you went without a word, why you never looked back.'

It was like taking the cane to the palm of your hand with every blow. But each one deserved. 'It wasn't like that, Leo.'

'No? So tell me how it was then.'

'I hate what I did.'

'And yet you did it anyway.' He took a step closer as she did the same. As well as the dark hair that might one day go grey like his dad's she could see the green eyes that had held hers captive plenty of times before. The eyes she'd looked into when she said *I love you, Leo,* the eyes she'd never been able to imagine filled with sadness when she left because it hurt too much to think of the pain he'd be in at her departure.

Nina had never really talked about her leaving with anyone, not even her grandad, not her brother either. She'd locked her feelings away, lost herself in her job as a nurse and a whole new place to live away from here. 'I can't do this right now, Leo. I need to get back to Grandad.'

'Of course.' He fixed her with his stare, no sign of the flirty smile she remembered where it reached his eyes and told her his feelings without the need for extraneous words. 'Do what you do best, Nina . . . leave.' And with that he turned and marched back to the boathouse without so much as a backward glance.

Chapter Five

Leo

Seeing Nina yesterday after all this time had left Leo in something of a bad mood that had lasted the rest of the afternoon, the evening and overnight. And continuing on today, he'd burnt his mouth on his morning coffee, he'd stumbled over the piece of wood in the car parking area that he'd been meaning to chop up and use in his log burner for ages when he helped a customer secure his new kayak to his car, and he'd almost sold a penknife to a kid without checking for identification – and he definitely wasn't old enough.

Nina had been on and off Leo's mind over the years, but he'd learned to get on with it. She'd hurt him when she fled the bay and him without so much as a goodbye, let alone an explanation. His calls had gone unanswered; begging with Walt had led to nothing other than to know that she was all right and that she wasn't coming back. Leo had felt sorry for the old man because he had turned up at Walt's bungalow many a time when she first left, hoping she might be there. Walt and Elsie had comforted him with their words and their cups of tea, told him Nina didn't know how to help herself, let alone be with anyone else. Their allegiance had of course been with Nina, but they'd never turned him away and always assured him that they'd let her know he asked after her every single day.

As time wore on, his visits to Nina's family became less frequent. Nina had left, so had Adrian, the two most important people in his life. Leo had had an image of his future in his head for as long as he could remember. Part of that image was him and Adrian running the boathouse together, brothers in arms. The other part was his happy-ever-after with Nina, and yet when she left and so did Adrian, he threw himself into the business that he was managing and running on his own and did so with such passion, and if he was honest, obsession, to make it work. He'd always seen himself settling down in the bay, being like his grandparents and his parents, happy with one another, a couple of kids or maybe more, content with life on the south coast and fulfilled. He'd thought he'd settle down with Nina, but since she left he hadn't met anyone else. Some days he thought that a good thing – less chance of being hurt that way. And Nina turning up now was like throwing a grenade into what he'd built after the tragedy that sent some people running. He'd long since buried his feelings about a future with a family of his own – it was still on the periphery, but no longer front and centre, the boathouse had become that. But Nina O'Brien? Well she had the power to change everything.

Leo couldn't relax at work, his mind on other things apart from the business. He spent his time with one eye out the window because from there, the side of the boat-house, you could just about see beyond and through the trees to both his cabin and the one which still caused him grief even to this day. He wasn't sure whether he was wary of another glimpse of the woman who'd broken his heart or whether it was actually what he wanted. He'd been rude to her last night but given he hadn't heard a word since she upped and left, he wasn't going to be overly nice. Why should he be? He'd never stopped hurting but he'd learned to bury that pain and deal with it and the boat-house had become his one true love. Somehow he'd carried on and he didn't much appreciate her being back now, dragging up the past to rub his face in it. He could do without it.

At lunchtime Leo turned the sign on the door to Closed so he could duck out to the bank and for some lunch. The rain had come this morning, the cooler temperatures too, a true reminder that another summer was as good as over. Business-wise it had been a good season, and despite being at the tail end of it plenty of people still wanted to make the most of the calm waters and being able to have lessons before the season was completely over for the less experienced. Leo had run classes throughout the summer with school holiday programmes in demand, so it was nice to take a step back and be able to do things like close for an hour in the middle of the day and head into town. And he needed the break because tonight he had an eighteenth birthday party coming for a kayak session. It would be manic, he expected and he only hoped they saved the drinking and crazy behaviour until well after they'd left here. He knew the hard way how dangerous it could be out on the open water; the whole town did.

Salthaven was very much within walking distance from the old boathouse, but Leo took his truck for speed because it would give him the chance to drive up to Adrian's place afterwards and check up on his brother. He'd do it under the pretence of wanting company for lunch although he knew now that his brother wouldn't believe that for a second.

He parked halfway between the pier and the shops, the only place he could find a one-hour free space in the popular town, and after he'd been to the bank he picked up some supplies for the boathouse and for home and collected two baguettes from a local bakery, both stuffed with chorizo and halloumi and salad leaves.

Back at his car Leo was about to pull away from the kerb when he saw Rhianne's mum, Bridget and although he was pushed for time, he could never ignore either her or her husband Elijah. He turned off the engine and wound down the window and answered her questions about the boathouse and the calm now the summer holidays were over; they discussed the roadworks a few miles out of Salthaven that created a tailback a couple of miles long and you regretted joining as there were no shortcuts. They touched on the reason she had with her a whole bag of oranges – she was making marmalade later today – and inevitably they talked about Rhianne.

'She hated oranges and never could understand why anyone would spread marmalade on their toast,' Bridget smiled before telling him that Rhianne's go-to for her morning toast had been real butter and a tiny scraping of Marmite.

At least the woman could smile. Leo wasn't sure whether he'd be able to stand up ever again if he'd endured what she had. Every parent's worst nightmare, burying their own child. After Rhianne's funeral Leo had avoided any interaction with her parents, whether it was conversation or even eye contact until one day he'd talked to his mum about it. She'd explained their pain from a parent's perspective: she talked about him as a baby, how she'd felt about her sons over the years, what Rhianne's mum and dad must be going through. That day he'd cried for the first time since the drowning, like a toddler who'd fallen and cut open his knee and his mum had cradled him like she must've done when he was little. Ever since that conversation with his mum, Leo had made a point of always being available to talk to Elijah and Bridget whenever they wanted.

'I got myself a good recipe for chocolate orange cake,' Bridget informed him.

'That sounds mighty good to me.'

'I got it from Jo at the café.' She adjusted the bag onto her other arm. 'I wanted to talk to her for longer, but you know what the café at the end of the pier is like, busy even out of season.'

'I sure do. And I'll bet it's a delicious recipe. You enjoy it.'

'I will,' she smiled. 'I'd better get going.' But before she did she said, 'Your mum told me Adrian has come home.'

'That's right.' Although he wasn't sure 'come home' was the right phrase. He was living back this way but so far hadn't ventured far beyond his front door, let alone down to the water he'd loved for many years.

'Do give him our best, I hope to see him around.'

'I will.' Leo waved goodbye, but his smile soon disappeared. He'd pass the message on, but he doubted very much that Adrian would want to hear it because it was Adrian who'd been in charge of the boat the night Rhianne drowned and he'd never forgiven himself for what happened. He blamed himself; he hadn't been able to save her. And she wasn't just someone on board, she'd dated him for a while, although Leo always got the impression she was more keen than he was. He wondered how much of his brother leaving the bay and avoiding the water was down to guilt and how much was grief, when he'd known Rhianne better than any of them.

Leo pulled up on the driveway at Adrian's place. His brother had rented a top-floor flat with floor-to-ceiling windows overlooking the cliffs and the sea. He couldn't see Salthaven from his flat but he could see a part of Stepping Stone Bay and a good chunk of the rest of the coast. Somehow it felt better that despite his brother's reluctance to get involved with the boathouse again or venture near to the sea, part of his heart still lay with the ocean in this view his new place afforded.

He pressed the buzzer at the bottom of the substantial detached period residence which had been renovated from a family home into three separate dwellings, with what was once the garden out front now allocated parking spaces.

'Card for tomorrow,' said Leo, handing over his brother's birthday card the moment Adrian answered the door. 'And a chicken and chorizo baguette in here,' he smiled, holding the carrier bag aloft as the waft of the food announced its arrival anyway.

'Is that my birthday gift?' Adrian enquired.

'We've talked about that,' said Leo. 'I'm willing to give you one hell of a thirty-fifth birthday gift if you'll let me. Come into the boathouse business with me, like we always planned. Otherwise it's a six-pack of beer or a few nice bottles of wine unless you can think of another present.'

Adrian pulled two plates from the walnut wall cupboard in a kitchen so sleek Leo hoped he didn't mess it up merely by sitting there on the high stool. 'We have talked about it. And I'm still not interested. I'm a teacher.'

'There's a sentence I never thought you'd say. But I'll bet you're good.' He always had had patience teaching people to sail or kayak or paddleboard. Leo just never thought Adrian would've exchanged the open air for the four walls of a classroom.

'It pays all right, don't have to worry about the weather apart from snow days.'

'How's the job hunt going?' Adrian had left his permanent teaching role in Leeds without a job to go to.

'I'm going to do supply teaching for a while, probably get my name down at a local school soon enough, but no rush.'

Leo supposed a break would do his brother good. He still wasn't himself. He'd left the bay on a bit of a high that the rest of the family had seen through. It had been a front to mask his pain, all the enthusiasm about a new future, a new wife, the promise of a completely fresh start. And now he was back it was as though he'd finally returned to earth from his mission and needed time to slowly readjust. He'd been through so much – the summer tragedy they'd all been there for, getting married, divorcing, quitting a job, moving here. Just thinking about it was enough to make anyone's head ache.

'Your neglected boat is still waiting for you at the marina,' Leo told his brother. 'I take it out now and again, you know, just so it doesn't get upset.'

Adrian managed to at least find that mildly amusing. 'Cheers, bro. Say hello from me won't you?'

'Yeah, sure.' He'd give the nagging a rest for now – at least his brother hadn't mentioned again about selling his boat. Leo knew that boats and the boathouse were in his brother's blood as much as his and always would be no matter whether he acknowledged it or not. He placed a baguette on each plate and laughed at Adrian's appreciative groan on his first bite.

Leo and Adrian were similar looking – roughly the same height, although in their younger years Leo had constantly felt that at three years his brother's junior he was trying to catch Adrian up height-wise. They'd both inherited their fair skin from their father's side, skin that meant they were careful out on the sea and rash vests were a must, particularly in the height of summer. Their green eyes they got from their mother, Anne, their muscular physiques from their father Jimmy, who'd spent so many years working with boats that it had given him a certain longevity. All that fresh air and moving around was good for the body and mind. While Leo's hair was dark without any greys yet and longer on top, Adrian's had the salt-and-pepper look and he kept it cropped short, a bit army-like Leo always thought. The well-trimmed facial hair softened the look though, they wouldn't allow that in the forces, but it made Adrian seem more himself than the version who'd fought to get away from the confines of his life all those years ago.

Adrian paused halfway through demolishing his baguette. 'My divorce is final at last.' He rescued a piece of chorizo that had escaped onto the plate.

'Finally. Any regrets?'

Adrian grunted. 'About marrying or divorcing?' In tracksuit bottoms and a scruffy faded t-shirt Leo was pretty sure had said INXS once upon a time, Adrian seemed a far cry from the guy who'd left the bay with Harper, lived an entirely different life as a teacher where he wore a shirt and tie every day, been in a marriage where he was one half of a power couple who weren't interested in family life but preferred eating at fancy restaurants or heading away for weekend countryside escapes.

'Both I guess.'

'We had fun for a while. But we shouldn't have got married. And we shouldn't have dragged our heels getting a divorce either.'

'Why did you wait so long?'

Adrian shrugged. 'She was and still is busy partying and flying high in her career, I just didn't bother. I've not always been in a good place.'

'I know.' At least his brother could see that. He didn't need anyone to say they told him so. 'But you're back now.'

'Yeah, I'm back.'

'Talking of marriage, the gift is all lined up for Mum and Dad.' The joint gift the boys were organising was for Anne and Jimmy to spend two nights at The Dorchester followed by tickets to see a show in the West End. Their first date ever had been to see a musical in London and so it had seemed a fitting gift to try to recreate the memory in some way. 'And of course we'll have the family dinner, we'll give it to them then.' At least Adrian lived closer now, because before he moved back this way he'd rarely come to visit and Leo had had no idea whether he would turn up despite the occasion. 'You still going to cook?'

'I am.' At his brother's raised eyebrows Adrian shook his head. 'I have managed to survive on my own you know, cooking for myself.'

'Yeah, but anniversary dinner and all that.'

That had his brother laughing. 'I've got a few tricks up my sleeve. Don't worry, it won't be toast and boiled eggs.'

'Nothing wrong with that.'

'I think forty years of marriage deserves a little more.' Adrian put both plates into the dishwasher and leaned back against the counter when he was done. 'I just hope the topic of conversation isn't that they made four decades and I couldn't even make four years with my wife.'

'Hey, this is about their success not your failure,' Leo joked.

Thankfully Adrian took it the way it was intended, as brotherly banter.

Adrian should never have married Harper, but today was the first time Leo had heard his brother say it out loud, even though he'd suspected Adrian had thought it for a while. Marriage had been a rash decision – no doubt about it, Harper was stunning, a whole lot of fun, and probably everything Adrian had needed at the time to get over what happened. The trouble was, a whirlwind romance followed by a wedding had been a short-term solution. Now he was back, maybe Adrian would finally work through his emotions and try to make this town and the bay his home again. Mind you, Leo was one to talk when it came to dealing with his feelings. It seemed he'd buried a lot of them, just like his brother, and while he appeared to most people to have forged ahead with his life, Nina's return had caused him to wobble at the reminder of the heartbreak, the dent in his pride when he'd lost the woman he loved. And that was before you dug deeper and found that while Leo might never admit it, he had never fully let go of the desire to settle down and have a family. Nina being here after all this time was a reminder of what he'd never achieved, and that was one of the biggest frustrations of all.

'Cup of coffee?' Adrian offered.

'Yeah, thanks.' Time to stop feeling sorry for himself, focus on his brother.

Coffee made, they took to the easy chairs positioned beside the floor-to-ceiling window. 'Bloody fantastic view,' Leo approved.

'Why do you think I rented this place?'

'At least I know you don't totally hate the sea.'

Adrian paused. 'I never hated it, I hate what it can do, what it did.'

Leo got it. He wasn't sure he'd get much more out of Adrian, but he didn't want to let him get so wrapped up in his guilt now he was back that he couldn't see past it. 'You do realise Rhianne's death wasn't your fault, don't you?'

'So everyone tells me.'

'You couldn't control the weather, Adrian.'

'No, I don't suppose I could.'

It was all he was going to get right now. Time to change tack. 'So Nina's back.' Leo could feel the weight of his brother's stare as Adrian turned in his chair to face him. 'I spoke to her, but I was a bit of an arsehole.'

Adrian waited before he answered. 'I'll never understand why she left.' He swigged his coffee and winced at the heat of it. 'I mean, me leaving was one thing, but she had you, a whole life here for her.'

'You had a life too.'

'Not the same. And life for Rhianne ended that night,' he added more gruffly.

'It didn't mean it had to for you too.'

Adrian looked like he was about to reply but instead advised, 'Drink your coffee.'

After a pause he added, 'Seriously though, you and Nina need to talk. Properly.'

'I'm going with the ignoring her approach. Works for me,' he shrugged.

'Bit hard to do that given the proximity of your home and work to their family cabin.' Adrian ran his hand across his head the way he used to do when he was thinking, his shaved hair so short now that there was nothing to tug his fingers through, nor many strands for the salt water to cling to if he ever ventured back into the sea. 'I wonder if she's back for good, I wonder why now?'

'No idea, bro. No idea.' Part of him hoped she had come back on a permanent basis, he couldn't deny it, and it frustrated him no end that he thought that way. She'd hurt him so badly, he'd glued himself back together, and he hated that here she was undoing him all over again despite his determination not to let her. She'd stirred up feelings he'd convinced himself he'd moved on from and he didn't like it one bit.

Leo remembered what he was meant to do. 'I saw Rhianne's mum earlier.' His brother visibly stiffened in his chair. 'She said to pass on a hello, she's glad you're back.'

Adrian simply nodded. Rhianne had been only twenty-two years old when she died, younger than Adrian, and given they'd dated a while, that must've made it even harder for Adrian to deal with his grief. How could it not?

'I dread bumping into them you know,' Adrian admitted.

'I avoided them for a long time as well.' Again Leo felt his brother shift his focus from the view to him. 'I talked to Mum about it a long time ago. The boat was yours, you were the skipper, but I was there, I'm a Magowan, boats are our business.'

'You've got nothing to feel guilty about.'

He finished his coffee. 'And neither have you. Remember that.' And with a brief clench of his brother's shoulder as he took his mug to the kitchen he said, 'I'd better get back to the boathouse. Join me anytime you like.'

But Adrian didn't move from his spot, he merely kept his focus on that view.

Back at the boathouse Leo was straight into work when he found local surfer Steve waiting for him outside. He climbed out of his truck. 'Not been here too long I hope?'

'Ages.' But good-humouredly Steve lifted up his coffee cup. 'Don't worry, only five minutes and I'm still finishing this anyway. I came to collect the wetsuit I ordered.'

The keys jangled as Leo reopened the boathouse and let them both inside. 'It came this morning.' He found the delivery and pulled back the clear wrap so Steve could check the size.

'Looks good to me,' Steve approved and as Leo rang up the purchase on the till he admired the surf watches in the display cabinet, behind glass because they were way too expensive to lose to wandering hands. 'Might put one of these on my Christmas list.'

'I've sold four already,' Leo told him. That was another reason to put them right by the till. As he packaged up purchases the watches caught the eye of the buyer and some hadn't been able to resist. 'I don't think any of them actually came in for a watch specifically.'

'Neat trick.' Steve looked closer at the purple one, a more basic model that would do the job. 'Jess needs a new one and it's her birthday coming up.'

Leo took the watch out and went through its specifics. Jess was Steve's girlfriend, they'd been together for a while now and since he introduced her to surfing she'd been hooked.

'I'll take it,' said Steve once he had the details. He was already brandishing his card.

'Good man. Love an impulse purchase. And I've seen her surfing, she's pretty good, she'll love the gift.' As he popped the watch into another bag he asked, 'Has she persuaded you to try winter skiing yet?' That had been more her thing before she fell for Steve.

Steve raised his eyebrows. 'The lure of the sunshine is too much and let's hope it stays that way. Falling in the water is one thing, but falling on snow? Not for me.' He winced as though he could predict the sort of pain it might involve.

Leo took payment for both purchases as Steve talked more about surfing, using terms Leo was vaguely familiar with – well you had to be, working in the boathouse. Not that Leo was a surfer himself. He was much more of a kayak enthusiast or a paddleboarder. And he knew that with so much beauty around Salthaven and Stepping Stone Bay he'd never walk away from it all, no matter what life threw at him.

'You seen much of Adrian since he got back?' Another of Steve's usual questions when he'd exhausted the surfing conversation with a mere novice. He and Adrian had always been friendly.

'Just had lunch with him as a matter of fact.'

'Nice. I'm surprised I've not seen him down here though. Don't suppose he got that much surf or time out on a boat when he lived in Leeds; he needs to make up for lost time.'

'He certainly does.' And hopefully he would, eventually.

'When you next speak to him tell him I'm up for a beer any time. He needs to rediscover his love of living here.' The avoidance of the bay clearly hadn't gone unnoticed by Steve.

'I wouldn't phrase it quite that way when you see Adrian.' And then more seriously he added, 'Thanks for not giving up on him.'

'Never would. He's a local, a good mate, well thought of around here. But don't you go telling him I'm not giving up on him either or he'll think his little brother is trying to get people to be his friend.'

Leo laughed. 'You're probably right.'

Steve held his bag aloft. 'Better get home and hide Jess's present.' But he stopped before he reached the door. 'Talking of rediscovering the love for the bay, I'm sure I caught a glimpse of Nina yesterday.'

Any uncertainty disappeared when Leo nodded. 'It's very likely. She's around.'

'Back for good?' Steve wondered, leaning against the open door.

'No idea.'

Steve blew out from between his cheeks. 'That's three of them come back then.'

'Three?'

'You heard Maeve was back, right?'

'Actually I didn't, no.' Salthaven and Stepping Stone Bay were big enough that you could go about your business without everyone else knowing what it was, but if you kept your nose to the ground you could find plenty out. The problem was he was so busy he didn't have a chance to do that very often and relied more on people coming in here to keep him up to date with local goings-on.

'She's working in the café. The whole family is back in town,' Steve announced. 'They all had enough of the snow apparently,' Steve joked before he left Leo to it.

And after the door fell closed it made sense to him. His little helper, Jonah, with his Canadian accent was Maeve's son. Somehow she'd found a happiness and he was thankful that at least one of their friendship group had.

Leo had a steady afternoon after Steve popped in, but he managed to sweep most of the shop floor between customers, not lingering long near the front of the boathouse in case Nina walked past. And when Jonah came flying through the door just before four o'clock it was good to have the company. The boy chucked his backpack behind the counter as usual and talked at a rate of knots about how boring school was today. If Leo wasn't mistaken he was trying to avoid the inevitable question of whether his mum had given her permission for him to be here.

'Mate, slow down.' Leo stowed Jonah's backpack further under the counter so neither of them would trip over it. 'How was school really?'

'As I said, Boring. With a capital B.'

'Sometimes boring is good.' Leo would humour him for a bit before he started with the lecture. 'It's better than being terrible, awful, unbearable,' he added clutching his chest, making them both laugh with his amateur dramatics playing out as though he'd been seriously wounded.

Jonah reeled off the lessons he'd endured, although he also shared a funny story of one of his friends emerging from the toilet cubicle with toilet paper coming out of the back of his trousers. Poor kid, he'd never live that down.

'I told him before he went in the playground,' said Jonah. 'The other boys weren't going to, but I know what it's like being a bit different.'

'You seem normal to me.'

He shrugged. 'Still hard being the new kid.'

Jonah hadn't said much about anything other than he had come to live on the south coast after living his whole life in a completely different country and that he loved the water and one day wanted to learn as many water sports as he could.

Before Jonah persuaded him to allocate him a chore Leo asked, 'Did you talk to your mum?' He knew the answer as soon as he asked. 'We've talked about this. Call her, now.' He decided not to let on that he knew Jonah's mum was Maeve as it would sound as though he'd been doing some digging and didn't trust Jonah.

Reluctantly Jonah took out his phone and while he called his mum Leo saw to the couple who'd borrowed kayaks for a session who came upstairs to let Leo know they'd returned the water craft downstairs at the shed. Leo booked them in again for the same time next week and then went over to Jonah who took the phone away from his ear.

'She's busy and will call back,' Jonah told him.

'OK.' Leo could always call the café where he now knew she worked, but he'd give Jonah a bit longer, give him the benefit of the doubt, and then he'd have to take matters into his own hands. 'We'll try your mum again after I've sorted out the kayaks. Want to help me clean them?'

Jonah didn't need asking twice, he went and positioned the wooden sign out front of the boathouse while Leo locked up and they both headed down the internal stairs and through the shed to where the kayaks were waiting for them.

'You get the hose,' Leo instructed his young helper, 'pull it all the way out and you can be in charge.'

'Awesome!' Jonah yelled over his shoulder as he ran to grab the hose reel. He needed both hands to carry it back, but wasted no time unravelling it and connecting the appropriate end to the tap, ready for the job in hand.

Leo almost wished the kayaks were dirtier, Jonah was so obviously in his element. Once he'd hosed down the first and moved to the second, Leo took a cloth to work on the first one to dry it off and wipe up any remaining stubborn dirt, although there wasn't much at all, just a couple of odd bits of seaweed. It kept him occupied while Jonah took charge of the hose and it stopped him thinking too much about Nina, which was next to impossible to do. He was trying to tell himself that he was fine with seeing her last night, that his gaze out of the window of his own cabin hadn't stubbornly been drawn towards her place, that he wasn't wondering every minute since he'd seen her whether she was still there inside, or when she'd come back again.

'Le-o,' Jonah whined his name as though he might have had to do that a couple of times to get his attention.

'Sorry mate. You done?'

'Done.' He picked up another cloth and wiped over the second kayak the way Leo had done with the first.

'Let's carry them back in, you take one end, I'll take the other.'

'We could carry one kayak each. I'm strong.'

'You take that one then.' Leo pointed to the smaller of the two in a brilliant turquoise. And although he could tell Jonah was surprised at the weight, he let the boy do it by himself all the way over to the racks. Leo lifted the one he'd been carrying into its rightful place and when he pointed out the rack for the kayak in Jonah's grasp he could tell the boy was looking at the vessel and contemplating whether it was the right size for him. It was; Leo was expert at looking at someone without asking their height and knowing which craft would suit them the best. And if Jonah was anything like Leo the boy would start in something that size and quickly progress to the bigger kayaks when he got too tall for that model.

Leo was well aware that if you learned to be happy in the water at a young age, it gave you the confidence that could keep you safe in the years to come. He crouched down. 'Do you want to try calling your mum again?'

Sheepishly Jonah admitted he'd left his phone in the shop.

'Jonah, I don't want to be mean, but this is the last time you can come in until I speak to a parent. I know you like coming here and I like it too, you're great company and the best helper I've ever had.'

'I know, but you have rules.'

The way he said it made Leo laugh and he ruffled the boy's hair as Jonah's head dipped and he refused to look

Leo in the eye. 'I'll talk to your mum and if she's happy you could even stay longer on some days.'

But Jonah was shaking his head. 'Mum won't like it, I'm too close to the water being here.'

So that's why he was so hesitant to call his mum. And hearing those words saddened Leo more than he'd ever thought they would. Adrian had backed away from a life near the sea involving boats, Nina had left the bay behind and now it seemed Maeve had been affected in the same way. He was the only one who'd stuck around. He was the only one whose passion for the sea had never waned, and sometimes that made him sad, other times angry. Sometimes it made him guilty at the joy he got out of it despite the tragedy he'd witnessed. And he could've done with his brother, his girlfriend and friends nearby after it happened too. Yet they'd all dispersed and occasionally he resented them for it.

As Leo realised the gamut of emotions he swayed between on occasion Jonah told him, 'She's always happy for me to go into a swimming pool. She likes it and thinks it's safer with a lifeguard right there watching us. And I can swim too.' He managed a smile. 'Mum says everyone should learn to swim.'

Leo let out a breath. 'Your mum sounds like a clever lady.'

'She is,' he shrugged matter-of-factly. 'And I have a swimming lesson tonight once Mum finishes work. She's just funny about the sea.' A frown formed. 'It's not fair. Not when I really want to do things.'

The other couple who'd taken paddleboards out returned their boards and Leo put them in the appropriate rack spaces as they wrestled off the wetsuits they'd hired. They had a good laugh about it, the girl struggling so much even Jonah was giggling with her as she finally broke free. Jonah took the wetsuit over to the rack at the end of the shed and Leo hung it up with the others that were ready for cleaning, as the couple set off laughing along the sands.

'Why do they make them so tight?' Jonah wanted to know.

'If you wear a wetsuit that's too loose, cold water would constantly flush in and out and make you very cold,' Leo explained. 'There'd be no point wearing one. When they fit snuggly the rubber lets in a small amount of water which is heated by your body and becomes a layer of protection as it stays there. So between you and the sea you have the warm layer and the suit.'

'Can I try one on?'

'I need to get back up to the boathouse in case I have customers.'

'Pleeeeease Leo,' he begged, 'I'll try this one, it's my size.' He already had his hand on one of the wetsuits hanging on the drying rack, as though he didn't want to let it go.

And he was right. Leo had lent that particular one to another boy about his age who'd come here this morning before school with his dad. 'Go on then,' Leo relented. 'But quick, then I'd better get upstairs and unlock the boathouse again. And you can bring in the sign.'

Jonah immediately stripped off his shorts and t-shirt and with swimming trunks beneath in preparation for his lesson at the pool later on, he wasted no time stepping into the suit and trying to hoist it on. Leo didn't even have a chance to tell him that it was best to turn the top half inside out and sort the legs first. Jonah barely got it over one calf before his face began to turn a curious shade of pink with the exertion, he got it over his knee on one leg and then halfway up his thigh before he was laughing uncontrollably and unable to find strength from anywhere. He'd attracted a couple of onlookers too and by now Leo was laughing at Jonah who, as he'd tried to get the suit on, had hopped around so much he was out on the ramp in the sunshine.

'Take it off and start again,' Leo advised, although Jonah seemed to be having so much fun doing this and the laughter was a panacea to the mood Leo had been in last night and first thing this morning.

Eventually Jonah agreed and the wetsuit was off once again. 'Do I need a bigger size?'

'Nope, this one should be fine,' said Leo. 'Remember what I said.'

'Should be snug,' he recited, 'so it traps some water to keep you warm.'

'Basically, yes.' He'd turned the top half of the wetsuit inside out and handed it back to Jonah. 'Take it slowly, don't try to yank on the whole suit at once.'

Jonah still struggled, but it was far easier this time and with a bit of jumping up and down and jiggling it was on.

'Now you can zip it up yourself.' Leo took Jonah's hand to show him where the zip was.

Jonah pulled up the zip and his chest swelled as though this was the best present anyone had given him. And he was looking at the sea as though all he wanted to do was run down to the water's edge and straight into the waves to test it out.

Leo checked his watch. 'You only have twenty minutes before you need to leave here. You'd better start trying to take it off,' he joked.

'I want to test it out.'

'Not until I've spoken with your mum.' And now he knew who she was and that she was funny about the sea Leo wasn't sure how that conversation was going to go. 'If you get permission I'll take you into the water or in a kayak, whatever, but not until then.'

Jonah looked like he was going to sulk, but reluctantly nodded.

And Leo saw an opportunity. 'Back in a sec.' While Jonah was still transfixed by the water, at each wave crashing to shore, Leo went to grab the end of the hosepipe and turned it on him.

Jonah let out a yelp.

'You're testing it out!' Leo laughed. 'You'll be able to see how warm you are in it despite the water temperature!'

Jonah couldn't stop giggling, jumping about as the initial cold water hit the suit.

He and Leo were still laughing and Leo was about to help him off with the suit and get back up to the boathouse when Jonah's smile disappeared.

'What's wrong, mate?' Leo wiped his brow as he'd managed to splash himself quite a lot too.

And when Leo turned to face whatever had made Jonah go from fun-seeking to extremely worried, he saw a dark-haired woman marching across the sands. Maeve. And she looked furious as she tried to walk over as fast as she could, her feet unable to get proper purchase on the sand. Her sunglasses pulled down initially, she flipped them up as she drew closer.

She glared at her son. 'What on earth do you think you're doing?'

It was then Leo realised she wasn't angry, she was upset. She was shaking. 'He's all right, Maeve.'

'I've been worried sick, Jonah. Why didn't you answer your phone?'

'My bag is upstairs.' His voice quivered as he pointed up to the window of the shop area above the boathouse.

Leo was about to speak again but sensed he shouldn't, not yet.

'You're supposed to be at home after school before you come to meet me from work. I got off early and phoned you to tell you I was walking home and I'd be there soon.'

'Why did you finish early?' Jonah asked and Leo wondered whether the boy was worrying this would be the new arrangement rather than the fun he'd found himself without her knowledge.

'I'm working late tomorrow.' She shook away the question. 'And right now, my working hours aren't the concern. I panicked, Jonah. When you didn't answer, imagine how that made me feel.' She breathed in deeply either to calm herself or find patience from somewhere. 'You didn't text me to say you'd got home after school either.'

Jonah's voice trembled. 'I'm sorry. I forgot.'

'You can't forget! Ever!'

'How did you know I was here?'

'I tracked your phone when I didn't hear from you. At first I thought the location must be wrong but then when you didn't answer either I knew you'd come down here.'

Leo tried again to soothe the situation. 'It's OK, Maeve. He's all right.'

'Did you take him in the water?' she snapped as though she didn't even know Leo, as though he hadn't been part of a group of friends all those years ago, friends who'd been through a tragedy that had splintered them apart. The sea had changed everything that day and it had taken a little piece of all of them in one way or another.

'I promise you, I didn't,' Leo assured her. 'He just wanted to try on a wetsuit so I let him.'

She looked about to lose her temper with Jonah but instead pulled him in tight and whispered into his hair. 'You're safe.'

'Of course he is. I always keep him safe down here.' She might be wary of the sea but Leo begrudged her thinking he'd ever let a boy come to harm.

Maeve pulled back from her son and directed her question at Leo. 'This isn't the first time?'

Oops. 'I told him I needed to speak with you or he couldn't come down again.'

'Don't be angry at Leo,' Jonah begged. 'He asked me to tell you and I didn't.'

'Take off the wetsuit, Jonah,' Maeve ignored her son's pleas. She looked as though she was barely holding it together and she'd pulled her sunglasses back down, perhaps so nobody would be able to see if she was crying.

'I'm really sorry, Maeve,' Leo tried again as Jonah wrestled the suit off better than he'd pulled it on, and slunk off to put it on the rack with the others. 'I did ask him to contact his parents, his mum. He stalled.'

'He's good at that. It's a tactic I've learnt to look out for.' Her shoulders fell a little.

'I didn't really put two and two together when he first stopped by because I never knew you were back. I keep myself busy, but Steve told me you were in the bay just today. Welcome home.'

He ran a hand across his jaw, unsure what to say to defuse the situation. 'He's a great kid.'

'I know,' her voice wobbled. 'He's my whole world.'

And although he wasn't sure whether it was the right thing to do, Leo pulled her into a hug and felt her body relax against his as she sniffed away more tears.

Chapter Six

Nina

Walt was up and about before Nina and had been every morning since she'd arrived. She was staying with him for the time being, and then perhaps she'd go and stay at the cabin once most of the redecorating and cleaning up had been done. She loved his company and she was sure the feeling was mutual, but she never wanted to be an annoyance, so giving him some space might be nice all round. Staying at the cabin would also mean she was on site to show any potential buyers around when she listed the property for sale.

'Everything all right, love?' Walt asked when she finally surfaced and set about making herself some breakfast. 'I hope you're not wearing yourself out already.'

'Of course I'm not.' She dropped two piping-hot crumpets onto her plate ready to spread with butter. 'I'm enjoying time off work to be honest. It's been a while since I had a decent break and lie-ins seem to have become a habit already.'

He returned her smile. 'The sea air is doing you good.'

She spread the second crumpet before popping the lid back on the butter. Grandad might think her sleeping in was all about the fresh air down on England's south coast, but last night it had been more the tossing and turning and thinking about Leo since she'd bumped into him that had led to a lack of sleep during the night and therefore a bit of a catch-up in the morning. Being back here and seeing Leo after all this time had knocked her sideways in a way she'd perhaps known was coming, but had still taken her by surprise.

Walt sat down with a cuppa opposite Nina. She always felt as though she was about ten years old when she was here at his bungalow that had a sea view if you stood in the converted loft room and peered out of the very top left corner of the window. As a kid she'd loved to get a stool, climb up and see the sea. And now, at a modest five-foot-one, she could manage without the stool as long as she stood on her tiptoes. She'd looked last night, catapulted back in time when she caught a glimpse of the water. It reminded her so much of her childhood, being in the bay, at the cabin, here with her grandparents in their home. It brought back the good times, but also the sad times when she'd missed having a normal, intact family so much it hurt.

Nina's mum and dad had split up when Nina was almost an adult. Despite all of that moving around together and wanting to give their kids a stable future by not dragging them here, there and everywhere, they hadn't even lasted just the two of them. They'd made the announcement they were splitting up and each of them moved into separate houses with neither Nina nor William having any desire to go live with either of them. They were settled with Walt and Elsie, they had lives, they were no longer interested, especially if it meant choosing between parents. Nina and William had talked about it and neither of them wanted the drama that could occur if they chose one parent over the other, and Walt and Elsie had agreed – besides, they loved having both of them around and hadn't wanted them to move away. And Nina was glad she hadn't back then. And true to form, her parents had got on with their lives – their dad stayed in the forces and went away for long periods of time, their mum turned her attention to new relationships that never seemed to last. And Walt and Elsie, well they stayed the same, and Nina was pretty happy about that.

As Nina ate her crumpets and Grandad flipped through the newspaper at the table, Nina's eyes wandered over to a photograph of her with her gran. It was on the pinboard Grandad still had in the kitchen, the board that had been up for so many years Nina was surprised it was still hanging on by its hooks. Upon it were plenty of old pictures lingering along with postcards, little reminders, random bits of paper Nina wasn't sure all needed to be there. In the photograph with Elsie, Nina was holding an orange glass jar with a screw-top lid that her gran had bought for her at a time when she was missing her mum and dad, when school became a struggle, when she didn't feel good enough for anyone, when she had no idea of her place in the world. Grandma Elsie had told her that whenever she had a worry she should write it on a piece of paper, fold it up and slot it into the jar. Then when she screwed on the lid she would know she didn't need to think about the problems inside. Instead she was sup-posed to set aside a time to worry about everything she'd written down. They'd adopted a pattern of doing it reg-ularly at the start – Grandma Elsie would empty out the jar's contents, some bits they'd throw away as the problem had gone, other worries they talked about, and over time Nina found she needed the designated worry time a lot less and then eventually, not at all. But she'd kept the jar and its contents for a long while afterwards, adding in her worries whenever she needed to. Even though she didn't necessarily go through them again after the worry went into the jar, she'd found the very act of writing down the things that bothered her therapeutic and like ridding herself of a weight she no longer needed.

One day Nina and Leo had been playing Jenga at her cabin and when it had been him who pulled out the block that caused the tower to come tumbling down he'd crawled under the bed to retrieve the few pieces of wood that had been scattered beneath and discovered her orange jar.

'What's this?' Leo had asked, pulling out the orange screw-topped jar filled with little pieces of paper.

'It's nothing.' She took it from his hands and ran to the kitchen, where she pushed it into the back of the cupboard.

'Why won't you tell me what it is?' he'd asked, mouth downturned. She hated keeping a secret from him. She never usually did. They'd told one another everything back then.

'If I tell you, you promise not to laugh?'

'Promise.' He held out a little finger for her to link with her own, their promise between friends.

She mumbled just loud enough for him to hear. 'It's a worry jar.'

'What's a worry jar?'

She hardly knew what to say. She was embarrassed. She was nine and she'd let him see how bad a swimmer she was when he glided through the water at twice her speed, he'd seen her cry when she fell over, which happened at least once every summer and usually left a big graze on her knee that took time to heel. He even knew she wet herself once when he'd made her laugh too hard. But she'd never told him her deepest thoughts.

'I worry about things a lot,' she shared eventually. 'Grandma told me if I write down the worry and put it in the jar then I don't have to think about it any more, not until the special worry time.'

He contemplated her explanation. 'Does it work?'

Nina shrugged and flicked her long blonde plaits over her shoulders as she sat cross-legged opposite her best friend in the whole wide world.

Leo went over to the little table in her bedroom and tore off a piece of paper before locating a pen and wrote something.

'What are you writing?' she asked him.

'A worry,' he said as though it were obvious.

'Are you going to put it in my jar?'

He folded the paper up and looked at her. 'Am I allowed?'

She paused, but then unscrewed the jar and held it out to him.

'When will worry time be?' He still clutched the piece of paper.

'It used to be once a day. But I don't have it any more. I just write my worries and put them inside. It helps,' she added and it seemed to do the trick because he dropped his piece of paper into the jar.

After that day Nina and Leo had used the jar, but swore to one another they wouldn't look at what was inside without both of them being present, and gradually the jar had been used less and less and then one day they'd decided the best place for worries was the bottom of the sea and so they'd got rid of it for good.

Nina finished her crumpets. She hadn't thought about that jar in a long time. If she had it, she'd definitely have put a piece of paper or two inside about seeing Leo after so many years. Not only had she bumped into him and had the most awkward conversation ever, but she'd seen him on the beach with a woman and a young boy. Her grandad had never said he'd settled down but maybe he'd wanted to spare her more pain. And after twelve years she really shouldn't expect anything different. She should be pleased for Leo, he'd always talked about a future with family in it, but given their history it wasn't easy to accept now, even though she knew she should try.

Over at the pinboard Nina looked at more of the photographs and everything else pinned to this spot on the wall. 'How many of these pieces of paper have been on here for years, Grandad?'

Walt chuckled. 'Probably too many to count. I should have a clear-out, shouldn't I?'

She peered at one long piece of paper. 'You've got what has to be a receipt here that's so faded all I can see is the name of the supermarket at the top.' She plucked it off. 'Permission to chuck?'

'Go ahead.'

'And here's another, and another!' She shook her head as she moved along from left to right retrieving useless pieces of paper. 'Grandad, this is shocking.'

'You're here to sort the cabin, not this place.'

'I can make myself useful though. Earn my keep.'

'You're better use at the cabin, the sooner it's done, the sooner we can get it sold.'

The reality sunk in that little bit more with his eagerness. 'Are you really sure about this, Grandad? I mean, are you really willing to part with it after all this time, given what it means to you, to the family?'

'Nina, we've been through this. It's the best way. It's not used anywhere near as much as it should be and with your brother living in another country it'll be used even less.' She couldn't disagree. He cleared his throat. 'I want to be prepared, Nina. Me and your gran talked about this a lot, what would happen when only one of us was left.'

Nina could well imagine. If there was an award for being practical it would've gone to her grandma, who had a no-nonsense way of looking at things. When Christy left her children in their care so often and it seemed as though she had a new boyfriend every five minutes, Grandma Elsie hadn't moaned about it, she hadn't tried to change matters; she and Walt had carried on with Nina and William and injected as much happiness into life for them both as they could.

Grandad was right. It did make sense to sell the cabin when it wasn't used much at all and when Walt could have the extra money to ensure he stayed right here in his bungalow. But Nina found she veered from being happy it was going and that the past would be the past, to wanting to cling on to it and keep it in the family the way they'd always talked about. Grandma Elsie may have wanted both her and Walt to live in the bungalow for the rest of their days and do whatever it took to make that happen, but Nina could also remember a time when her grandma had said it was a real shame Christy wasn't interested in the seaside cabin because it would always be special to all of them. As a young girl Nina had assured her gran that nobody would ever take the cabin from the O'Briens, she was adamant that one day she would take her own children there to play out their own adventures the way she had. But that had been when she was able to dream, when life didn't seem to have any consequences, before she'd left the bay behind.

Nina moved along to the next space on the pinboard and found a couple of menus for restaurants that no longer existed in Salthaven or Stepping Stone Bay and when the doorbell went, Nina threw those into the recycling bin along with the old receipts. 'I wonder who that could be.'

'If we answer, we might find out.' Walt barely looked up from his newspaper.

Nina went to answer the door and broke into a smile when she saw who it was. 'Camille, it's so wonderful to see you.' She'd barely got her words out when Leo's grandma wrapped her in an enormous hug and a pleasant amount of summery floral scent. Nina sensed Walt had left her to get the door on purpose.

'It's lovely to see you too.' She had hold of both of Nina's hands now, looking into her eyes. 'You look well.'

'Is that Camille?' came Grandad's voice.

Camille bustled inside and Nina closed the door after her. Although she'd seen Camille a handful of times when she'd come back to see her grandad, she still didn't have much of an idea what to say to a member of Leo's family because the cloud of her leaving Leo hung over her on a permanent basis. But Camille didn't seem ruffled by her reappearance in the bay this time, or indeed the previous times, and in fact seemed to be carrying on as usual chatting away to Walt, which was nice. Her grandad had a good friend in Camille. He might have lost his wife but he had company and the thought warmed Nina right through that Camille had stuck around rather than drifted away as she so easily could have done when things didn't work out between her grandson and Nina.

As Walt and Camille continued to talk at a speed Nina couldn't quite keep up with – they were talking about someone's rabbit that had gone missing but was found this morning, alive and well – Nina put the kettle on, and from the assortment tub of biscuits she'd brought for her grandad, she laid out a selection onto a plate.

'Do you still live nearby?' Nina asked Camille as the kettle reached its crescendo and she positioned mugs and dropped in teabags. It occurred to her that every time they'd seen one another she'd never really asked Camille many personal questions. She'd felt it too prying when she wasn't a part of their family any more. Of course she never had been officially, but she'd been with Leo for so long she'd honestly felt a part of it and when she left him she'd had to walk away from the rest of them too.

'I'm around the corner in a little bungalow now I'm all on my own. No sense having that big house when there's only me.'

'You must miss Malcolm.' She'd sent a card when she heard from Walt that Leo's grandad had passed away. She'd donated to their nominated charity too, but apart from signing her name on any correspondence she hadn't given any extraneous details. All she'd wanted to do was let them know she thought of them despite her absence.

'Thank you, dear. It's been six years now, but the pain of loss never goes away completely. It lessens a little and for that I am grateful.' Camille shared a look of understanding with Walt that told of the dedication and depth of love they'd both felt for the people who'd been taken from them.

Nina remembered something special about Camille. 'How's the fudge-making going?'

Walt laughed. 'I'm surprised I've got any teeth left the amount I eat. She's forever bringing over new flavours for me to try. Some better than others.'

Camille laughed along with him and looked to Nina. 'Yours and Leo's favourite was always—'

'Salted caramel,' Nina and Camille finished together.

'Oh his mum used to have a fit that I gave you both so much,' Camille chuckled. 'She said you'd both have cavities before you were ten, false teeth by the time you were thirty.'

Nina pointed to a full set of teeth she'd had straightened in her mid-twenties. 'Still all there and happy to report no fillings.' In her mid-teens she'd resisted all attempts from an orthodontist to straighten her teeth and finally decided to go for it after university when she realised he'd been right all along. The braces had been off for some time now, but she still appreciated the difference they'd made.

'I'll make some fudge and bring it over to you,' Camille decided, her matronly figure a testament to her love of the kitchen and the delicious food she created in there. 'If you're hanging around in the bay that is.'

'I will be for a while yet.' She wasn't sure whether Camille was fishing for information or not. 'I've the cabin to sort.' But she didn't miss the look between Camille and her grandad, a look that suggested they'd talked plenty about her and Leo and what might have been.

'Talking of the cabin,' Nina went on, gathering herself and leaving them where they sat. 'I'd better get down there. There's plenty more to clean before I can even think of getting out a paintbrush.'

And all she hoped was that she wouldn't bump into Leo again for a while, never mind his girlfriend or son. It still felt odd that Walt hadn't told her, but again she realised perhaps he'd done it to protect her, although a heads-up might have been nice.

Chapter Seven

Leo

Leo kept looking at the door to the boathouse as he stood at the counter, having just closed it to take payment for a surf leash, but Jonah still hadn't come in after school the way he usually did. And the hour Jonah usually spent at the boathouse went slower than ever as Leo wondered whether the young boy would ever be allowed to come down here again.

Maeve had taken Jonah home yesterday as soon as Leo had walked them both inside to retrieve Jonah's bag from beneath the counter and reopen the shop. Maeve had barely said another word to either of them and Leo had kept his mouth shut too. That night of the party on the boat was a part of the past they all shared – Leo, Maeve, Adrian, Nina, others too although they'd drifted on with their own lives, and they were forever bonded in a way none of them had either predicted or wanted.

Despite Maeve's fury, or fear, or a combination of both emotions yesterday on the beach, Leo had hoped Jonah would show his face again today. In fact, Leo's mood sank that little bit more every time the door opened and it wasn't Jonah. He'd grown accustomed to the young boy's company and chatter and help around the place. And so once he'd turned off all the lights at the end of the day and locked up, instead of going home he decided he'd make his way to the little café at the end of the pier. He could do with a long walk anyway and hearing Maeve say yesterday that she was working late he thought he'd go and talk to her, not just about Jonah, but because she was back in town after all this time and with the drama on the beach it hadn't really been the time for a normal catch-up.

The drizzle continued as he walked away from Stepping Stone Bay, down the hill into Salthaven town and turned left to head along the pier. The Victorian lamp posts elegantly lined the way and Leo passed the ice-creamery now closed for the evening, the shop that sold beach bits and bobs, and carried on all the way towards the end and the café that had sat here for as long as he could remember. Come winter this place would be a cosy escape, and even now, as summer faded away for another year, it was a place of solace for the locals. Save a paintwork touch-up and a new sign, as well as a few little alterations inside the café, not to mention a change of ownership, this place was a town favourite and felt the same as it always had.

What Leo hadn't expected was to see Jonah sitting inside the café as he arrived. He'd assumed Jonah would be at home under the watchful gaze of a childminder or grandparent, but here he was sitting in the corner with school books opened out in front of him; but when his eyes lit up at Leo's arrival Maeve intercepted any interaction between the pair.

'What are you doing here?' She was a pretty young woman with dark hair, eyebrows neatly shaped and a naturally olive complexion. The frown she had on her face now didn't suit her at all.

'I've come in for a coffee and a pastry after a hard day at work.' He hunched his shoulders as though it were obvious. She hadn't been back all that long, so she wasn't to know he didn't do this all the time. He did it occasionally but to be fair, he wouldn't be here now if it wasn't for their strained encounter yesterday.

'I'm sorry.' She closed her eyes briefly, a dirty plate in one hand, a glass with the dregs of a juice in the other after she'd cleared a table. 'I'm being rude. Forgive me and please, sit wherever you like.'

He waved at Jonah but sat closer to the counter away from the boy until he knew what was what. And Maeve didn't miss it.

She wiped down his table. 'You can talk to Jonah, I don't mind. He likes you.'

'You sure?'

She managed a tentative smile. 'I'm sure. Go ahead.' She motioned to Jonah that it was all right to come over and reminded Leo that there was a specials board to broaden his choices of what to eat and drink.

Leo smiled at Jonah as he came and sat with him. 'What would you recommend?' They looked over to the board next to which was another board filled with postcards from locals' holidays over the years. It was jam-packed as it was and Leo wondered how they ever fitted anything new on there.

'I had a chocolate brownie – Jo's are the best,' Jonah advised.

'You know, I think I've earned a brownie today . . .' Leo recited his order to Maeve and added on a coffee. 'I had to work doubly hard with no helper.'

Maeve seemed about to lecture him but her lifted shoulders dropped down. 'I worry about him, he's eleven, spending time with a strange man definitely wasn't on my radar. Not that you're strange.' She pulled a face, and shaking her head went off to fulfil the order.

'I'm glad she doesn't think I'm strange,' he said conspiratorially to Jonah. 'Do you think she'll ever let you come back to the boathouse?' he asked more quietly when Maeve disappeared into the kitchen section at the back of the café which was compact but well-organised with a counter at the front, a selection of different-sized tables with chairs and a window seat with plenty of scatter cushions.

'Don't know, she was pretty mad.'

When Maeve brought over the chocolate brownie she must've sensed what they were talking about. 'He can come down after school,' she told Leo.

'Are you sure?'

'He can go to the boathouse but I'm not ready for him to go in the sea with anyone.' She gave Jonah a look that suggested she wouldn't tolerate any protest. 'He's having swimming lessons, I'd like him to be a really strong swimmer before he tries out anything else.'

'Understandable,' Leo replied.

When she went to fetch his coffee Leo turned to Jonah. 'So it's not a case of *never*.'

But Jonah had spotted a friend outside when there was a knock on the café's window and was already on to his next request. 'Mum. Can I go and hang out with him? I've done all my homework.'

'Go on then,' she softened as she brought over Leo's macchiato. 'But stay on the pier, don't go down to the beach,' she called after her son.

Leo admired the fancy shape drawn in the froth on top of the coffee. 'It must be hard.'

'What, the design on the coffee?' She was toying with the cloth in her hand, one eye outside beyond the window watching her son.

'Coming back, settling in to a new town for Jonah, parenting. Is his dad around?' He already knew the answer and he'd obviously hit a nerve, because she muttered that no he wasn't and that was it, conversation over. And so while Jonah was outside he devoured the brownie which was as good as he remembered they'd always been when Molly had been in charge, and enjoyed the coffee, failing to catch Maeve's attention again until finally she walked past at the same time as Jo served the next customer and Jo told her to take a ten-minute break. She had no choice but to sit with Leo now or seem rather rude.

'I should make sure his homework is in his bag.' She looked over at the table her son had abandoned in his haste to sit with Leo.

'Or let him do it when he comes in. Not many people in here and plenty of tables.'

Finally she slumped down in the chair, her excuses exhausted. She looked shattered, perhaps from the move, or the day at work or attempting to juggle parenthood with everything else. 'Again, I'm sorry.' She covered her eyes with her hands but took them away when Jo, without having asked, delivered a big mug of milky tea and set it down in front of her new member of staff. 'I'm being really rude to you, I know I am, Leo,' she went on when Jo left them to it. 'I really don't mean to be.'

'Are you going to blame it on being used to a big city

rather than a small town and bay on the south coast?' But he was smiling when he said it.

Sighing she said, 'No, I'm going to blame it on being a miserable cow.'

'Glad to hear it, the honest truth.' He got a smack on the arm for that but it broke the ice and they talked about her time away from here, her time in Canada, about Jonah and her desperation for this to be the right move for the both of them.

'I know I'm not the only one who left Stepping Stone Bay,' she said when they'd exhausted the topic of schools and problems with kids settling in when they had to change from one to another.

'You weren't. Nina left. Adrian too.' And now they were both back.

'I think a few of us bottled things up.' She shook her head. 'There was plenty left unsaid.'

He didn't pry into her remark. But she was right. As a group of friends, they'd been happy one minute and then the next? They'd all tried to move on in whatever way they could.

'You never left,' she said to him. 'You've stayed all this time.'

He nodded. 'I'd always wanted the boathouse my parents ran, my grandparents before them. I didn't see how I could pick it up and take it anywhere else. So I stayed.'

'It must've been hard for you when none of us did.'

He didn't want to lie. Now seemed a good time for honesty. 'I resented all of you for a long time.'

'And now?'

If it had only been Nina to leave he might've found it even more difficult to think about it logically, but over the years, especially watching Adrian's life evolve as he became this different person to the brother he knew, he'd managed to see that they had all coped in whatever way they could. It hadn't been easy to think of it in those terms; it had taken a bit of coaxing from his parents to understand everyone else's points of view, a bit of accepting he might need to think more deeply about the very people who'd left him to it. Eventually he'd come to realise that his way of coping had been to stay, whereas theirs hadn't been, and thinking that way kept him relatively sane.

'Now I'm not interested in going backwards and making demands.' Not with Maeve anyway. 'I'm not going to give you a hard time, don't worry.' When she looked relieved, rather than question her and her motives he offered up more details about his own life, his brother's. 'Adrian wanted the business once upon a time.' He shrugged as though he couldn't do much about it. She'd always been easy to talk to and it was one of the things he'd missed when the group of friends fragmented. Maeve might not have been a close friend prior to that night but talking to someone else who had been on the boat was always going to mean more than talking to someone who hadn't witnessed the same tragedy.

She set down her mug, the tea all gone. 'It's sad he no longer wants it. I know you're both close. Everyone in the bay kind of assumed you'd both be running it together for the rest of your days.'

He smiled. 'Me too. But it was always something there for us in the future. You know what it's like when you're young, you're having fun, you're not making solid plans. It's as though we all took tomorrow for granted, then with one night, one terrible night, we all got to see what a privilege growing up actually is.' They shared the understanding that Rhianne hadn't got the promise of tomorrow, her life was over before she got to do much at all.

'After the accident I was numb,' Leo confided. 'I didn't know what to do, but staying in the bay was easier than going. And then my parents were heading into retirement and it was time to take the reins. And so I did it solo.'

She fiddled with the handle of her mug. 'You must be glad Adrian is back in the bay though.'

'Yeah. The family is pretty happy.'

'But . . .'

Leo met her gaze. 'He's here, that's the main thing for now, but he's not back to his old self. I'm not sure he ever will be.'

She cleared her throat. 'When I was in Canada my mum heard that he was in a really bad way after what happened.'

Word had travelled across the miles. 'He was a mess, I can't deny it. Don't tell him that if you see him – even though he knows it, he won't like gossip.'

'I get it.'

'He took a long while to get his head straight, a really long while, and as I said, he's not totally back to the Adrian I remember, it's as though he's being cautious even after all this time.'

She contemplated what he'd told her. 'I suppose the only advice that feels right is to not give up on him.'

His words to Steve echoed in his ears, the way he'd thanked the man for not giving up on his brother. 'I won't.' He relaxed some more. 'Coming here was a massive step, so it tells me he's going to be right in the end.'

'It sounds like it,' she smiled back at him.

'I'm hoping he'll come into the boathouse business eventually.'

'Isn't he a teacher these days?'

With a grin he said, 'Yeah, and I think he's probably good at it. But I never thought he'd take an inside job when he could be out there.' He tilted his head towards the window that had an idyllic sea view no matter the season. 'I worry about him all alone in his flat, not venturing out much.'

'Alone?' She seemed confused. 'I heard he got married.'

'He did. Divorced now though.'

She pulled a face. 'I'm sorry to hear that.'

'Don't be, it wasn't the best match with his wife.' Adrian and Rhianne had never been a good match either. Rhianne was a bit of a wild card and she'd even given Leo a few clear signs she was interested in much more than friendship with him despite her involvement with his brother. She might have meant it as harmless flirting, but Leo hadn't been comfortable with it at all and it wasn't exactly the makings of a relationship when one of you was attempting to play around with someone else in your group of friends, never mind their brother, no matter whether it was only ever meant to be a bit of fun.

Talk turned to Maeve's parents, his mum and dad, extended family and then Stepping Stone Bay and Salthaven and what had changed, as well as what had stayed the same, as though frozen in time. 'This place for one,' said Maeve looking around them both. 'It's had a bit of a facelift but it's as sturdy as the pier. I hear the town still gathers to watch the fireworks on bonfire night every year.'

'That they do,' Leo smiled. 'I usually make it down here, but the boathouse is a pretty good vantage point to watch too and I can also see the big bonfire up in the fields beyond the bay.'

They moved on to talking about the boathouse, the shop part of the business and the tuition he offered.

'You must think I'm helicopter parenting with Jonah,' she said, a bit embarrassed.

'Hey, it's not for me to judge. He's a great kid, so all I know is you're doing a good job as a mum.'

'You don't think I'm crazy for being so worried about him and the sea? I mean, he's a good swimmer, getting stronger by the day.'

'We all cope differently when something bad comes our way.' He stopped short of telling her that Adrian, three years older than him, never went in the sea any more despite it being ingrained in him through family and his upbringing. Adrian was a strong swimmer, a proficient sailor, but what had happened had left an emotional scar that cut deep and his way of coping was to stay well away from the water in case it swallowed him whole.

'I'd better get on,' Maeve got to her feet. 'Thanks, Leo. For the chat. I felt terrible the way we left things yesterday after I lost my temper. And then again today I was rude when you came in. Forgive me?'

'Forgiven already.' He followed her as she took her empty cup out to the kitchen and he waited at the counter until she emerged. 'Is Jonah in a lot of trouble?'

She made a face to indicate Jonah coming through the door. She took payment from the boy Jonah was with for a can of cola and dropped money in the till for Jonah to have an orange juice and with them both ensconced at the table at the rear where Jonah shoved all his books and papers back into his backpack, she told Leo, 'Not too much trouble, no. But as well as emptying the dishwasher each morning which is his usual chore, he has to help me prepare the dinner every night next week and he's to come to the café straight after school rather than go home on his own.'

'Sounds fair.'

She made sure they wouldn't be overheard by her son. 'As I said, Jonah can come to the boathouse again, but he'll have to see out the week first. And I really don't want him in the sea, not yet, and certainly not with the nights drawing in and the—'

'Maeve.' Leo stopped her, his voice low like hers so Jonah wouldn't know what they were saying, 'I heard you when you asked me not to take him in the sea earlier. Whatever rules you have, I'll abide by them, you don't have to worry. But I like his company, he's welcome any time. As long as you are ready.'

With an air of relief she smiled. 'Thank you, Leo. That's good to know.'

He waved across at Jonah who gave him a hopeful wave back and when he winked he thought he might have seen Jonah's eyes twinkle as he hoped the same, that he might soon be back at the boathouse.

Chapter Eight

Nina

Nina started her morning by washing down the walls in the lounge area with sugar soap. She couldn't even remember the last time they were painted, let alone cleaned. Then again, who cleaned their walls on a regular basis? She certainly didn't. There were cobwebs in the corners, dirty marks here and there, and outlines from where a couple of pictures had been. Those pictures were now stacked ready to take to a charity shop. Both scenes of the sea with boats, they were too dated for the look Nina wanted to give the place ready for sale.

She screwed up her face at the sight of the filthy water lurking in the bucket, the same it had been on her last cleaning stint here. Three walls down, one to go. She left the cloth on the kitchen bench top, retied her ponytail that kept working itself loose and picked up the bucket to get rid of the water. She'd tip it outside this time, watering the small patch of grass at the front of the cabin that didn't add all that much, but at least injected a nice green if the grass was looked after.

At least being busy stopped her thinking about Leo and whoever he might be involved with now and her face broke into a smile the moment she stepped out onto the veranda because not only had the sun graced them with its presence, but her grandad was meandering down the slope towards the cabin arm in arm with Camille.

Nina tipped out the water. 'I thought I was crashing here to give you some space.' She gave him a big hug. 'Don't tell me you're missing me already?' She'd come here armed with an airbed and a sleeping bag along with a pillow so she could sleep here from now on and get cracking this morning with an early start.

'We thought we'd come and support you,' said Camille. 'We parked at the top of the track and walked down.' She let Nina link Grandad's arm instead of her and brandished a container.

'You've brought treats?' Nina quizzed.

They stopped by the cabin and Camille opened up the lid of the container she had to reveal what was inside. 'Salted caramel, especially for you.'

Nina's tiredness she'd felt after tackling those walls abated at the sight of the fudge. 'You didn't have to go to any trouble.'

'No trouble at all. I enjoy making it and I can't very well eat it all myself. Well I could, but I shouldn't.' She indicated a second plastic container in the bag looped over her shoulder. 'I'll just take this lot over to Leo's, he loves it too, remember.'

How could she forget? And when she heard his name it made her think of his reaction when he'd seen her for the first time in so many years. She hated the hurt she saw, the resentment. And she couldn't blame him at all.

She led Grandad inside the cabin. 'I'll get cleaned up and we'll have some fudge and a cup of tea. Sit on either sofa,' she encouraged. With a re-cover they'd look good as new and she could spruce the furniture up even more if she added cushions in a variety of designs.

In the bathroom Nina scrubbed her hands clean, and back in the kitchen wasted no time flipping the brand new kettle she'd bought yesterday on to boil before taking a crumbling block of fudge from the container to pop in her mouth. She closed her eyes as she chewed and when she opened them again Camille was back. 'As good as I remember,' she complimented.

'It's been a few weeks since I came here to check up on the place,' said Grandad as Camille accepted Nina's offer of a cup of tea. He looked around. 'It always brings back such wonderful memories whenever I'm here. It smells clean already.'

'Funny that,' Nina chuckled. 'And we did have some wonderful summers didn't we?'

'You kids had a ball down here,' Camille put in as Nina handed her a cup of tea. 'Me and Malcolm were busy running the boathouse most of the time when we were in charge, then helping out when we passed it down a generation, but I remember spending my lunch hours and the after-school hours making sure none of you got up to too much mischief.'

Nina hoped she wasn't blushing at the comment. As youngsters it had been a case of watching her and Leo so they didn't get into trouble in the water or so that neither of them climbed the trees that were so high that if you fell it would be a disaster. But Leo and Nina had also been caught making out when they first moved from friendship to something more and Nina would rather forget the look of absolute horror on Camille's face walking in on her and Leo in bed together.

'I was exhausted most of the time,' Grandad chuckled, rescuing Nina from any further scrutiny from Camille. 'We'd watch you here, playing outside or we'd take you to and from the beach. But it was good for us. Elsie and I always agreed that having you kids around so much kept us young.' He winked. 'I loved every moment.'

'Me too.' She proffered the container of fudge.

'Oh no, you enjoy all of that. I've had plenty.'

She treated herself to another piece. She supposed there were benefits to your parents being so busy with this, that and the other that your grandparents took over. It formed a bond that was everlasting, special and something Nina had always treasured in the absence of a closeness with either of her parents. They weren't estranged, they spoke, albeit infrequently, but something had been lost along the way. Or perhaps it was because she was so close to her grandparents that it was hard for anything or anyone else to measure up ever again. And whereas Walt and Elsie had always been a support and encouraged her with whatever she wanted in life, Nina had always felt as though she had to strive to be better for her mum and dad. She'd always blamed herself that she must've done something along the way for them not to want her enough.

Nina took her grandad through her plans for the cabin. She'd already talked about what she planned to do, but with him here now it was far easier for him to visualise.

'Seems a shame to be doing it all for someone else,' said Camille as Nina described the changes she envisaged.

Nina agreed but she didn't want to make her grandad feel bad. 'If Grandad wasn't selling up then the cabin would probably stand here neglected for even longer. It wouldn't be doing its duty as a beautiful abode by the sea.'

Walt nodded. 'It wouldn't, you're right Nina. And I wholly approve of your ideas, it's going to look wonderful. We'll get a buyer in no time.' When he exchanged a look with Camille, Nina had to wonder whether he was really as OK with the sale as he claimed to be when he spoke to Nina or William, or whether he'd confided something different to his friend. She really hoped not. It was all well and good going down memory lane inside the cabin and wishing things were different, but that wasn't going to pay the bills. The sale was a practical solution, it couldn't be emotional, not when he really needed the money for his future, if it would make him feel safe and secure. And there was a lot to be said for anything that could make you feel that way.

As they drank their tea they moved out onto the veranda to discuss the cabin some more, its surroundings, all the while Nina conscious Leo might be close by if he was home, although Camille's speedy visit suggested she might have left his container of fudge at his door because he wasn't around.

Walt recalled a particular game of hide and seek with the kids and the time Leo and Nina had hidden so well he'd begun to panic when he couldn't find them for almost an hour.

'My heart was in my mouth,' he admitted, 'it wasn't a good feeling at all.' Hand on his chest he advised her never to try it with little ones. 'I only found you in the end because Elsie had the bright idea to call out "Doughnuts!" at the top of her voice. That got you coming out from your hiding places and we took you straight to the bakery in town to buy you the biggest doughnuts we could find. I've never felt so relieved seeing your little faces.'

'I remember,' Nina laughed. 'I was wearing a white t-shirt and it it was filthy on one arm from where Leo and I had hidden beneath an overturned boat and then I got jam from the doughnut all down the front.'

'Leo was always getting dirty,' Camille shared as she looked over in the direction of the boathouse. 'He's never been a neat freak. Neither has Adrian.'

Nina had heard from her grandad that Adrian was back. 'How is he?' Camille was looking out at the bay and Nina sensed that much like hers, Adrian's return hadn't been a case of coming back and picking up where he left off.

'He's not too bad. Divorced, although those two were never right for each other anyway, and at least he's home. Leo sees a bit of him but he's yet to come down here to the boathouse or the beach.'

As she listened to the lapping of the waves against the shore in the distance Nina understood his reticence to come this way. It must've been a huge step to return to the area as it was. She wondered whether he'd ever be able to enjoy sailing the way he once had. She wondered whether he'd battled the water in the way she had herself, not wanting to go in, knowing how treacherous the sea could be, how it could change just like that. She could still remember how distraught he was the night Rhianne drowned, because he'd been the one to try to save her. They'd all told him not to jump in the water, it was dangerous, he could've died too, but he'd ignored all of them and had tried in vain to find Rhianne, but couldn't. It was the coastguard who'd finally dragged her body from the water. And by then it had been too late.

'I hope he makes his way down here eventually,' said

Walt diplomatically, a support for Camille whose eyes misted over.

'Me too.' Her sprightliness had given way to a dulled version of the usually upbeat woman. 'It's a shame, a real shame. That boy was all about family. All about the water, sailing, boats.'

'He still is,' Walt assured her. 'He's just a bit further away from it all at the moment. Not physically, but in his head. He'll get there, I know he will.'

Camille patted Walt's hand that had landed on her shoulder. 'I admire your certainty, so I'm going to choose to believe it too.'

'Grandad is right, I think he'll get there too,' Nina encouraged.

When Walt asked whether Nina wanted to join them both for lunch in town Nina shook her head. 'I really want to keep going with the cabin today. I've got the walls to finish, scrubbing the kitchen, the bathroom. All the boring stuff has to be done before I can even think about painting.'

'Don't you forget to eat properly,' said Walt as they took their empty cups inside.

'Grandad, you worry about me too much. I'll probably treat myself to afternoon tea at the café on the pier.'

'That sounds like a good idea. You might catch up with Maeve.'

'I will do if she's there.' She wouldn't mind seeing someone else who'd left and then come back. Perhaps the solidarity would help her feel less like she was sticking out like a sore thumb around here.

Walt picked up the light grey jacket he'd worn here and pulled it back on. It was still decent weather for September but catch the breeze in a certain direction and it was nippy. 'There'll be storms later on though, could you call me to let me know you're safely back at the cabin.'

Nina was about to assure him that of course she would when Camille patted him on the arm and said, 'She's a grown woman.' But she understood. 'A text message will be enough, don't you think?'

'It will,' Walt admitted. 'And I'll see you for dinner tomorrow night?'

'Of course.' She kissed them both goodbye on the cheek and turning to go back into her cabin, she caught a glimpse of Leo's place and thought of the fudge Camille had left there. The veranda was a sun trap no matter the mild temperature and the fudge might be ruined if Leo didn't collect it soon. And inside, when she sneaked a piece of her own fudge, she didn't want Leo's tub of sweet treats to spoil and waste Camille's hard work.

The least she could do was go and make sure it was in the shade. She was being kind, neighbourly.

Outside she stepped onto the first stepping stone that linked her cabin with his and although they were only steps, thirteen in total, it was like a tiny piece of her heart cracked that little bit more at what she'd lost when she moved from one stepping stone to the next. When she got there she took the steps up and pushed the container to the farthest part of the table which was out of direct sunlight and she smiled at the little paper note his gran had left on top of it beneath an elastic band. It simply said *To my Leo*. Like Nina, he was close to his grandparents. The only difference was, he had his parents too, whereas hers were disinterested at best.

As she turned to go back to her own cabin, Nina's eyes

fell on the windowsill the other side of the window, or namely what was sitting on top of it, angled enough that she could see what it was. It was a photograph of *The Wildflower*, Adrian's boat, the same boat they'd all been on that night for the party. Nina wondered whether it was still kept at the marina a short distance on from Stepping Stone Bay. She wondered, did Leo go out on it? She shuddered at the thought as the past washed over her once again, at the same time as the crashing waves she could hear beyond the cabins and the boathouse where Leo must be now, either in the shop or down below, instructing, cleaning craft, working with his hands the way he'd always wanted to. She admired him for his strength, the way he'd been able to stay here when she, Maeve, Adrian, all three of them had left the bay behind. Nina couldn't remember everyone who'd been on the boat that day; some of them she'd not known well at all, and she wondered whether part of the reason was that she tried to blank out the memories as much as she could.

Back in her cabin Nina finished wiping down the lounge walls; she scrubbed the kitchen surfaces, put bleach in the sink to get the chrome clean and shining once again, and it was time to sort herself out a bit.

She pulled on a pair of jeans that didn't show the dust and grime from this morning and grabbed her teal cardigan, given the slight chill in the air that came along with September as the onset of autumn approached. It was time to get out and about in Salthaven, head held high, and stop avoiding it the way she'd been doing up until now. If she was going to enjoy her time here even a tiny bit, she had to get used to people seeing her face. And so, car keys in hand, she went to the car and set off up the road to where it joined the main street that would lead down and into Salthaven and all the way to the little café at the end of the pier.

Nina should've known when Molly and Arthur weren't in their home in Spain, they would be here in Salthaven, even though they'd retired from the café and left their granddaughter Jo in charge. And she should've known they weren't going to let a local who'd been away for more than a decade get away with a simple passing hello.

'I thought they'd never let you go,' Jo laughed when Nina finally went inside the café.

'Your grandparents are lovely, I don't mind at all.' And it was true. In fact, it was something she hadn't had in a really long time, having locals interested in what she was doing, and she found that although she was hungry and couldn't wait to see what was on Jo's menu, talking to Molly and Arthur had given her a tiny sense of coming home. Up until now she knew of course that this was where she'd grown up, but feeling it, absorbing the warmth of being welcomed back, was another thing entirely.

'When are you due?' she asked Jo, looking at her healthy baby bump.

'Mid-December, so a way to go yet. But thank goodness I've had Molly and Arthur stepping in over the summer when it's crazy busy, and I've taken on some full-time help.'

'Good for you.' Nina knew Jo had her hands full with this place and with one-year-old Ava because Molly and Arthur hadn't only asked about Nina, they'd volunteered lots of updates on their own family and shared their own stories since their retirement – the way they lived between Spain and the UK, rotating every six months; how they couldn't believe how much Ava changed even between FaceTime calls, let alone visits.

'Now what can I get you?' Jo asked her.

Nina put a hand to her tummy as she perused the specials board and decided on the cheese and bacon quiche along with a garden salad and an apple juice. As Jo went off to make the order she picked up a magazine from the collection on a shelf at the side of the main counter and sitting back with her fresh juice when Jo brought it over, she flipped through the pages of the glossy gossipy publication and began to relax.

Every time the door opened she could hear the sea, the cry of the gulls, locals chatting their way up and down the pier. And when the door went yet again as Nina finished her last mouthful of quiche she realised this time it was the newest member of staff arriving. The woman hurried behind the counter, then hung a cardigan in the cupboard to the side of the kitchen and tied on an apron as she had a brief conflab with Jo who soon afterwards, bag slung over her shoulder, smiled at Nina and told her she was nipping into town to meet her husband, Matt.

'Say a hello from me,' said Nina. Everyone knew who Matt was, his family owned the local fruit and vegetable farm and he was a familiar face in town.

'Will do.' And with that she left her assistant to look after the café.

'Can I get you anything else?' A voice came from over Nina's shoulder.

Nina turned. 'Maeve,' she smiled, 'it's me, Nina.'

'Nina!' She finally registered who her customer was;

obviously Jo had had other things on her mind other than updating her employee on specific clientele. She flung her arms around Nina as Nina stood. 'I heard you were back, it's great to see you.'

Nina felt her own emotions surge. 'And you too, welcome back. Although I'm sorry to hear your mum's sister wasn't well. How is she?'

'She's getting better, I think having Mum around has helped a lot.'

'Good to hear.' They smiled at one another as Nina sat down again and straightened her cardigan.

'I meant to come and find you and say hello before now but I've been crazy busy, what with the job, Jonah . . .'

'Who's Jonah?'

Maeve smiled, long, dark hair that was tied back into a low ponytail snaking across her shoulder until she pushed it away. 'He's my son.'

'Of course, I knew that. Grandad keeps me up to date,' she explained. Life really had moved on. Maeve, a mother; it was hard to fathom. And when Maeve took out her phone to show Nina a photograph of her little boy Nina's mind clicked. 'Were you both down at the boathouse yesterday by any chance?'

Maeve pulled a face. 'You didn't see me screeching at poor Leo did you?'

'I didn't see that, no.' She'd only seen them hugging and that had been enough. To think Leo had a son had been a shock to the system, to see a mini-Leo standing right there with him, wetsuit on and ready to go in the water. But now she realised the boy couldn't be Leo's because Maeve had left around the same time as Nina had and everyone had known how Leo and Nina felt about one another. Nobody else had been responsible for destroying that other than Nina herself.

'I mean, I really overreacted,' Maeve went on, talking hurriedly as other customers filed in. 'I didn't want Jonah in the sea, it scares me, because . . . well you know.'

'I do know,' she said sympathetically, her heart still fluttering at the realisation she'd jumped to a pretty huge and incorrect conclusion when she'd seen Leo and Maeve together. And although she had no right to lay any claim to what Leo did or didn't do, she felt nothing but relief. Which made her a bit selfish, and for that she was slightly ashamed. 'Go, serve your customers, we'll catch up once they're sorted.'

'Can I get you anything first?'

'A glazed doughnut please, you've no idea how much I've missed those.' Molly and Arthur had always done such wonderful doughnuts and Jo's were likely to be equally as good.

'Coming right up.' Maeve seemed just as pleased to see Nina as Nina was to see her.

Nina's first bite of the doughnut brought back the memories of sitting in here many a day after school, a hot chocolate or a coffee along with a doughnut, plain glaze or with sprinkles added. And the sweet treat now, after all these years, still made her tastebuds dance with every bite.

When the rush of customers eased, Maeve wiped down the table that was vacated next to Nina and with one eye on the door for anyone else coming in they caught up, told one another a bit about their lives since they'd left the bay. Maeve told her all about the cold in Canada, how she'd loved the feel of an exciting new city to live, but how her parents had missed Salthaven and the bay and her auntie's call had come at the right time. She told Nina that her parents had also, bizarrely, managed to buy back their old house.

'Obviously meant to be,' said Nina, looking out of the window as the sun went in and ominous clouds began to gather. The rain wouldn't be too far away. She wrapped her hands around the mug of tea Maeve had made her and looked across at her friend. She wondered why Maeve hadn't mentioned Jonah's father as they talked. Was he even in the picture? Was he still in Canada and missing out on being a dad now they'd left?

'We've both been away for so long,' Maeve sighed as though the weight of it all was still on her shoulders.

Nina nodded. 'Twelve years. And I still occasionally dream about that night.'

'Me too. Why do you think I'm so scared to let Jonah in the sea?'

'I would be too. Whenever the weather clouds over, whenever a storm rolls in, no matter whether its close by or the other end of the country, it reminds me of that night and I breathe a sigh of relief when it's over.'

'Leo says he'll keep Jonah safe at the boathouse if I let him go down there.' She briefly explained how unbeknownst to her her son had found something to occupy himself after school. 'He sounds as though he loves it there, he helps out too.'

Nina's heart lifted at the mention of the kindness from Leo, the man who had once been the love of her life and who would make an amazing father one day. Already with Jonah it sounded as though he was getting some practice in. 'Leo wouldn't let anything happen to Jonah.'

'He'd be careful, I know,' Maeve nodded. 'But I'm not ready yet.'

'So don't rush, take it slowly.' She knew it was hard, she hadn't wanted to go back in the sea for a long time after that night and she only had herself to worry about. She couldn't imagine what it must be like to have the responsibility of a child, especially given what they'd all witnessed.

'That's one of the reasons I left, you know,' Maeve said absently as her gaze drifted to the window. 'This town, Stepping Stone Bay, both are beautiful. But every time I looked at the sea and its beauty I was reminded of its cruelty and how it took someone from us.' Her voice caught and it was a few beats before she said, 'I didn't know Rhianne as well as you and the others, but it still got to me. I still wonder how it could've happened. Should one of us have noticed she'd gone overboard before we actually did? Would it have made any difference?'

'It's always easy to ask those sorts of questions.'

'Not so easy to answer them though.'

Nina sighed. 'No, it really isn't. I bet Adrian asks himself whether he could've swum harder and found her.'

'He did his best. The water was treacherous that night; there was no way, she was found quite a distance from our boat, as the current had taken her.'

Nina shook her head, closed her eyes. 'Out of everyone, the tragedy had to have affected him the most, it was his boat, he'd jumped in the water and couldn't find her. I can't imagine what that would've felt like for him.' She'd been too busy trying to fathom her own feelings, her own need to get far, far away from everything.

'He should never blame himself.'

'No, he shouldn't.' And just like that, as though both

of them had needed to for a really long time, they finally talked about that night. Nina hadn't discussed it with anyone, not in detail, and yet here they were in a local café after all this time recounting the night that had haunted them both ever since, the process surprisingly cathartic.

Nina and Maeve both recalled Rhianne making a huge fuss about wearing a buoyancy vest. 'She said the colour didn't match her top.' Nina smiled now in the confines of the café with Maeve. 'She made me laugh, you know what she was like about fashion, she always liked to look her best. I'd always ask her opinion on clothes if we were going out, her advice on an outfit if I was unsure. Anyway, I told the boys she had a point when she said the orange clashed against the red, but I stopped laughing when Adrian clearly didn't find any of it funny.'

'I don't remember him being annoyed.'

'He wasn't annoyed so much as frustrated. Understandable, he was skipper, safety was his priority. Rhianne was out for fun, she thought it was a bit of a laugh talking colour schemes.'

'She was a bit drunk, but then we all were. I remember someone making a joke that we were at a party and we weren't exactly white water rafting.'

Nina didn't remember that. 'Like I said, it might have been a party, but safety was his main concern.'

'Rhianne seemed like she was a lot of fun,' said Maeve, 'but I didn't know her all that well.'

'She was what I'd call high-spirited, she'd always see the best in a situation, I'll give her that. She never took life too seriously and I often wished I was a bit more like her rather than worrying about things all the time.' She pulled a face. 'Do you remember her laughing as she walked the narrow edge of the boat from the deck at the front around to the cockpit at the back? She made it look so easy, but none of us dared to try.'

'I would've fallen in for sure.' Maeve's smile turned to a frown. 'I've never forgotten the fear in Leo's voice as he came from the helm where Adrian stood to tell us all that a storm was rolling in from nowhere.'

'Me neither.'

'When I saw the way he was reacting, Adrian too, I started to get really worried.'

Nina nodded. 'I figured we'd get wet and maybe feel a bit unwell if the boat rocked. I don't think any of us were prepared for how quickly weather conditions would change and what that would do to us.'

Adrian had wasted no time turning to head back to shore after that, but trying to tell a party of youngsters who had beer in their bellies as well as a desire for fun that they had to make a sensible choice was next to impossible. Half of the party-goers had removed their buoyancy vests and Leo was picking them up from the cockpit, handing them out, imploring people to put them on, telling them the water was getting rough, hold on to something or you were going to go in.

'I'd been out on the boat with Adrian and Leo plenty of times before,' said Nina. 'It had always been wonderful. I'd lie on the deck in the sun, or I'd read a book, we'd been rained on before but it had been refreshing rather than scary. But that night . . .'

Maeve shivered as though she were right back there. 'I loved a good storm before that night, I'd get excited watching the grey clouds tumbling over one another in the sky, the flashes of lightning, the rumble of thunder. But now I hate it.'

'Adrian and Leo kept us as safe as they could.'

Everything had happened quickly once the Magowan brothers both grew more serious and conveyed the urgency to get back to shore. Up until that point the boat had been gently rocking side to side in a way that felt almost pleasant, like kicking back in a hammock after too much fun and food and being able to drift off a bit. But then suddenly it had been replaced by a fierce movement, yanking them one way and then the other and everyone on board had started to realise the seriousness of the situation; a few of them had looked close to vomiting with the motion of the craft. Nina remembered gripping the rail closest to her so tightly her knuckles turned white. Her hands were cold, wet, slippery, and she'd closed her eyes hoping she could hold on. And she'd only opened her eyes when she heard yelling. At first she'd thought it was a girl screaming and then she realised it was Adrian. He'd seen Rhianne go over the side. Leo had taken control of the boat, he'd killed the power, he'd called the coastguard, yelling above the din of the storm and all of them, knowing Rhianne was missing, had scoured the waters from onboard.

'I told Adrian not to jump in after her,' said Maeve. 'If he'd been quicker . . .'

'We all told him not to,' Nina assured her, 'don't think it was you who delayed him, your fault he couldn't find her. She went over quick enough and the current was too strong. It's a blessing he's as strong a swimmer as he is, or at least was, otherwise he might've died that night too.'

Maeve covered her mouth and tears sprang to her eyes as they both remembered the shouts, the voices muted when gusts of wind made yelling inaudible, the rain lashing against their faces making it next to impossible to see, the instability of the boat making everything that bit worse as the brutal seas did their best to capsize the rest of them.

Nina could remember the moment Leo stumbled over the buoyancy aid Rhianne had eventually put on and that he'd found sloshing about in a pool of water at the back of the boat. She was most likely so inebriated she'd taken it off, and while it had been a joke that it didn't match her outfit, the way they'd laughed along with her suddenly hadn't been funny at all. And all they could do was stare at the murky depths as Leo and a couple of the others helped Adrian back onto the boat when it became obvious that the water was winning against them and it was up to the coastguard now, as their boat drew closer, the lights almost blinding them with their beams searching out for the missing member of their party. They'd sent out a helicopter too but it was all in vain.

Rhianne had gone. In the water far too long to be revived by the time she was found.

Nina took a deep breath, fingertips stemming tears in the corner of her eyes when she realised she was about to cry. 'I'm sorry, Maeve. I didn't come in here today with the intention of upsetting either of us. I haven't seen you in forever, this was supposed to be a nice catch-up.' She smiled at the irony. 'This is the total opposite.'

Maeve wiped her eyes too. 'I'm just glad the customers haven't needed me.' She looked around to check that was still the case. 'And I think I actually needed to talk, so

I'm glad we did. Plenty of time to catch up after today, if you're hanging around.'

'Yeah, I'd like that.' Nina wondered whether Maeve had kept this all bottled up just like her. 'Have you talked to anyone else over the years? Your parents?'

Maeve shrugged. 'Not really. Not since the day after it happened when I told Mum and Dad. None of us lot really even talked at the funeral either, did we?'

'We were all too messed up, numb even.' Nina had felt like an imposter that day, like she had no right to be there with Rhianne's broken-hearted parents who surely must put some of the blame on the rest of the crowd on the boat that night.

'I can't get my head around what it must be like for Rhianne's parents,' said Maeve. 'Rhianne has gone, we're all still around. It doesn't seem fair.'

'No, it doesn't. But they've managed to stay living here and according to Grandad they seem all right, happy even. I've no idea how. And perhaps "happy" isn't the right word.'

Maeve's face contorted. 'I don't know how any parent could possibly carry on after that. I mean, if anything happened to Jonah . . .' She went over to turn on the lights inside the café as the skies darkened beyond the windows.

'It doesn't bear thinking about.' And Nina felt terrible too that she'd upset Rhianne that night on the boat, having a go at her when she looked like she was making a move on Leo. They were friends, she should've known Rhianne was doing nothing other than flirting, but the alcohol had gone to Nina's head and she'd been quite spiteful with her words. It broke her heart that their last conversation hadn't been a nice one. And whenever she'd looked at Rhianne's parents on the day of the funeral the argument had echoed in her ears and she'd felt wretched.

Maeve went over to serve a local who requested a slice of carrot cake and when she came back she asked, 'Have you seen Adrian since he got back?'

'No I haven't, but then again I've kept myself to myself. His gran told me he's not been near the sea or the boatshed though.'

'His whole life was boats, the water.'

It was incredibly sad to think that not only had Nina hurt Leo, he'd had the pain of losing what he had with his brother. She had no idea whether Adrian would ever get that part of himself back, but she hoped so for his sake and for Leo's.

Nina smiled. 'You've got customers again.'

'Won't be a sec.' Maeve served a group of teens who came in for takeaway milkshakes.

Nina switched the topic of conversation from tragedy to something more pleasant when Maeve came back over: 'I still can't believe you have a son.'

'Neither can I sometimes.'

'Are you with Jonah's dad?'

Maeve looked a little panicked, but answered pragmatically, 'No, we're not together.'

Married? Divorced? Nina's eyes naturally fell to Maeve's left hand and her ring finger which had nothing on it.

'Talking of men,' Maeve smiled before Nina could ask much else, 'What happened to you and Leo? You were love's young dream, I always thought you and he would get married, have kids; you know, the whole white picket-fence dream.'

Nina was glad of the light-hearted tone even though they were talking about Leo. It was easy with Maeve, they'd both been away, they both understood the pain from that time, the need to escape. It helped that they'd talked so openly already, not something Nina had expected coming to the café today. 'It was my fault,' she said. 'I left without much of an explanation.'

Maeve nodded as though she understood that it wouldn't have been easy. 'Are you back for good do you think?'

'I'm not sure what I'm doing to be honest. I came to sort out the cabin, but with my brother living abroad, I already realise that I'd like to be closer to Grandad.'

'That makes sense.'

'I don't know,' Nina shrugged. 'I need to think about my options.'

Maeve looked out beyond the window. 'I wasn't sure about this move myself but I didn't want to be without Mum and Dad and I knew deep down it was the best thing for Jonah. I can't avoid the sea forever.'

'I loved it as a kid, being so close to the beach, so for what it's worth I think you've done the right thing for your little boy.'

Maeve smiled but soon flipped the conversation back to Nina again. 'I heard from Jo that Leo is still single.'

'Don't get any ideas.' And Nina wanted to hug Jo for coming in right at that moment and Maeve rushing to her side to take all her bags.

'What on earth have you bought?' Maeve asked her boss.

'Baby clothes. Matt made the mistake of leaving me at the shops.' She shrugged, smiling across at Nina before announcing she'd be broke if anyone let her go near any baby clothes shops again.

Nina left them to it and before she headed back to her car she ventured along the pier right to the end. This was a great vantage point to look out to sea, and although her heart thumped at the sight of the weather changing around her, she suddenly felt compelled to be out here, to take it in a while longer, to face a fear of a weather change she'd once found fascinating, stunning even.

Aside from one fisherman who was packing up, his wax jacket flapping in the wind, there was nobody else around and Nina stared out at the sea as the waves became more choppy, white-tipped as they answered the skies up above. Seeing the sea always brought with it memories, and as the wind picked up some more and the fisherman bid her a goodnight she knew it was time for her to go too. She wanted to be tucked up in her cabin by the time the storm arrived and so she waved at Maeve and Jo as she passed the café once again and set off along the pier before climbing into her car and heading for the road that would lead down to the bay and the two cabins.

And this time when she reached the first cabin she didn't feel quite such a pain stabbing away inside her chest. Going to the café today had been the best idea and it felt good to have rekindled a friendship with Maeve already.

But when she saw Leo's cabin beyond she knew she had a long way to go to feel comfortable around here. She'd hurt him terribly and wondered whether he'd ever let her be a friend after what she'd put him through.

Somehow she seriously doubted it.

Chapter Nine

Leo

L eo woke up in the middle of the night drenched in sweat, the sound of a branch from the nearest tree banging against his window in the ferocity of the wind. It had been a long time since he'd dreamt about that night on the boat, but the nightmare had left him spent the way it always did when it came to haunt him. And it had a different ending that left him reaching for the glass of water beside his bed, the images fresh in his mind as though it were yesterday and as though the ending were real.

When the weather had turned that night, the partygoers had had enough alcohol to find it funny at first, not entirely taking it seriously, but as conditions rapidly worsened all of them realised it was no joking matter. He remembered taking control of the boat while Adrian insisted everyone put their buoyancy vests back on – some of them already had, thanks to the rocking of the boat – and then Leo had found Nina and sat next to her. She'd had her eyes closed tightly, clinging on to whatever was in reach. He wanted to hold her and comfort her, but it would've been stupid not to hold on to something himself. A couple of partygoers looked as though they were about to spew, and Leo suspected a few of them would before they got back to the marina. Things had rapidly got worse. Adrian was yelling Rhianne had gone over the side. Leo picked up the radio and called for help, Adrian had chucked the life ring over for Rhianne, although nobody could see her, and then Adrian jumped into the water himself.

Their carefree trip with friends had turned into the stuff of nightmares.

The nightmare Leo had just woken from had finished not only with losing Rhianne, but his brother too, Adrian unable to make it back to the boat.

Now, safely inside his cabin twelve years after the event Leo could hear the storm that had probably seeped into his psyche despite his dry bed, the safety of the cabin's walls, the stability of the ground, and caused the dream to resurface.

He went into the kitchen area and ran the tap to fill another glass with water and when he heard another crash outside he looked out to see one of the branches from the tree he'd climbed as a kid had been ripped off and smacked onto the table on his veranda.

He looked over towards Nina's cabin, knowing there was a tree right next to her bedroom window. He had sudden thoughts that it might crash through the glass, but was she even there? His gran had left him a note with the fudge to say they'd brought Nina some too, implying she was, but was she staying overnight? Was she having a nightmare like he was? Did she even do that any more, or had she put the past behind her and was able to sleep like a baby through a storm?

His heart pounding, he pulled on a pair of tracksuit pants, a fleece over his bare chest and ventured outside.

He took the thirteen steps from his cabin to hers, steps that had never meant so much as now, when he thought she might be in danger. He'd take a peek inside, see if there was a sign she was there, and if not he'd just go back before the wind knocked him sideways. The rain had already soaked him through even on the shortest walk known to man.

And then he heard a yelp, and when he looked in the window her face was right up close on the other side. He wasn't so bad at lip reading that he couldn't tell what she'd said and it almost tickled him that she'd said the 'f' word when she hated it. It had always made him laugh when they were teenagers, the age everyone thought it was funny to use foul language, and still she'd insisted on saying 'fudge' or at worst, 'flipsters'.

'I'm sorry!' he yelled, but she'd disappeared.

He was about to head back to his cabin when he heard the door to her cabin open and when he turned she was peering out at him from her position on the veranda, a long mauve cardigan wrapped around her body, her bare knees showing.

'I'm sorry,' he called out again, 'it's just, the storm . . . I didn't know if you were here.'

'What are you doing creeping around in the middle of the night? I heard something and you scared the crap out of me.'

Another funny thing was the day she announced to her grandparents that she knew what the C word was – their faces had fallen until she spelled it out – c-r-a-p. And they'd collapsed into laughter, hugging their granddaughter to them.

'Once again I apologise.' This time he yelled it louder,

as the wind howled in protest at anyone daring to come outside while it had its say. 'I couldn't sleep, thought I'd check on you.' But he shook his head. They were nothing to one another any more, she'd made that clear when she left without a word. He held a hand up to wave and began to retreat, embarrassed he still couldn't rid himself of the nightmare that came back now and then like an old reel of film stored in the attic brought out and replayed when you least expected.

'I couldn't sleep either.' Her voice stopped him from stepping onto the first stepping stone and he turned to face her, her smile coy, her expression cautious as though she didn't know how much to reveal. 'The storm,' she added by way of explanation as if he needed it.

'Yeah.' By now he had rivulets of water running down his face, and his fleece would need squeezing out when he got to his cabin. 'The storm.'

He wasn't sure how long they stood that way, him getting drenched, her in the relative safety of the cabin's veranda, slender legs showing out of the bottom of her cardigan which was firmly held against her body by her arms folded across her chest. But long enough until she said, 'Goodnight, Leo. Thank you for checking on me.'

'Goodnight, Nina.'

He turned and took the stepping stones back to the safety of his own cabin where he left his sopping clothes in the bathroom, dried himself off and slept an uninterrupted sleep until the sunshine woke him in the morning as though nothing had ever happened.

Since the night of the storm Leo had seen Nina on and off, and rather than dirty looks or avoidance, they'd slowly begun to wave at one another, sometimes offering up a cautious smile, and there was even a cordial hello the time he was putting out his rubbish and she'd just come back from a walk. He hadn't tried to make her talk other than those brief greetings and she hadn't encouraged him either, but with their tentative exchanges Leo had begun to feel less angry at her for leaving or at least more comfortable in her presence now, he wasn't sure which. He'd even begun to think fondly of the days as kids when they'd first met, nostalgia winning with the reminder of the day they'd met by the water when they were six. Nina had made a magnificent sandcastle and the waves rolled in and destroyed it. He'd seen her, this girl crying beside the sandcastle's remains, and he hadn't said much other than asking her whether he could help rebuild it. She'd accepted the offer and they'd been friends ever since, way before it got more complicated.

What Leo was asking himself now was whether he was only interested in friendship with her or did he still have deeper feelings, the feelings he'd thought he'd buried a long time ago? And would she ever explain why she left him the way she did? Did she regret doing it and wish she hadn't now they'd seen one another? He supposed he'd always known that one day she'd probably show up in the bay again, or at least he'd assumed she would, but he'd also thought he'd have no problem ignoring her and not questioning much about her and her life the way it had turned out.

In the boathouse he refocused on his customer. He didn't have time for daydreams, to think of what might have been and what could still be, only time for business, something he could control to a better extent. 'Good choice,' he told the woman who'd come in today and picked out a neon green buoyancy vest he'd only just had delivered. 'Nice and bright, it'll keep you safe.'

'Hopefully I won't need it,' she smiled, 'I'd like to stay in the craft if I can.'

The kayaker went on her way from the boathouse and Leo removed the plastic from the other vests he'd got out of the box but hadn't had a chance to sort through. He hung like colours together, in size order, even though they wouldn't stay that way for long, and by the time he'd finished Jonah had shown up.

'Good to have you back, sport.' They high-fived and Jonah's smile was as bright as the buoyancy vest Leo had just sold.

Leo, comfortable to have Jonah here now he not only knew that a parent was aware of his whereabouts but that that parent was Maeve, reiterated that Jonah would be helping out, but staying away from the water until his mother was ready. Jonah seemed happy with the arrangement and knew he had to be patient, and while Leo had promised Maeve they wouldn't go near the water, he wouldn't hold back on his enthusiasm for the sea and talking to Jonah about whatever he wanted to know.

'Let's get to work,' Leo told his young helper. He took a pair of scissors and slit open the top of another of the boxes, this time a smaller one, that had come in the delivery. 'Could you hang these waterproof phone covers up for me?'

'Sure.' Jonah took the box while Leo unpacked a box of t-shirts and organised those on a rail. It was good to have his comrade back, he'd missed the company.

Once the new stock was sorted Jonah swept up and

wiped down the glass cabinet by the till, Leo took a couple of calls and bookings for paddleboards, and by the time he had to lock up the boathouse to go down and take return of a couple of kayaks it was almost time for Jonah to go. But not before he positioned the sign outside to let customers know where to find Leo.

Leo locked up the top of the boathouse and was about to wave Jonah off before he went to retrieve the kayaks when he saw Nina, the sunshine highlighting her blonde hair in a way that was a sudden reminder to him of what it had been like when they'd take a boat out, just the two of them, not a worry in the world it had seemed.

'Did you walk to the paint shop?' he asked her as Jonah shrugged on his backpack. She looked as though she was struggling with a couple of paint tins, one in each hand, tugging her arms downward with their weight.

'Yeah,' she sighed. 'Could've been a mistake,' she added, shifting each tin in her grasp.

It was the most they'd really talked since they'd begun to be civil to one another. The dream he'd had, or rather the nightmare, had acted as a bit of a reminder that no matter how much he'd been hurt since she left, he was alive and so was she, so was Adrian. And knowing that had the power to rein in any anger and allow him to be much more of a glass half-full guy rather than the opposite.

He didn't ask permission, just stepped towards her and scooped both paint tins from her hands. 'Let me.'

'Thanks. I thought the exercise would be good,' she said, 'but it turns out paint tins that don't feel too heavy at first, really do after twenty minutes.'

Jonah had followed Leo over to Nina and Nina smiled. 'Hello Jonah.'

'You two already know each other?'

'We met the other day near the end of the pier when I was out walking.'

'I was meeting Mum,' Jonah explained. 'What are you painting?' he asked Nina.

She pointed to her cabin. 'This place. I need to get it all shipshape ready to sell.'

'Why are you selling?' Jonah rambled on as Leo led the way over to the O'Brien place.

'I have to, it's for my grandad and he needs the money now he's a bit older.'

'If this cabin were mine,' said Jonah as they reached the steps leading up, 'I would want to keep it forever. It's right near the sea.'

'If I could, I would.' As she said it her gaze locked with Leo's and he wondered whether she'd been thinking of all the memories they'd made there too.

As talk turned to what colour she was painting the walls and the ceiling Leo set the paint tins down inside the front door.

'I love painting,' Jonah went on. 'I could help. I helped Mum paint my room in our apartment in Toronto. I want to paint my room here but we're renting so I'm not allowed.'

'No, I don't suppose you are.' Nina looked to Leo. 'Can you spare him from the boathouse? I've heard he's been your little helper.'

Leo smiled. 'He's finished up with me. But you'd have to check with Maeve as he's supposed to go and meet her.' He looked to Jonah who was hovering, waiting for an answer. He suspected all the kid had lined up was sitting in the café waiting for his mum to clock off.

'I'll give her a call.' Nina had already pulled her phone out from her back pocket. 'We had a long talk in the café the other day and swapped numbers.'

'That's nice.' What else could he say? That he wished they'd been able to do the same?

'It was really nice to see her after all this time.' She scrolled through her phone contacts.

'I'm glad you talked.' Leo told her. 'Can you believe she has a kid?' He ruffled Jonah's hair and the boy ducked away but laughed. 'A good one too.'

But all Jonah was interested in now was stopping the grown-ups from talking and having Nina call Maeve for permission.

The fact that Nina had been to the café, a local haunt, pleased Leo. It meant she hadn't completely written off the town and the bay. Part of him knew he was leaving himself open to hurt by being hopeful, by being kind to her, but being an arse wasn't going to help, was it? Especially when he didn't really know how he felt any more, something he wouldn't have laid claim to this time a few weeks ago when Nina O'Brien had been gone long enough for him to assume he'd never have feelings about her again.

'I'm sorry, Jonah,' said Nina when she'd called Maeve's number and heard it ring a number of times. 'I don't want to leave a message on voicemail, best to speak with her first. Make sure she's happy for you to be here.'

Jonah shrugged and took out his own phone from his backpack. 'She's working, she'll answer if it's me.'

Nina smiled at Leo. 'Didn't think about that.'

Jonah made the call and passed the phone to Nina. It was nice, hearing the relaxed tone of Nina's voice, the way he remembered her.

'She says yes,' Nina told them both when she ended the call. 'She'll pick you up from here in an hour and a half.'

'Cool.' Jonah zipped his bag up again after popping the phone inside.

'There's some orange juice in the fridge,' Nina told him, 'go help yourself and we'll get to work.'

When Jonah went inside Leo leaned in closer to Nina so he wouldn't be heard and did his best to ignore the smell of the same perfume he'd inhaled up close for years. She was still wearing it and it was still just as tantalising. 'Are you sure about this? You don't mind?'

'Don't worry,' she confided, her blonde hair brushing against his face, they were so close, until she realised and took a step back. 'I won't let him loose on anything major until I know where his talents lie. Nothing that can't be painted over again very quickly and easily.' She put her thumb up when Jonah called out that he needed to use the toilet in her cabin.

'By the sounds of your phone call you and Maeve are getting along well.'

'She's nice, I can't believe we lost touch.' And she looked at the ground when she realised what she'd said.

'Nina, it was a long time ago. I wasn't pleasant when I first saw you—'

'I took you by surprise.'

'You could say that.' A moment hung between them. 'But we're both adults. And I don't want things to be unpleasant while you're here.'

'Me neither.' Clearly relieved she asked, 'Any sign of Adrian coming down here?'

He shook his head. 'Unfortunately not, but him being back in town is a start.'

'It sure is.'

'Mum and Dad still worry about him a lot but I know they're relieved to have him down this way.' It felt good to have someone to talk to about Adrian, someone who understood. He tried not to say too much to his parents as he didn't want to worry them any more than they already were, so he kept up the positivity about his brother whenever they asked. And it wasn't a lie, he felt sure Adrian was on a good path now.

'You know,' said Nina, 'the three of us couldn't have timed our returns any better, we've all shown up in the space of a few weeks.'

He began to chuckle. 'That's true. Funny how life works out sometimes . . .'

'Yeah.'

'I'd better get back.' He hooked a thumb over his shoulder to indicate the boathouse.

Leo left Nina and Jonah to it and headed down to take return of the kayaks. He gave them each a good clean and once they were safely stowed in the shed headed back up the grassy slope to find Nina and Jonah carrying out a small bookcase.

With no customers waiting outside the boathouse Leo went over to join them. He'd be able to see the entrance to the shop from here anyway so he could run over if he was needed.

Jonah was kneeling on the groundsheet Nina had laid out flat beside her cabin and he was already dipping his brush into the tin of paint Nina had opened.

'It'll need a couple of coats,' Nina instructed before reminding Jonah that there was another glass of juice on the step for him when he got thirsty.

'He's not afraid of a little hard work is he?' Nina confided as Jonah got to work. 'Maybe you could come back tomorrow if Mum agrees,' she suggested to Jonah.

'Can I?' He was delighted with the suggestion.

'Of course. You could do the second coat yourself if you do.'

'Cool.' He said it without looking up this time, his forehead creased in concentration.

Leo and Nina sat down on the steps of the cabin so that Leo could see the boathouse from his position and they could keep Jonah company. Nina had offered to take over but Jonah was having none of it.

'I was going to paint the bookcase at the same time,' she said quietly to Leo so Jonah wouldn't hear, 'but he insisted I let him do it himself. I've plenty to get on with inside but I thought I'd supervise out here for a little while first.'

'He's a great kid,' said Leo. 'He's meticulous when he's helping me at the boatshed, I reckon he'll do a good job with whatever he turns his hand to.'

The sun warmed their backs as they sat there and Nina turned a little so her body was almost facing him so she could lean against the railing. She had on rolled-up jeans exposing slender ankles, a white shirt that looked old and well-suited to painting and with the buttons undone at the top he could see the softness of the skin on her neck, skin he knew what it felt like to kiss.

'It must be tough being a single mum,' Nina contemplated as they watched Jonah, whose enthusiasm didn't wane.

He ran a hand across his jaw. 'I can't imagine how Maeve does it.'

'Do you know anything about the father?' Nina wondered.

'That's girl talk, she's not likely to tell me is she?'

'Good point. I wonder if he wasn't good to her, maybe she had to get away, that's why she's back.'

'We shouldn't speculate. But again, it's not something she'd talk to me about.'

'Maybe in time she'll talk to me,' said Nina. 'For now I guess she's making the best of it, doing what she can for Jonah.'

'Growing up here is great for a kid like him.'

'More independence than in a big city, although she's wary of the sea.'

'I think her being here is good for that too. I think slowly she'll fall back in love with it.' He gulped at his choice of words that could easily be referring to Nina and him, not just Maeve or the mighty ocean.

But Nina didn't seem to have picked up on his discomfort. 'Maeve seems scared of the water and I get that. I was for a long time. I hope you don't mind the question, but is Adrian scared too?'

'I don't mind. But no, I think his avoidance is more about guilt than fear.'

She nodded, understanding. 'It must be really hard for Maeve, as I know she doesn't want her fear to become Jonah's.'

'She and I have talked and cleared the air, but did you know she went off at me when she found Jonah trying on a wetsuit on the beach?'

'I heard she lost her temper. I think she was a bit embarrassed.'

'I should've asked him more questions. It's a bit odd, a

young boy coming to help out a man in his shop when the man knows nothing of him.'

'It's not odd if you know you, Leo. You're not some weirdo.'

'Thanks for the vote of confidence.'

'So why did you let him help if you thought it was odd?'

Leo shrugged. 'Because he reminds me of myself at that age. I loved going in to help Mum and Dad, especially if it got me out of doing any school work. Like Jonah I was happy sweeping up, doing the boring jobs, as long as I was around anything related to the beach or water craft. Adrian was the same as a kid too. I think we once fought over who took out the rubbish from the boatshed.' That made her laugh, and it was a pleasant sound after all this time.

Leo turned his focus back to Jonah. 'He's desperate to try everything – kayak, surf, paddleboard, sail – it's like he was born for it. But he knows he has to be patient about going in the sea, wait for his mum to make the decision. He's good like that, most boys would ignore it and go in anyway.'

'You and Adrian would have. I can't imagine the Magowan boys accepting the word "no" when it came to the sea.' And then more seriously she asked, 'Does Jonah know why Maeve is so frightened of what might happen?'

Leo shook his head. 'I get the impression Maeve doesn't want to tell him, not yet anyway. It would be a lot for a kid to hear, especially when it was the reason she left.'

'We all had a great childhood here; it'll be wonderful if he gets to enjoy it the way we did.'

She wasn't wrong there and you fast learnt to respect

the sea when you lived somewhere like Stepping Stone Bay or in the town of Salthaven. 'Maeve probably knows she can't keep Jonah in a bubble forever; sooner or later he'll be in that water. Maybe coming back here was a way to force herself to move forwards.' He paused. 'Talking of returning, I know you're here to do up the cabin for Walt, but is he all right?'

Nina's gaze drifted beyond the cabins, the boathouse, the sea beyond, the white frothy tips of the waves you could just about see in the distance. 'He's in good health apart from the odd niggle, he's happy, but he's a planner and I guess he knows it's inevitable that he'll slow down. He wants a financial cushion if you like, an assurance he won't have to leave his bungalow.'

'I can understand that, it's his home.'

'He knows he'll have to make some alterations.' She began to laugh. 'Last night he told me it needs some changes to make it old-fart-proof.'

'Now that sounds like Walt, always did have a bit of a sense of humour.'

She put one hand on top of the other, slotting her fingers together on her lap. 'My brother is living out of the country now so it's just me. I'm not sure what to do about that. William helped Grandad a lot and I love to help him too, it's why I came here. But long term . . . well I can't stay off work forever.'

'Are you worried?' Silly question, he could see she was; her knuckles alternated between pink and white when she squeezed her fingers together and then released them.

'I'm too far away to see him on a daily basis. And if something happens one day . . .'

'What about your mum? Could she help out?' Her

look told him the answer to that one. 'Still looking after number one then?'

'Yup.' She sighed.

'Well you have to work, I get that. I'm one of the very few who work so close to home and in such close proximity to parents and grandparents. But I can see why you worry with nobody else being around for Walt. He has us all though, and Camille, they're great friends.'

'I know.'

'But it's not the same.'

She shook her head and then on a breath he suspected she'd been holding until deciding whether to tell him she said, 'I'm considering transferring my job closer down this way.'

If she'd told him that when she first arrived he would've told her to pack up and go away, but now, he didn't want that. He wasn't sure what he wanted, but friendship might be a start.

'I think it's time, and although Grandad says I shouldn't uproot my life for him, I want to. I want to be near him. It'll be good for us both. He's my family.' Before he could ask her more about where she intended to live – would it be here in the bay? Would he see her all the time? – she added, 'But even if I do work closer to Grandad, I still won't be around all the time. I do shifts, and although I'll be able to check on him every day, that might not be enough as he gets older. And I don't have enough money to cover his care, to pay for someone to go into the bungalow each day for him. He's really worried the government will tell him to sell his house to fund care.'

'That can't be nice to have hanging over you.' He understood more about the sale of the cabin now.

'He really, really doesn't want to leave that bungalow. I don't know what the law is, I've no idea how it all works, and it wasn't a problem for my grandma thank goodness. But the man has a right to live out his days in the place he calls home.'

Leo put his thumbs up to Jonah who'd done a grand job with the top of the bookcase and now moved to doing the sides.

'He's made up his mind that he wants some extra money as a safety net and in order to have that it means selling the cabin.' She put a hand to the step she was sitting on as though it connected her with the history, the memories, the possibilities. 'It felt like the right thing to do, but . . .'

Wait, she was hesitating?

But he didn't get to ask the question before she looked him straight in the eye. 'It doesn't matter how I feel. I don't have a choice.' And then she turned away, as if remembering they weren't together any more, that she did things on her own now and had for a long time, or at least he assumed she had.

'I can't offer a magic solution I'm afraid.' Although he found he really wanted to. 'All I can offer is that if Walt needs any jobs doing around the bungalow then make sure he asks me. I'm not bad at DIY remember – and recently I fitted a handrail for my gran beside her front steps that get a bit slippery when it's wet, I fixed my parents' fence that fell down in the high winds – I'm a man of many talents. I can do things around his bungalow as needed and I can even help out with his garden if it gets too much, keep it shipshape for him.'

'Why are you being so kind to me?' She gulped.

And he smiled, nudged her gently. 'Don't worry, I'm not. I'm being kind to Walt.'

She looked back at him as though she was sorting through their personal history in her own head but didn't know what to tackle first. 'Thank you, I mean it.'

'You're welcome.'

When Leo saw a man up at the entrance to the boathouse waving across to them he hoped he hadn't kept him waiting long, his mind and his focus on something else entirely. 'I'd better head back over there.'

Nina got to her feet. 'And I'd better start painting. Jonah is working harder than I am. Maeve might not let him back down this way if she thinks we're both after slave labour.'

'I think he's loving every minute,' Leo assured her before leaving her to it.

After Leo unlocked the boathouse and let the customer inside he hooked the doors open and looked across at the cabins again, the cabins that had been a feature of his life ever since he could remember. It didn't feel right that soon one of them would be under different ownership, would belong to a stranger.

But he understood why. Walt needed the money and Nina needed the reassurance that Walt would be financially secure and able to stay in his bungalow for as long as he wanted. He just didn't want Nina's time here in Stepping Stone Bay to come to an end.

After all this time he finally felt he might be able to put his anger and resentment behind him, and thinking that way felt better than he ever would've imagined.

Chapter Ten

Nina

Nina worked hard over the next week to finish most of the work at the cabin. Jonah had helped much more than she'd expected and Maeve had even come in one evening after work when he asked to stay on for longer to finish a skirting board they'd started painting together. Nina wasn't sure whether Maeve had noticed Jonah doing it but more than once Nina had seen him glance out of the window, over at the water, his longing to go out in the sea evident. Nina would've bought him a kayak lesson to say thank you for all his help but she knew she couldn't and so she'd settled on buying him a doughnut and a hot chocolate.

Nina finished the sandwich she'd made quickly in the kitchen, still revelling in how bright and fresh the place looked with its new cooker, the cool white paint on the walls and the chrome polished to a sheen, all part of the cabin-by-the-sea feel she wanted to create. She'd just washed up her plate, smiling at the sleek new kitchen tap and her mind casting back to it being fitted earlier that morning when she heard a call from the steps that led up to the cabin and went to see who it was.

'Camille, come in,' she told her visitor, 'I was just about to make a cup of tea.'

'Wonderful.' She came in from the late September sunshine. The weather could trick you in the autumn – some days were a reminder that winter was around the corner, others were clinging on to that summer buzz with bright days and clear skies that made you want to make the most of them.

'Is it just you? No Grandad?' She got a second mug down from the cupboard.

'He's outside soaking up the summer a while longer.'

When Nina went to the front door she looked this time to the big tree stump over past the bins and close to the water. Her heart went out to her grandad. No doubt he wanted to soak up the memories of the cabin too, while he still could; the sun-filled days he'd spent with her and William, the rainy days when they'd played board games all day, even the winter time when Nina and William had begged to come to the cabin and they'd all piled down here with armfuls of blankets because there wasn't any heating in the cabin.

Nina could only really remember the boathouse and the two cabins being the way they were now, but watching her grandad, his back to them as he looked towards the sea, she knew he'd remember what it had been like long before she was born, and the passage of time that had brought such change. Stepping Stone Bay Boathouse had once built and repaired huge boats, but over time Leo's family had responded to the market and the growth in population down this way, as well as their personal preferences, and altered their business model.

As Nina carried on making the tea Camille spotted the shiny mixer tap at the kitchen sink. 'This is new.'

'It is, put it on this morning.' And because she knew a

question was bound to come her way she added, 'Leo did it for me.'

'It's nice to see you two together again.'

'We're hardly together.'

But Camille pulled a face that suggested she thought otherwise.

Yesterday Leo had walked over when she was sitting on the steps of the cabin scrolling through search results on her iPad and he saw she was looking at taps. He'd also noticed how bored she looked.

'Why do there have to be so many?' she'd grumbled to him. 'If there were a couple to choose from it would be so much easier.'

He sat down next to her as she moved over. 'May I?' He had his hands out expectantly.

She handed him the iPad. 'Be my guest, hardly riveting stuff. All I want is a kitchen tap that hasn't got any scratches or damage – it'll be that little extra to lift the kitchen that's all.'

He'd laughed, scrolled himself. 'Let's see what we can find.' Nina had leaned back on the step above and closed her eyes, but when she felt him looking at her she opened them and he snapped his head back round telling her, 'Go for this one. Sleek, contemporary, it'll look good.'

'Is it easy to put in? Do I need a plumber?'

'Don't be daft. I'll put it in.'

And so she'd gone to pick up the tap, and catching him helping a customer in the car park on the way back, he'd headed over shortly afterwards and fixed the tap on for her. And watching him helping out had brought with it unexpected sadness at what might have been.

But now, today, it was on to thinking about sofa covers

146

rather than Leo's company, as Camille took out those Nina had ordered from the big department store in town and her grandad had volunteered to pick up today.

'I hope you don't mind but I ironed these for you,' said Camille.

'Mind?' Nina shook her head. 'Of course I don't mind. But you really didn't have to do that.'

Camille dismissed the concern. 'Your grandad said you didn't have an ironing board when I suggested they'd be full of big folds from where they'd been wrapped around pieces of cardboard and shoved into plastic. So we unwrapped them to check and oh they were ever so creased. I live right near town, it only took me a moment. I know for a fact Leo doesn't have an ironing board, so it's not like I could borrow his.'

It was easy to forget Camille was Leo's grandma, she was more like her grandad's companion these days and it was good to know their friendship was so strong. More than once Nina had wondered whether it was anything else, but it seemed disrespectful to suggest it might be.

Nina headed outside with a cup of tea for Walt. She walked over to her grandad's side and as he saw her in his peripheral vision he shuffled up on the stump so she could sit down too.

'I sat here last night,' she told him. She'd nursed a hot chocolate as it grew dark, able to see the lights on at the bottom of the boatshed, Leo's form as he dragged in a couple of kayaks that must have been hired just before dusk from the ramp all the way into storage. She'd almost walked over to say hello but somehow going to his place of work felt intrusive. Instead she'd admired his build, remembered what it had felt like when he was hers, their bodies pressed close together night after night with their whole lives ahead of them until everything had changed.

'It's a beautiful spot.' She shielded her eyes from the sun so she could take in the view. She didn't want to make it obvious, but she'd already glanced over at the boathouse to see whether Leo would emerge round the side from the shop part at the top to follow the path to the bottom, or whether he'd emerge from the boathouse beneath with a kayak or paddleboard, in a wetsuit, ready to give a lesson.

'Why do you think I had the tree cut down but the stump left behind?' Walt smiled, sipping his tea and Nina focused on him rather than looking for what might've been. 'I never thought I'd see the day our family had to say goodbye to this place.'

'You're talking like you won't ever come down here again.'

He made a face she wasn't sure how to read. 'You know we almost didn't buy the cabin. Elsie wanted a beach hut instead.'

'You never told me.'

'Desperate for one, she was. And I wanted to be on board. I very nearly was, but then these cabins were being sold off. I was having a pint in the pub with Leo's grandad when he got the call from Camille to say the two rickety cabins that were at the edge of their boatyard were up for sale. He'd asked what anyone would want with one of those, they were only fit to knock down, and when he finished the call I told him how much beach huts go for. He was floored and agreed the cabins were a far better option. Anyway, by mutual agreement we walked down to take a look at them. As soon as I saw the cabins I knew Elsie would fall in love with them and if we could buy one it would give her a real slice of privacy, right here at the beach. Oh, she loved the beach.'

'I know, Grandad.' She put a reassuring hand on his arm at his melancholy but acceptance that Elsie was gone now and only memories remained. 'So the Magowans didn't want to buy both of the cabins when they knew how profitable they'd be?'

Walt shook his head. 'I think Malcolm still thought it was a bit crazy to invest in one, but he'd have done anything for Camille and it turned out she wanted one as desperately as your grandma did. They're similar in a lot of ways. And it worked out for the best. Camille always says that her fondest memories of the family are at their cabin, same as ours.'

Nina smiled in agreement.

'And now her grandson lives in the cabin that brought them so much joy. It's nice that, don't you think?'

'It is,' she agreed, refusing to be drawn into another conversation about Leo. She sensed that was what he was trying to do in a roundabout way. 'You know you could always move into the cabin. Leo would be next door if you needed help, it's beautiful down here.'

'What and have to negotiate that big hill every time I wanted to go into town?' he laughed. 'Not too bad now I'm able-bodied but it's a young person's game down here, or a place to visit. My bungalow is perfect for me. And Leo shouldn't have to look out for an old man either.'

'He said if you need any jobs doing at the bungalow then he's very happy to help.'

'He's a good man.'

'I know.' He always had been. And she'd never thought she deserved a man like Leo Magowan. She hadn't thought she was good enough for him and when she was so mixed up she made the decision that it was best if she left. She'd been lost, scared, grieving over the tragedy as they all were, but most of all she was tired. Tired of not believing her self-worth, of doubting herself and thinking she wasn't good enough for even her own parents.

'I always thought you or your brother would bring your kids here for endless summer days,' Walt reflected. 'It's a shame we can't keep it in the family like the Magowans have. But such is life. We do what we can.'

'We do.' She didn't want to tell her grandad that although she'd stayed away for so long and had only come back to do up the cabin, since she'd got here she'd been hit by an unexpected surge of nostalgia that felt like more than just memories. The task of getting the cabin spruced up and arranging the sale was now accompanied by an array of emotions about the bay and the town. And rather than longing to find a buyer quickly, already she felt trepidation at the thought of even letting a stranger inside.

Walt stood up and finished his last mouthful of tea. 'Come on, let's go and see what Camille is up to.'

But before they made it over to the cabin Leo intercepted them after spotting Walt first. 'Lovely day,' he said, reminding Nina of their previous polite greetings that she'd been grateful for since initially Leo hadn't been at all impressed she was back. But now, now she knew she wanted more than the odd exchange and she longed for better conversations like the one on the cabin steps.

'It most certainly is.' Walt looked as though he might be thinking of how to leave them alone when they heard a yelp from inside the cabin.

'What was that?' But Leo's question was asked as they all hurried into the cabin. 'Gran, whatever are you doing?'

Sofa cover half on, half off, she'd slumped onto the sofa. 'I've been wrestling this wretched thing on! I swear they're made too small.' She got up. 'And now I'm putting creases in them again,' she groaned.

'Come on, girl,' said Grandad, making Nina smile because that was the way he'd talked to her grandma when she needed a bit of encouragement. 'It can't be that hard.' But then he changed his focus and looked at Nina and Leo. 'Maybe we need a bit more strength and should leave it to the youngsters.'

Leo stepped forwards. 'Come on, Nina, we'll show them how it's done.' And he winked at her, actually winked. And it looked as though he realised a fraction too late that it felt too familiar.

'We'll give it a go,' she agreed.

Leo took one end of the material and she took the other, Nina standing level with the middle of the sofa. 'Let's pull on the count of three,' he suggested.

'Count of three,' she agreed. And they counted together.

On three, hands on the material, they pulled with all their might but when the sofa cover still didn't go on Nina fell backwards onto the floor – she'd been sitting with her feet up against the edge to get a bit more power behind her pull – and she was laughing hard. 'Camille is right, they're too small!'

Walt and Camille were chuckling away, Leo too. Walt wouldn't be defeated though. 'Between four of us, surely it'll go on.'

All four of them took positions and pulled as hard as they could when Walt called, 'Now!'

And with the light blue waffle-weave sofa cover pulled on they stood back to admire their handiwork. Bows tied at the bottom of each arm created the shabby chic effect Nina was after. She could feel the warmth from Leo's bare arm against hers and his hand was so tantalisingly close as they stood there that she almost reached for his fingers, to feel the connection they'd always had.

But Camille interrupted her thoughts. 'You know what we need to do now?' she said.

'What?' Leo asked.

And Camille turned at an angle. 'We have to do the other sofa.'

And with that they all complained but with an edge of amusement. Leo leaned closer to Nina. 'I should've legged it back to the boathouse before she realised.'

And Nina revelled in the conspiracy.

The next cover was way easier with four pairs of hands and when Leo left, although Nina wanted to watch him until he was out of sight, she turned back to admire the lounge.

The painting was finished, the furniture was ready, all there was left to do was accessorise.

Which made it all far too real. The cabin would be up for sale before she knew it and things were going to change yet again. And this time she wasn't at all sure she wanted them to.

Nina met Maeve in Salthaven town centre mid-afternoon and as she hooked her bag over her chair and sat down she had to wonder whether Maeve got fed up with cafés, given she worked in one.

But when she posed the question Maeve insisted, 'Not

at all. It gives me a chance to size up the competition and report back to Jo.' She laughed. 'I'm kidding. As long as I'm sitting down and people are waiting on me rather than the other way round, we're all good.'

The waitress brought over their hot chocolates and a lemon and poppyseed muffin each and talk turned to the cabin, the decorating and Nina's recounting of the sofa cover saga. 'Honestly, I thought Camille was going to keel over she was working so hard to get the thing on, it was like they'd made it two sizes too small.'

'I'll bet they look lovely.' And then she began to smile. 'It was nice of Leo to help. He seems to be around a lot lately, he's hardly avoiding you.'

'No, and for that I'm glad. And Jonah might've enjoyed the sofa cover saga if he'd been there.'

Maeve seemed hesitant. 'I do hope he hasn't been in the way.'

'What? He's helping!'

'You're sure?'

'I really am.'

'He loves helping Leo too.'

Nina wasn't sure how to interpret her tone, there was a hestitation there. 'Leo doesn't mind either. He really doesn't.' And when Maeve said nothing she added, 'He isn't letting Jonah in the water, if he says he won't, he won't.'

Maeve shook her head as though ridding herself of her worries. 'I'm sorry, I'm worrying, that's all, part of being a mum.'

'I'm sure it is.'

'So the cabin is coming along?'

'I can't believe it's all taking shape so quickly. I still need to shop for accessories today which seems a luxury compared to scrubbing, cleaning and painting.'

Maeve mentioned a few places that might have what Nina was looking for accessories-wise as she'd been buying things for her flat since she arrived. 'And if you're going for the nautical theme try that new shop on the corner near the supermarket, they've got some lovely little seaside prints in beautiful frames.'

'Thanks for the tip. Oh, and I've decided to organise a little party for Walt.'

'Is it his birthday coming up?'

'No, but now the cabin is redecorated it feels right to have a bit of a gathering there. I want to do it for him and I'll get pizzas – Grandad loves a Hawaiian.'

'Great choice. But it's sad though, a final party.'

'Sad, but Grandad is pragmatic.' Although Maeve had planted a small seed of doubt to add to the other seeds that had already been sown. She was just doing her best not to let them grow too much. 'Oh God, do you think I'll upset him by putting on a party?'

'Don't be daft. He'll recognise it as the kind gesture it's meant to be. Let me know when, and I'll be there. You could put up white and blue balloons to keep the nautical theme.'

'Great idea,' Nina smiled. 'And it's tomorrow night, is that too short notice?'

'I'll see if I can get my parents to look after Jonah.'

'Don't do that, the more the merrier, he's very welcome. He can tell Grandad all about the bits that he painted in the cabin. Go on, bring him, I need to say thank you for helping, so he can have as much pizza as he likes.'

Maeve began to laugh. 'I'll warn you now, he'll be

asking for chicken wings as well as pizza, since he tried those from the shop just up from the cabin he's addicted to them.'

'Chicken wings can be arranged too,' Nina smiled.

Maeve scraped the top of her chocolate froth off with her spoon. 'Doesn't all of this talk make you want to hold on to the cabin?'

All Nina had to do was look at her.

'And there's no way you could?' Maeve asked.

'Not really.' She shrugged. 'I don't know, maybe it's for the best if I don't keep it. It's less of a tie, it'll be empty a lot of the time. It's not like I have a family to bring down here.'

'You might do one day.'

'It's been good to have Jonah there, see another kid enjoying the cabin. He likes the stepping stones, I always did too.' She'd watched him leap across the stepping stones plenty of times, welcome at either cabin whenever he liked or was allowed.

'Has he been to Leo's cabin too? You know, if he's jumping across the stepping stones?'

'I don't actually know.' Nina was a bit confused at the question. 'You do trust Leo don't you?' It bothered her more than it should to think maybe she didn't.

'Of course. Just interested that's all.' She smiled, her dark hair and olive skin so much like her son's. 'He gets bored waiting for me when he has to come to the café. He's eleven but just that little bit too young for me to be happy with him spending hours at home on his own.'

'Has Jonah made many friends?' Perhaps that was what she was worried about, that her son was spending his time with adults rather than kids his own age.

Maeve's shoulders relaxed. 'He has. He's got a couple of buddies he kicks a football around with at the weekends, they don't live too far, and the school just sent out details of a trip planned for next June, a week away. The boys are already talking of sharing a room so . . . well it's great that he's settling in so quickly.'

'And you? How are you finding being back here now you've been here a while?' Her hot chocolate had barely touched the sides, all of the manual labour of the last few days had Nina almost as hungry as when she was on her feet as a nurse for a day.

'Sometimes I miss the noise of a big city – crazy I know, but I think I got used to hearing neighbours so often, or cars on the street. Here I have my windows open when it's warm and hear the breeze when it's dark, the gulls as they swoop overhead. I've spent so long wanting to stay well away from the sea that being so close, waking to the smell of it even, was weird at first but it seems to be changing something in me.'

Nina nodded. 'I know exactly what you mean. I've been back this way several times, but being at Grandad's is totally different to being at the cabin. At first I wanted to get in and get out as quickly as I could, then I started to enjoy the transformation – and if I'm honest, the time off work – and slowly it's become a nice place to be again. That's why I thought a party would be really lovely for Grandad.'

'It will be. I'm looking forward to it already. It'll be good to get out of the flat for the evening.'

Maeve tucked into her lemon and poppyseed muffin, her talk keeping her from eating thus far. 'Jonah told me that when he's been over to help you, Leo has walked him over to your place.' She said it with a smile. 'I'm pretty sure he could manage to get from the boathouse to your cabin safely without Leo's help.'

'He probably could.' She refused to rise to the bait.

Maeve persisted, even though she was getting barely anything from Nina. 'You two were love's young dream back then.'

'The key word there is *were*. It's been a long time since we were those people. I hope we'll stay friends though.'

'More than friends?'

Nina shook her head. 'I'm not even going to get into that discussion.'

Maeve caught a crumb that fell from her muffin. 'You're right when you say we're all different people now.'

'You're a mum for a start.'

'Leo seems the same though.'

Nina nodded. 'Yes and no. He's matured, having his own business and responsibility, I can see that without asking too many questions. But it suits him, being here.'

'Have you seen Adrian yet?'

She shook her head. 'Not yet.' She'd thought about visiting but she didn't want to make him feel uncomfortable. He'd emerge when he was ready, and she knew she would've hated people to descend on her and ask questions when she returned, so she'd given him the same grace. He probably wanted to process things in his own way. And she knew Leo well enough to know he'd bring his brother back, he had to.

'I never really talked to him after that night,' said Maeve.

'Adrian?' And when Maeve nodded Nina took a deep breath. 'I did, he was a mess.' It shouldn't surprise her that his homecoming was very different from Maeve's, from her own. Neither of them had galloped back in and picked up where they left off, but Adrian had it much harder. 'That night he and I walked back to the cabins ahead of Leo. Leo wanted me to get him away from everything, home, warm, calm.' She met Maeve's concerned gaze. 'I've never seen a grown man cry the way Adrian did that night. Great heaving sobs like he was in pain,' she remembered, 'this big strong man was broken, it was horrible.' And she remembered rocking him the way her grandad had rocked her when she fell over in a rock pool and grazed her knee, the way her grandma had pulled her into an embrace when she was upset her parents seemed to have less and less time for her and her brother as the years rolled on.

Maeve let the information sink in. 'I wonder if he's scared to go in the sea like I am.'

Nina shook her head, repeating a similar conversation she'd had with Leo. 'Leo thinks not; it's the guilt he feels, the sense of responsibility, more than any fear.'

When Maeve's phone pinged she sighed. 'I totally forgot I've got a delivery coming to the flat today.'

'You need to get back?'

'I'm afraid so. It's only a parcel of new books but I don't want them to dump the package on the doorstep and walk away. If they do that what do you think the chances are of seeing those books ever again?'

Nina laughed as they picked up their bags and made their way towards the front entrance. 'Pretty much zero.' She was still smiling as she pulled open the door, and as though their conversation had conjured them up, they came face to face with the Magowan brothers.

Nina paused, but barely for a second, before she flung her arms around Adrian. 'It's so good to see you.' She took hold of his upper arms as she pulled away. 'Really good. Welcome home.'

'Thanks, and likewise.' It was then he spotted she wasn't alone. 'Maeve?'

Maeve's jaw had dropped and she seemed to be grappling with words that refused to come out of her mouth. She hadn't been quite as shocked the first time she'd seen Nina at the café, but then again Nina had just told Maeve what a mess Adrian had been that night, given her a graphic description of a man who was broken.

'It's good to see you, Maeve.' Adrian was still looking at her. 'You're doing well?'

'I am.' She revealed a glimmer of a smile but it was short-lived, and she gathered herself and quickly added, 'I have to go, I'll see you around. Maybe. Soon.' Flustered, she hugged Nina goodbye, and then Adrian excused himself to go inside and grab them a table.

'And then there were two,' Leo smiled in the unique way he did with his eyes and lips that felt like flirting. She'd told him that once, and he'd said it was impossible for him to smile any other way. 'Twice in one day. How are the sofas? Comfortable?'

'They're fine; thanks for the help earlier.' She ignored the tug of desire in her belly. He looked handsome in a pale grey t-shirt and cargo shorts, his usual smooth-shaven look pleasantly marred with faint stubble. 'It's good to see Adrian out and about.'

'It's time. He's almost a hermit.' Leo raised a hand to his brother on the other side of the window. 'And he probably knows we're talking about him right now.'

'Then I'll let you go. But not before I tell you that I'm having a party for Grandad tomorrow night at the cabin. I thought it might be nice for him to enjoy one last gathering there before it goes up for sale.'

'Sounds like a fine idea. He'll be able to appreciate everything you've done, although the new tap is clearly the standout.'

'Clearly,' she laughed. 'Your gran noticed it so it must be. So you'll come?'

'I'm invited?'

'Of course. Adrian too.'

'I'll be there, wouldn't miss it. But Adrian, I'll work on him.' And with that he headed inside.

Nina walked on fifty metres or so until she reached the estate agents. Meeting Maeve hadn't been the only thing on her agenda when she came into town. And this was it. The cabin was ready. It was time to list it for sale.

The estate agent was so keen they arranged for an agent to come out in a couple of hours. Nina was happy to take charge of this side of things after Walt had said he'd rather not be involved until he had to be, and so she spent the rest of the afternoon shopping for accessories. She bought scatter cushions in cream and ocean blue, framed pictures of the beach and the seaside. She found a cute storage organiser with a beachside fabric that she'd put in the bathroom for surplus loo rolls and some novelty coat hooks to hang just inside the front door to the cabin, a place for people to hang their coats or an umbrella until they needed it.

By the time she headed back, her arms were laden with goodies for the cabin to add to its décor. Her job here was heading towards the finish line.

The question was, was she really ready to cross it?

Chapter Eleven

Leo

Leo finished up the kayak lesson well before the skies grew dark. It seemed like one minute you were wondering whether the endless summer nights would ever end and the next, you wondered how the darker evenings and mornings had crept up on you. The shorter days would be here soon, but for now he'd enjoy the opposite.

With the shed shipshape, the way he liked to leave it every evening, he made sure everything was in order in the shop area above, turned off the lights and locked up and set off on the short walk from the area out front down towards the cabins.

The lights were on at Nina's and this evening he wouldn't need an excuse to go and see her because he had an invite to the party.

Nina had been gone for twelve years and Leo hadn't been a saint in that time, he'd had girlfriends on and off and hadn't thought too deeply about whether they would last long term or whether he felt as strongly about them as he had Nina. But now he knew without a shadow of a doubt that he hadn't. None of the women he'd dated over the years had made the hair on the back of his neck stand on end if they accidentally brushed past him, he wasn't held captive when they spoke like he was with Nina, wanting her sentences to continue, wanting her to share whatever she was thinking. He hadn't felt a rush of excitement if he'd bumped into them unexpectedly the way he had with Nina at the café in town. He'd been rude the first day she turned up here again, but since that day it was as though with every little wave, every polite exchange, not to mention the longer conversations and looks they shared, as well as laughs and proximity, something inside him gradually woke up and it was like he could finally breathe again. He was opening himself up to a whole world of hurt when she left the bay after the cabin was sold, but he couldn't help himself. His feelings were still there and rather than accept her leaving, perhaps it was high time he told her how he still felt. Maybe she'd finally tell him the truth, why she'd run, why she'd left the great thing they had together. The lack of explanation had been one of the hardest things to accept, and seeing Nina back here in the bay made him realise that even after over a decade, he still needed to know everything.

He was about to pass Nina's cabin and head to his for a much-needed shower before the party for Walt when Jonah poked his head out of her front door. 'We're having pizza! And chicken wings!' he announced.

Nina appeared behind him, cheeks bright red as she blew into a balloon that expanded until Leo couldn't see her face any more. A quick show of dexterity and she tied the rubber in a knot. 'Done. Thank goodness.'

'I helped,' Jonah claimed.

'Now why doesn't that surprise me? Am I last to arrive?' Leo asked.

'Not at all.' Nina reeled off some of the names of people

who were coming – Walt, Camille, Jonah and Maeve, Molly and Arthur.

'Don't forget Surfer Steve,' said Jonah.

'That is indeed his full name,' Nina laughed. 'Is Adrian coming?' she asked when Jonah went back inside to help Maeve tie balloons up high wherever they could.

'He said he might pop down later.' He shrugged.

'You don't think he will.'

'He hasn't been near the boathouse or the bay or my place since he got back.'

'Well you never know.'

'Yeah.' He doubted it though, not with all these people. He'd barely said hello to Maeve outside the café as it was, although he loved the way Nina had given him little choice when she'd flung her arms around Adrian yesterday. It had taken him by surprise, but in a better way than Leo thought it ever would.

'Shall we go get the pizzas and chicken now?' Jonah's interest in the balloons had clearly been shortlived.

'Yes, we'll go, your mum can stay here for any guests who arrive.' She checked her watch. 'Which should be any time now. And they'll be nice and hungry for the fresh pizza.'

'And chicken.'

She playfully dug Jonah in the ribs. 'You and your chicken.'

'The boy has good taste.' Leo high-fived him.

Nina grabbed her purse and came down the steps from the small veranda. She pulled on a cardigan over a figure-hugging navy top with a neckline that revealed sculptured collar bones. 'Jonah, do you want to grab your hoodie?' She looked at his t-shirt.

Jonah shrugged. 'I'm not cold.' And already he'd turned to go and jump from one stepping stone to the other, towards Leo's cabin, as though he was used to having to wait for adults to finish talking.

'He had homework after school and Maeve says he needs to burn off some energy,' she confided as they watched Jonah reach Leo's cabin, turn round and head back towards them. 'The walk up to the pizza shop will do him good.'

'Good idea. I'll come over once I've had a shower.'

She sniffed as she leaned closer. 'Yeah, you definitely need one.'

Her apparent flirting held him captive but he managed a laugh. 'Thanks.'

When Jonah ran over again, Nina asked Leo whether he had any requests for pizza toppings. When he said not really she added, 'Happy with most things, but no anchovies right?'

'You remember.'

'Extra chillies though,' she smiled back at him. Even in the fading light he could see a sparkle in her eyes.

'Lots of chillies,' he confided in Jonah, eyes wide.

'And extra chicken wings,' said Jonah, 'or Leo will finish them all. I saw him eating chicken the other day, he likes it as much as me.'

'Come on you, let's go. We should be back in half an hour-ish.'

And, with a smile beamed his way from Nina, off they went, while Leo whistled the rest of the way back to his own cabin.

Leo had a beer at home before he left for the party, partly to relax with the anticipation of spending time in Nina's company, partly in the hope that Adrian would join him. But when it seemed his brother wasn't coming he headed over to join everyone else.

'Head inside,' said Maeve who was coming out of the cabin as he put a foot on the first step.

'You've not run out of pizza and chicken already have you?'

She laughed. 'No, I just got a call about a delivery at the flat – another one . . . I guess one of the perils of relocating – so I'll nip home and collect it and then come back. My car's up top on the main road.'

'See you soon then.' He went up the steps and smiled at the sight before him. 'I'm not sure I've ever seen so many people inside this cabin before.' He greeted everyone at once with a general wave. He could see Camille and Walt and went over to them, eager to congratulate Walt on the cabin's makeover. 'Nina has done a spectacular job, you must be really happy with it.'

'She did a wonderful job, I'm proud of her,' Walt answered as he stepped out of the way of Nina and Molly who between them were arranging pizza boxes on the kitchen benchtops, a couple of containers of chicken wings too, and a big pile of plates as well as napkins.

'Everyone, help yourself,' Nina called to the room, 'plenty of pizzas to choose from, help yourself to drinks too.' She turned to Leo and almost pressed against his chest. 'You smell better,' she joked as they stood in close proximity.

He didn't mind the teasing one bit and held up the bottle he'd brought. 'Should I put it with the others?'

'If you can find a space.' She indicated the drinks lined up at the back of the kitchen bench which was chocka.

He found a space – just – and helped himself to a big slice of supreme pizza with extra chillies, Nina laughing at him when the stringy cheese seemed to refuse to break no matter how much his teeth pulled on it.

'Elegant,' she laughed.

Leo had told himself he wanted to have a heart-to-heart with Nina, but he'd also told himself that tonight was not the night to do it. And yet, with the cabin so busy, with her standing so close, it was all he wanted to do.

And so when she took a few empty bottles out to the recycling bins to make room inside the compact cabin, he sat down on the front steps to wait for her.

'You had enough already?' she asked as she headed back.

'Definitely not.' He wanted to ask her to sit with him, but he'd take his cue from her. If she didn't, then she wasn't ready to talk. And if she did . . .

She sat down.

'It's a beautiful night, I love the end of summer, the start of cooler days,' she told him as they both gazed out at the darkness now that night had drawn its curtain across the sky.

'Seasons have their perks.' He turned to look inside the cabin where everyone congregated. 'Walt looks made up to have everyone here together. Sad, but happy, if that's not too contradictory.'

'It is contradictory,' she grinned. 'But I know what you mean.'

'When are you due back at work?' he asked. Please let her say *not for a long while*.

He got his wish. 'I've taken a couple of months' combined holiday and unpaid leave to get the cabin sorted and spend time with Grandad, so I've got weeks left yet.'

'And are you still considering a transfer down this way?' This time, please let her say *yes*.

'I am. People move around a lot in my profession, so I'm hoping it's relatively straightforward.'

'Fingers crossed, eh?' He felt his pulse race and in the past few years it had only really done that with anger whenever he thought of Nina. Now it had nothing to do with that and everything to do with how he was drawn to her the way he had been ever since they met, first as friends, then as lovers.

'I've already had an estate agent here to value the cabin.'

'Already?' Her words stopped his excitement much like throwing a bucket of cold water over his head.

'I know, they were keen. They're sending a photographer around tomorrow.'

'That's quick.' Too quick, but then he shouldn't be surprised. She'd never dragged her heels when she wanted to get something done. 'I bet it'll sell after the first viewing,' he encouraged. Much as it pained him to say the words, he wanted to be supportive.

She was looking at him as though she believed, like he did, that the sale would signify the end; it would be the full stop to their story that had been written over the years and was finally finished.

And Leo hated she thought that way and that he did too. He hated that her family would no longer own the cabin, that their families would no longer be those two families who'd built so many memories.

He and Nina had talked about having a family more than once, including how many kids they wanted to have. He remembered stretching out on his veranda, both of them lying on their backs, their heads nearest the railing so they could look up at the stars above, just about peeping through the branches of the tree that reached almost to the roof of the cabin. She'd insisted she wanted two, he'd suggested four. She'd told him that was crazy, that they'd have to drive around in a minibus whenever they wanted to go anywhere, they'd never be able to fly off on holiday as it would be too expensive for six of them, and she'd joked that she wasn't sure she could pop out four. He hadn't really cared at the end of the day, as long as they were together.

'I hope you don't mind,' said Nina, back to talking about the O'Brien cabin sale, 'but I ordered some festoon lights like yours to put around my veranda.'

He liked that she'd taken note of what he'd done at his own place, at least with the outside. 'It'll be nice for you to enjoy them before someone else if you can. You can sit outside, blanket around you and make the most of it. Until the cabin is sold.'

Sold . . . he was beginning to hate that word. And was he really doing this? Was he really putting his happiness on the line again by asking her for the truth? His crazy broken heart seemed to be willing to risk it all for another chance.

'I suppose I should make the most of it.' She put a hand to the wood of the steps, her other hand clutching her glass, and her hair lifted in the breeze grazing the top of his arm where it wasn't beneath his t-shirt. 'Are you cold?' she asked when he shivered.

'No.' He was feeling something else entirely. 'I'm hardened to the sea air. It's in my blood.'

She laughed softly before she told him, 'I think deep

down it's in mine too. Maybe not in quite the same way, but it's there.'

Her admission gave him the opening he needed. 'You just upped and left.'

She looked shocked he'd come right out with it.

'I need to know why,' he said.

'I was a mess, Leo.'

'We all were.'

'You know what it was like for me growing up, never feeling good enough.'

He had known that, the problems she had with her parents who didn't deserve that title in his opinion. 'You were always good enough for me.'

He'd thought she knew, but her expression said even that had been something she doubted. 'I was lost, Leo. I felt like I didn't deserve happiness, and no, I didn't think I was good enough for you no matter how many times you told me I was.'

'You know that's crazy, right?' He wanted to put an arm across her shoulders, to pull her close, a contrast to how much he'd wanted to push her away when she first showed up again. 'We were so young. Everything that happened . . . it was a lot.'

'You mean the party on the boat, Rhianne?'

'And us,' he said, but had to clarify. 'We were so in love and that wasn't a bad thing. But we were serious so quickly and neither of us had had a chance to learn much about ourselves, had we? Perhaps we needed that. Maybe we needed things to end.'

'I'm sorry I did that to you, Leo. I'm sorry I left without a word.' She paused. 'I knew you wouldn't let me go if I gave you warning.'

He opened his mouth to tell her he'd have given her all the time she needed, but he knew that wouldn't have been the case. 'I just wanted you to let me in, let me comfort you and take away the pain.'

She shook her head. 'It was impossible. My mind was so full of everything from what happened with my parents and all the pain they've caused over the years, to the party and Rhianne's death. It was like I had someone screaming so loud in my head I couldn't hear anything properly. I couldn't deal with it on my own let alone let anyone else in.'

When Jonah came to warn Leo that there were only three chicken wings left, Leo knew that it was time to let Nina get back to hosting the party. He'd started the conversation he'd needed to have for years and when she smiled at him as she stood up and he gestured for her to go inside first, he hoped the look they shared meant she might have needed this talk too.

And hopefully it was just the beginning.

Chapter Twelve

Maeve

Maeve took in the delivery of pots and pans for the kitchen at the flat. She'd made do with the few the owner had left them, but she'd soon realised if she wanted to cook anything in bulk, she'd need something bigger. She'd gone for decent ones too, something that would last and they'd take to the next house when they eventually bought their own place.

She parked up on the main road again and with the light dimming it wasn't so easy to see her way down the track towards the boathouse, although she smiled at the sound of voices coming from the cabin drifting towards her as she got closer.

She could hear the sea too and on a whim headed down past the boatshed. Jonah would be more than happy at the party, she wasn't bothered about pizza or chicken wings right now, she wanted to go onto the sand and get a bit of headspace. For so many years, living in Canada had detached her from her life here and now she was back she wanted to be a part of it again, she had to be, for Jonah's sake.

Maeve had only been sitting on the sand for a few minutes when she sensed someone was behind her.

She turned to see Adrian.

'Mind if I sit?' he asked.

Her mouth dry at the unexpected interruption, she held out a hand to gesture for him to sit down too. 'You came for the party?'

'Yeah, just not brave enough yet I guess.'

'I get it,' she smiled. 'Starting a job at the café soon got me over any worry about seeing the locals.' Maeve wished she had a bottle of water on hand, and as though reading her thoughts Adrian passed a bottle her way.

'Thirsty?' he asked.

'Do you mind?'

'Not at all.'

Their conversation was stilted, how could it be anything but? They'd all been friends before they went their separate ways, but Maeve and Adrian had been a little bit more than that.

Adrian asked her whether she was missing Canada, she asked him if he missed living in Leeds. Both of them were grappling with threads of conversation, the bottle of water passed between them as though it might be a baton or an energy source to propel them forwards.

'Leo was surprised Nina ever came back.' Adrian looked out at the water and Maeve could see now that he wasn't scared of it the way she'd been. The way his gaze was fixed on the waves as they built up and then crashed to shore she could tell he had a love, but also a boundary he couldn't quite step over.

'It's nice to have her back too.'

'You get on well?'

'Always did.'

He smiled. 'I remember you and Nina sitting on the

sand round at Salthaven beach watching me and Leo surf.'

'You remember?'

He wasn't looking at the water now, only at her. 'Of course I do.'

'Do you still have your boat?' she asked.

'*The Wildflower*.' He smiled now. 'I do. Over the years I've been tempted to sell it. I walked down to the marina the other day.'

'You did?'

'Didn't get any further than the main entrance. I couldn't do it. My poor boat is still neglected, athough Leo takes it out now and then.'

'It wouldn't be right for you to get rid of it. You love that boat.'

He didn't deny it.

'Leo must be glad to have you back.'

'I think he gets frustrated with me.'

'The business?' she asked although she already knew from Leo himself that that was one of his worries, it was what he wanted, him and Adrian together running the boathouse.

'Yeah.'

'He misses his brother. You two were always inseparable, this place was your whole world.'

'Your son must be yours.'

She opened her mouth to speak but nothing came out.

'What's he like? Leo says he's a great kid, got a bit of a Canadian accent still.' He suddenly seemed a bit uncomfortable to be sitting alone with her here.

'He is a great kid. And that accent is fading already.' Her phone pinged and she apologised, but then smiled when she looked at the text. 'It's Jonah, he's at the party and asking when I'm coming back. That means he must be getting bored, he's usually happy if I keep my distance.'

When she stood up he said, 'I'll maybe see you there later.'

She nodded, turned but then stopped and faced him once again. He was watching her walk away. 'Come with me?'

He took a deep breath in. 'In a while.'

But she didn't move. And amused, he stood up. 'You always were bossy.'

And he shared a smile with her that reminded Maeve of the younger man on the beach all those years ago, the drips of water as he emerged from the sea and the huge crush she'd had on him for a lot longer than anyone knew. Even him.

They walked so close to one another over to the cabin that Maeve caught a hint of shower gel on the breeze, a distinctly male fragrance that mixed with the sea air made her feel a little giddy.

'Where were you?' Jonah asked when she got inside. 'You were ages.'

'I wasn't that long,' she grinned and ignored the look Nina sent her way when Adrian came in to the cabin so soon after her that it looked as though they might have arrived together.

Adrian greeted everyone with a raised hand as he said hello. His voice didn't wobble at all, as Maeve thought it might have done. He'd gone quiet the closer they got to the cabin and she knew, just like she'd had to do when she first came back, he was preparing himself for seeing these people after so long away. The reality was, they all welcomed you back, they had their own lives and knew you had yours. And Adrian was soon chatting away to anyone and everyone. He'd always been that way, one of his best qualities.

'How're you doing?' Nina came to Maeve's side.

'I'm good. How's the party going?'

But Nina wasn't fooled. 'Did you two arrive together?'

'No.' And then she added, 'I went down to the beach for a bit of space and he came down there too.' She grabbed a slice of pizza. Must be all the sea air making her hungry.

'I'm glad he came.'

And with her mouth full Maeve nodded. She wasn't sure how to feel about him right now.

Camille initiated a discussion about the sofa covers and asked Maeve whether she'd had to furnish her flat, and with Jonah happily talking to Surfer Steve about his surfboard collection she tried to put any worries about her son aside and talked about her new home. Every now and then she glanced around the room and her eyes fell on Adrian. He even looked across at her once or twice and smiled. She hoped he wasn't facing a barrage of awkward questions. She hadn't had to, so she doubted it, and he did seem relaxed.

'He's fine,' said Nina coming to her side.

'Jonah?'

Nina grinned. 'Yeah, Jonah.'

She must have been staring more than she realised. But lucky for her, Nina's questioning didn't progress when Camille came over to offer her thanks for the party.

'Are you leaving already?' Nina asked.

Walt came over and heard what she'd said and with a chuckle informed his granddaughter, 'We're old, we'll leave you youngsters to it.' He reached out and hugged

Nina. 'Thank you for doing this. I don't mean just the party—'

'Which you're running out on,' she said.

'I need my beauty sleep . . . and I mean it, thank you for everything, for coming here after all this time and doing up the place. I'll be sad to see it go.' He looked around at the newly painted walls, the gathering inside of family and friends, absorbed the laughter and the chatter, the way the balloons swayed in the breeze coming through the open door or perhaps from the movement inside. The whole cabin was alive tonight, welcoming and warm.

'You all right?' Leo asked when Nina had hugged her grandad and waved goodbye as he and Camille headed off into the evening air.

'Yeah. I always knew this evening would be a joy, but difficult at the same time.'

Nina might be on high alert for Maeve when it came to Adrian but she had her own story that definitely hadn't ended with the younger of the Magowan brothers.

Nina went back to hostess mode and got Steve and Adrian another beer and when Maeve realised she'd looked once too often at Adrian and that others might start asking questions, she pitched in and began to clean up, even though when she'd offered earlier Nina had said there was no need.

She filled the sink with hot water, added detergent and swished the water to get the bubbles going before she dumped a whole pile of cutlery into the depths.

'I'll dry.' Adrian had come into the kitchen and picked up a tea towel.

'Thank you.' Maeve wasn't sure she'd ever been this nervous washing up. It wasn't like she had to do it in a fancy way, but he was so close, her head was all over the place.

And now Jonah came to join them and he had other ideas that didn't involve cleaning up.

'Please play a game with me,' he pleaded with his mum.

'I've told you, not at a party, Jonah.' He'd asked her earlier because there was only so much adult-talk a kid could do. 'You could dry up if you like.'

Her suggestion was met with the expected grimace. And Nina must have overheard because she came in and said, 'Jonah has helped out a lot around here. I think he's off the hook for the clean-up. Did you bring your iPad?'

He shook his head. 'I wasn't allowed.'

'Fair enough.' She pulled a face as though trying to think of something and then smiled. 'Wait here.' She disappeared off but was back moments later. 'I found this when I was clearing everything out for the makeover.' She held out a game in a box – Frustration. 'It's old but it works.'

Adrian put another dry knife away into the drawer. 'I was champion at that back in the day,' he claimed. 'I can't believe you still have it.'

'It's a relic,' Nina grinned.

'Will you give me a game?' Jonah begged, his attentions on Adrian now, even though he was drying up.

'Too noisy,' Maeve warned, dropping another fork into the drainer, its bubbles running off and heading for the sink. She couldn't look at either of them. Her heart was pounding at a rate of knots.

'We'll take it in the bedroom,' Jonah announced looking at Nina.

'Fine by me,' Nina told him.

177

'You sure you want to play?' Maeve asked Adrian in a soft voice. 'You don't have to. I could play instead.'

'I'm happy to. Unless you're not.'

'No . . . no, I don't mind.'

'Then that's settled.' He looked puzzled at her hesitation but shook it off and turned to Jonah. 'I'll warn you, I'm good.' He put down the tea towel and followed her little boy out of the room. It was all she could do not to watch them both, their every move.

'He must be bored,' said Leo as he came to take over where Adrian left off with the drying up. 'Nobody else his age here.'

Maeve just smiled and turned back to her task, vigoriously scrubbing the remnants of pizza off the last remaining pieces of cutlery before she started on some of the glasses that were in a collection beside the sink.

'It's loud in there.' Already they could hear the incessant popping of the Frustration board coming from the bedroom, Jonah's excited yelps and Adrian's laughter. 'Good to hear my brother happy though. All it took was an eleven-year-old kid, eh?'

Maeve didn't say a word. She couldn't.

'Jonah seems pretty happy Adrian agreed to play – I had no intention of playing that game when I saw it, no matter how much I enjoy your son's company.'

'Fair enough,' Maeve laughed. 'I think I'd have a headache if I was in there.' She caught sight of the time. 'I should probably take Jonah home soon, it's getting late.'

'Want me to give him the ten-minute warning?' Nina asked as she overheard their conversation.

'Thanks, Nina.' It was easier than her going in there and trying to drag Jonah away. He was already attached to

Leo; now Adrian seemed to be getting a look-in. And all of it made Maeve as nervous as she'd expected.

When she felt Leo's attention turn to her she asked, 'Has Adrian mentioned whether he'll teach again soon?'

'He doesn't seem to be in any hurry. So who knows. I can cross my fingers that it means he's considering a different profession, I don't know, like boats,' he smiled, 'but I might be getting my hopes up if I did that.'

'Your family must be really happy he's here.'

'We all are. And talking of school and being back, how's Jonah doing? He always seems happy enough at the boathouse. He doesn't tell me much about school, although I did hear that there's a new boy called Murray and he picks his nose.'

'Lovely,' she giggled, appreciating the lighter banter. 'And I'm not sure "enjoying" is a word he'd ever use about school, but he's happy, he's made some friends and he just moved up levels at swimming club. He's learning butterfly at the moment.'

'Not a stroke I ever liked. I couldn't really do it to be honest; Adrian was way better, he was a machine in the water.'

The mention of water and Adrian had her looking behind her to see whether her son was ready to leave. It seemed he still wasn't, she could hear him protesting.

'He's still hassling me to let you take him out on a kayak or show him paddleboarding,' Maeve said when she turned back.

'The weather is starting to turn. If you want to do it, do it quick. I know it's hard,' he added. 'But I'm patient, don't worry. And I love him stopping by – he's good company and I'll always keep him safe.'

'I enrolled him in swimming lessons from a really early age, there was no question of me doing that. I actually thought it would mean I wouldn't be like this, that I wouldn't have a problem with him going in the sea. But it seems a pool is one thing, but the sea is another thing entirely.'

'They're different, that's why, and it's good for Jonah to realise that. And if it helps, he definitely doesn't seem scared. You haven't damaged him.'

'He started swimming lessons and he was hooked.' She smiled at the thought of her son every time he got in the pool. 'He was hungry for more, the water is his happy place.'

'Then start slow. I take it he's been in the sea?'

'I'm not that mean a mother,' she told him.

'Didn't say you were. But how about you come down to the shed tomorrow when he's helping out. You can sit on the beach if it's warm enough, watch the paddleboarders or kayakers in the bay – I'll even give you my binoculars – that way you can see what it's all about, and you'll see them, most of them, wearing buoyancy vests. Even the strongest swimmers should wear one, it's something I encourage, not that I always get my way.'

'You want to take Jonah in the water tomorrow?' She felt her insides churn.

Footsteps announced Jonah's departure from the bedroom and at last the end to the games. 'I won fifteen games, Mum!' he announced.

'I won four,' Adrian laughed coming up behind them, and Maeve didn't miss the look of admiration Leo sent his brother's way, because Adrian seemed happy, not pained to be here with everyone after all this time.

And Maeve sent a look of appreciation Adrian's way, but for an entirely different reason.

'Did I hear Leo say something about Jonah going out on the water tomorrow?' Adrian came so close to Maeve that she held her breath for a second, her eyes level with the top of his shoulder, the muscles beneath his t-shirt.

'I'm not quite ready,' she confessed to Adrian so that only he could hear.

'Why don't you start with yourself.'

'You want me to go on a kayak?' She didn't miss the way his eyes dipped to her lips as she spoke.

'Not quite. But start by getting down there like this evening, *you* go close to the water, *you* really remind yourself of the fun you can have in the sea.'

Was he flirting or was he being serious? She couldn't tell without staring at him so intently gossip would be bouncing off the walls of the cabin.

'I'll bet I'm right in thinking all you've done so far is catastrophise, thinking the worst would happen if Jonah was to go into the water more than knee deep,' Adrian went on as though he could see right through her.

'Something like that,' she admitted.

'It's a hurdle, that's all. And one you can get over. It doesn't need to be rushed, doesn't even need to be this side of Christmas, you could wait until next summer. If you're hanging around.'

'I am.' And then she braved. 'Are you?'

'I'd like to.'

And he had no idea how much she wanted, needed to hear that.

But as Jonah tried to persuade someone, anyone else to have another game with him while she was distracted, she changed topic. 'Leo and Nina are getting on well tonight.'

'He says they're friends again.'

'Somehow I think they're more than that.' And before Jonah could harass anyone else she found her bag and went to his side.

'Can we play again another day?' Jonah asked Adrian without hesitation.

'I'll see, mate. I'm not sure my ego could take that much losing again. I mean, I used to be good back in the day.' He pulled a face that made Jonah laugh and Maeve's heart melt.

'Why don't I walk you both home,' Adrian offered Jonah and Maeve.

'No need,' said Maeve. 'The car's parked at the top – I need to get this young man home to bed.'

He looked about to protest until Leo finished putting out the last of the rubbish and slung an arm around his brother's shoulders, clearly glad to have Adrian here as he insisted on a nightcap for the both of them back at his own cabin.

Maeve bid them all a goodnight and with Jonah still rambling on about Frustration and how he'd only just won the last game, they trekked to the top of the track.

Things were beginning to change. Should Maeve dare to hope it was for the better?

Chapter Thirteen

Nina

A couple of days after the party, Nina had only just finished sweeping the front steps of the cabin when she saw the postman coming her way. He usually left the post for Leo's cabin in the little lock-up mailbox at the top of the track and the O'Brien cabin wasn't often on his radar. All Walt would usually get was important correspondence, but that hadn't been for a very long time, at least not until today when the postman handed her a letter and told her how good it was to see her back in the bay. She didn't have the heart to correct him and tell him that really she was only here to ready the cabin for sale and leave Stepping Stone Bay all over again. Because even if she came back this way, to the south coast, it wouldn't be right here.

She walked back to the cabin and tore open the letter which was from the estate agents containing the formal valuation and contract ready for signature. The paperwork was pretty much there, the photographs were too and had already been emailed across to her. This was it. She looked around the cabin, all the effort she'd put in and she tried to think about it in a business sense, but that was easier said than done.

And so instead of sitting there getting all melancholy, she picked up her bag ready to head out. She'd take the contract to her grandad for his signature and the long walk would do her good, because it was scaring her the way it felt so much like coming home here, especially since the party for Walt, the company and how filled with happiness and laughter the cabin had been. It was as though that night the cabin had been resurrected from the past to the present.

The sun was out and so she didn't need much more than a light zip-up top over her t-shirt, but rain was forecast later and so she put her umbrella into her bag.

She was walking past the boathouse when Leo called over to her from the doorway. 'Great day,' he smiled. 'Been writing letters?' he eyed the envelope in her hand.

She lifted it up as though that would explain things. 'It's the contract for the estate agent, ready for Walt's signature.' She didn't miss the slump of his shoulders. 'They don't want to hang around.'

'That's because they'll be rubbing their hands together getting this place on their books.' And now she didn't miss the reservation in his voice. 'Did they value it fairly?'

She wasn't sure how much to share, but it was hardly going to be a secret when it would soon be advertised. She told him what price the estate agent suggested they could get and he whistled.

'And your grandad is happy with the valuation?'

She nodded. 'Very. And he's very happy with the photos, we both are. I sent those to him too so he's had a good look.'

'Don't you love technology.'

The word *love* seemed to have hovered in the air as he

looked over at the cabin wistfully. 'Another family is going to fall in love with it.'

'If they're half as happy as our family was down there, then that's a good thing.'

'And Walt doesn't want to hang on to the cabin for a bit longer, might go up in price?' he suggested.

'He doesn't want to leave it to the last minute. He keeps going on about being prepared, talks about if he needs a carer at some point and how pricey they are.'

'True.'

'He'll be fussy choosing one as well.'

Leo's laughter had her smiling. 'I can see it now, Walt interviewing carers to make sure they're the right fit.'

'I'm glad he has Camille.'

'Me too, the pair of them get along well, they're good friends.'

Nina wondered was that all she and Leo would ever be now?

'So may I see the photos?' he asked before she could go on her way.

'You've seen the cabin. You were inside two nights ago, for a long time.' Her pointing it out had her thinking about how close they'd got on more than one occasion, not much room with the party in full swing, and then the way they'd talked on the steps outside, the truths that had surfaced.

'Good point. Show me anyway.'

She took out her phone and brought up the email. He'd come closer to her and she felt the warmth of his skin when his arm pressed against hers as they both looked, him shielding the phone from the sunlight with his hand.

'They've done a good job, the pictures will sell it easy.

And that's before anyone comes to look at it in person.'

'Do you think so?' The photos were good; some images made the interior look bigger than it was of course, but they'd captured the new décor brilliantly with its blue and bright white colour scheme, the epitome of a beach hideaway.

'I know so.'

And as Nina made her way up the track she turned back briefly to see Leo still lingering outside the boatshed. And he wasn't waiting for a customer, he was watching her.

What was she doing? It'd been twelve years, she'd treated him terribly by walking away. He surely wasn't interested in anything other than being a good friend and perhaps talking some more to find out why she'd left him the way she had.

Nina wondered whether she needed to leave the bay before she got in too deep and they both got hurt.

At her grandad's, Nina showed Walt the photographs again even though he had his own copy, and they discussed the valuation when he signed the paperwork.

'At the party, Leo offered again to help out here at the bungalow if I need him to,' Walt told her. 'It's very generous of him.' He held out the open biscuit tin. 'I don't want to be a burden though.' He looked around at the tired appearance of the kitchen.

Nina plucked a Bourbon cream from the tin. The kitchen here at her grandparents' home had been the same for a couple of decades. The lemon-yellow formica surfaces had faded with age, the patch nearest the window and the sink that got the sun or the most battering from cleaning chemicals had a particularly bad spot Grandad had covered with a sink tidy holding washing up liquid, a brush and a couple of cloths poking out haphazardly from the top. The cupboards had handles – mostly – but they were old-fashioned swirls that were impossible to clean and half of those were loose too. Nina supposed she'd got so used to it over the years that she hadn't noticed it subtly changing. But now, looking around the kitchen and hearing Walt talk, she realised the whole bungalow needed some attention, a makeover or at least upkeep, and that would be the situation for ever, seeing as this was where her grandad resolutely wanted to stay.

'I'm sure if Leo says he'll help, then he doesn't mind. And I could help you out too. I'm not suggesting I could refit a kitchen, but I can help with painting and even wallpapering if that's what you'd like.'

'You have your own life. I don't expect you to leap in to do this place as well as the cabin.'

'I enjoyed myself, different to work at least.'

'True. Sometimes a change is as good as a rest.'

'You enjoyed the party then?'

'You know I did. It was wonderful, and all those balloons. I thought balloons were for kids, but take note, if I ever have another party I want balloons again.'

'My lungs are still recovering,' she chuckled. 'So if that's the case I'll have to get a special pump next time.' She thought of the mixture of joy and sadness she'd felt that night and ever since. 'You know, Grandad, if I could, I'd buy the cabin myself.'

'You would?' He seemed surprised, even though she'd already talked about moving down this way. Perhaps he didn't think it would be real until it happened.

'I'll admit I hadn't given the cabin much thought at all until I came back to Stepping Stone Bay. Life has been so busy for me I never stopped to wonder what it would be like if the cabin was no longer in our family. I guess even though I didn't stay in it or even visit, I knew it was always there in the background.' And she smiled at her grandad because the way he was looking at her told her he'd known this was coming. 'I'm afraid I just don't have the money. Even if I sold my place, I couldn't buy the cabin. If we took sentimentality out of the equation and then added in the commute I'd need to contend with to the nearest hospital a good fifteen miles away, it's not even an option.'

Walt covered her hand with his. 'I understand. Selling the cabin is the right thing to do, Nina.'

Nina had bought a small studio apartment five years ago, brand new, off-plan and right near her work. It suited her, she could manage the mortgage and the bills on her single salary, she had a decent social life and holidayed in Europe most summers, but she'd always known the studio wouldn't be forever. If she was lucky enough to meet someone she'd want more space, and then if she had a family one day maybe they'd want a garden, room for a family to grow and enjoy. Buying the cabin now, instead of another flat, when she made the move back to the south coast would be crazy. The cabin was a nice extra but not practical enough for her, and if it lost value, which could happen, then she'd be really stuck. She'd just have to get on with this, follow the process and support Walt in the sale none of them had ever wanted to happen.

After her grandad looked again at the photographs of

the cabin's makeover Nina remembered, 'Do you have some tools I could borrow?'

'Tools?'

'I know you have a toolbox in your loft. I need a drill to put up some novelty coat hooks just inside the door to the cabin. Buyers will love those, they're a real homely touch, and useful obviously.'

'Well as grand as that sounds I don't have a drill any more. These days I have to get someone else to do anything involving a power tool. The one thing I did let young Leo do was put up the new bathroom wall cabinet for me and fix my bookcase – the shelves aren't strong enough.'

'You have too many books.' Already there were several slotted in or balancing precariously.

'No such thing.'

She knew he was waiting for her to respond to his suggestion. 'I suppose I could ask Leo.'

'He wouldn't mind, it would take him a couple of minutes at most and if you want to borrow a drill and do it yourself he's probably the best bet for that as well.'

She didn't know anyone else who might have one so she'd go with it. 'I'll ask him.' And rather than filling her with dread, she felt a little lift inside knowing she had another reason to bother him again.

By the time Nina left Walt to it, he seemed content enough. It didn't have to be said out loud that neither of them wanted to let a piece of their family history go, but both of them were practical and knew it made the most sense. And once it was done, they'd move forwards.

Nina walked back towards the cabin, glad she'd thought to bring her umbrella when a few drops of rain turned very quickly to more as she left the café on the main road clutching a decadent takeaway hot chocolate, which kept her palm warm. She reached the end of the track about to turn left to head straight for the cabin, but with the boathouse shop on her other side it made sense to go and see Leo now. And yet going right in to his place of work, approaching him rather than the other way around, still felt odd when she hadn't been inside the boathouse for years.

She shook off her umbrella and propped it up outside beneath the small overhanging piece of roof that gave a little bit of shelter. Inside, the shop above the actual boathouse was far bigger than she remembered. Shelves lined some of the walls and from those hung ocean shoes in varying colours, on top were a host of accessories, things she knew were associated with water craft but that she couldn't really identify. There was a display of colourful ropes, several circular clothing rails, one with wetsuits, a smaller one with t-shirts, another with brightly coloured beach wear. Down the centre of the shop were more shelves and she saw buoyancy vests, fleeces, long-sleeved tops, and on the left-hand wall as she walked inside were paddleboards, surfboards, a couple of kayaks fixed up high that would require the use of a stepladder to bring them down.

When Leo spotted her he was clearly surprised to see her, but professional in the way she'd expected of him he finished helping a customer choose between a full wetsuit and one that would only come down to her knees. Nina knew full well that if it were her she'd go for the bigger one, she hated to feel cold in the water.

Nina looked through the clothes as she waited. Unlike Maeve she hadn't avoided the sea, and while she hadn't been to the bay in years or to Salthaven beach, she'd enjoyed the ocean abroad, she'd swum in it, even snorkelled. It hadn't been easy to go back in after avoiding it for so long but she'd managed to do it a couple of years after she left the bay. She and a few other nurses she worked with had booked a trip to the Greek Islands, and because nobody knew her history she hadn't had to put up with sympathy or encouragement or anticipation from anyone else other than herself. And so she'd got on with it. When the others donned their masks and snorkels she'd done the same, when they'd jumped from the side of the boat after the skipper took them out to sea she'd followed them. The shock of the water had almost knocked the life out of her as she went under but she'd emerged smiling, she'd taken out her mouthpiece and floated on her back to feel the warmth of the sun beating down on her. And for that day she'd been a regular twenty-something out for fun with no ties. She'd never ever forgotten what happened, but in other locations away from here, she was able to tap into another part of herself and let some happiness in, almost accept what had gone before, with the present being more important.

Nina swapped the hot chocolate into her other hand after taking a sip and realising it was still lovely and hot. She looked out of the window at the far end of the shop as she waited for Leo, at the bay that was serene beneath rainfall that would be pitter-pattering its surface, the deep depths of the water beyond.

Leo had eventually come up behind her so slowly she hadn't noticed, especially with her mind elsewhere. And now she could feel the body heat through her top as he stood close – or maybe she was imagining it because she knew what it felt like, even after all this time? Leo had always been hot, not only in looks — they'd often joked about how she'd climb into bed and warm her feet on his legs, which were like little portable radiators.

'What can I do for you?' he asked.

'I came to ask a favour,' she told him, glad of the friendly welcome that at times felt as though they were those same two people who had always been at ease in one another's company.

'And what might that be?' He coiled the orange rope he had in his hands and went over to slot it onto a shelf next to one rope in a bright yellow and another in striking turquoise.

She wondered whether he'd meant to sound flirtatious when he asked the question and it had her a little flustered. 'I have some hooks to put up in the cabin and I don't have a drill.'

'You want to borrow a drill?'

She hunched her shoulders. 'If you trust me to use it I'll borrow it.'

'Might be easier if I just did it myself. Not that I'm saying you're not capable.'

'Not offended at all. And you're right, it might be easier. I could easily master it, but the paintwork is so beautiful and I don't want any mistakes at this late stage, not when we could get a viewing any day now.'

'You trust me?'

The unexpected phrase took her by surprise, but there was only one response to his question. 'I trust you.'

He nodded. 'Then I'll come over after I finish up here in a couple of hours, how does that sound?'

'Perfect.'

When the door to the shop went again he said, 'Stay here a while, enjoy the view and finish your hot chocolate.'

There was a high stool right by the window and she climbed up on it, silently accepting his invitation. Despite the rain getting harder as she sat there and eventually lashing at the windows with accompanying sound effects, the hot chocolate and the feeling of calm she felt around Leo cheered her when she hadn't realised she needed a little bit of a lift. The emotions that came with being here in the bay, and the cabin itself sometimes had her all over the place.

Leo eventually finished with the customer and came over to Nina's side. He had his keys in one hand, a couple of buoyancy vests in the other. 'I'll need to lock up, I've got a kayak lesson booked so I have to get down to the boathouse.'

'No worries.' She finished up her drink and he told her to leave the cup on the counter so he could rinse it and pop it in recycling.

'It's not the best weather for a lesson,' she said as they made their way over to the door and he picked up a sign to put out front.

He positioned the sign. 'It's good to have lessons in different conditions, helps prepare for the unexpected. And there's no wind, that's the main thing.'

Nina picked up her umbrella and opened it as he locked the door behind them. And before she headed over to her cabin she looked back at Leo as he turned to go down the side of the boathouse to the bottom. 'Stay safe,' she called after him.

'Promise,' he replied.

*

The rain continued to hammer down for the next couple of hours and with Leo taking longer than she'd expected and the temperature outside cooling quickly despite the daylight lingering, Nina peeled, chopped and stirred and pulled together a chilli con carne that was slowly simmering away by the time he knocked on the front door.

'Something smells good.' Leo had a box in his hand, presumably containing the drill.

She motioned for him to come in as she stirred the meaty mixture and replaced the lid. 'I was going to wait until after you'd been, but then I decided I'd be eating at midnight if I did that. Not that I'm complaining,' she leapt in quickly not wanting him to think her ungrateful.

'The lesson went fine but they wanted some free time after. And I can't turn business down when it's offered to me like that.' He set down the box he had with him. 'Right, show me where these hooks are and where you want them.' He crouched down on his haunches and took out the drill which he laid on top of the open case.

Once she'd shown him the piece and the wall she wanted it fixed to he selected the correct drill bit and got to work while Nina turned her attentions to the chilli even though it didn't need it. Anything to stop her watching him, his taut behind in cargo trousers, the glimpse of skin she got when his t-shirt rode up as he reached to drill the holes. A knot formed in her belly as she took out the packet of rice.

'It's done,' he announced, his lips gently blowing away dust from the hooks.

She tried not to let the sight of it make her body tingle all over and focused on the hooks when she went over to admire them. 'They look great.'

But she could feel him watching her, and the tingling

sensation crept all the way from the tips of her toes all up her body. They were so close there was no doubt now that it was his body heat she could feel. His hands hung by his side and she felt his fingers brush against hers briefly as though unsure whether to or not. Unless it was a mistake.

She backed away and returned to the kitchen to measure out the rice. 'Thanks, Leo. Much better than me doing it.'

Leo returned the drill to its case. 'No problem, told you it wouldn't take long.' He snapped the case shut and she thought that might be it, that he'd leave her to it, but he left the case there on the floor and came over to the kitchen. 'I could stay, if you want the company?'

She'd put a pan of water on to boil and had been pouring the rice into a cup when his words jolted her and the rice gushed out all of a sudden, overflowing the vessel.

'Where's your dustpan and brush?' He side-stepped the rice that had landed on the floor as she told him it was under the sink.

Nina cleared up what had spilt onto the kitchen benchtop and before she could change her mind she asked, 'Do you want to stay?'

'I wouldn't have suggested it if I didn't.' He still had the dustpan in his hand and turned to throw the remnants away.

'If you want some wine there's a bottle in the cupboard next to the glasses. Actually there are a couple of bottles leftover from the other night.' Her nerves almost got the better of her, but a glass of wine might calm her down.

'Sounds good to me.' Leo got out the glasses, but paused before he opened the red wine he'd found in the same place. 'Are you sure about this?'

'The wine or the meal together?'

'Both. I mean, people might talk.'

'Stop.' He was teasing her, she could tell. 'And the gossip mill is already underway. Maeve says we're getting on well. So did your gran.'

'Well we are.' He poured the first glass and handed it to her. 'But you used to worry about what other people thought.' He poured a glass for himself.

'I never did.' With the water on for the rice and the chilli all right for now she leant against the kitchen bench.

'You did so. It was one of your worries.' The word *worries* had her interest. 'You put it in the jar, don't tell me you've forgotten.'

She stumbled over her words. 'I'd forgotten the worry, but I hadn't forgotten the jar.' She just never thought he would've remembered. It felt so long ago and she'd assumed Leo would've buried that memory about her along with the rest when she left the bay. 'I wonder if anyone ever found it,' she said, looking at him over the top of her wine glass.

'Who knows.'

'I can't remember half the things I wrote now.' She wasn't sure whether to be glad about that or not. 'I'm sure a lot of them were ridiculous.'

'They weren't.'

'I appreciate the vote of confidence.' Another sip of wine relaxed her some more. 'I hope nobody found it – what if they traced it back to me, to us? We'd be ridiculed. It could be all over social media.' But as she laughed and tried to joke she realised he wasn't doing the same. 'Leo? You know something don't you?' He kept averting his gaze, taking particular interest in the wine's label on the back of the bottle.

'You always could read me like a book.' He looked up. 'Ok, admission time. You know how we threw the worry jar in the sea?' She nodded. 'Well about a year after you left the bay my dad brought out the jar.'

'He found it?'

'He saw us throw it in the water that day and went to grab it before it was washed out further. He told me he hadn't ever looked inside but he'd seen us pushing pieces of paper into it before and he thought we might regret getting rid of them all. He was going to try to sound me out about it and throw the jar back into the water if that was really what we'd wanted – we'd never have had to know what he'd done he said – but he didn't get much out of me when he tried and then he forgot about it until he was looking for some old oars in the loft and found it again. He handed it to me and told me he'd never opened it.'

'He really didn't look inside?'

'He says not,' Leo answered. 'I think if he had, he might have thrown it back in the water. It would've all been non-sense to anyone else but us. I mean imagine if someone had found it thinking there was going to be a mysterious message inside or a treasure map and all they found was our crappy scribbles.'

When Leo leapt up and shot into the kitchen she realised the pan of water must've boiled over. It snatched their attention away from the worry jar. He turned down the gas, she grabbed some kitchen towel to mop up excess water and once the pan was topped up again and heading towards a simmer she asked, 'What did you do with the jar?'

'I kept it.' He pulled his key from his jeans pocket, set down his glass of wine and left her dumbfounded. 'Wait here.'

It seemed to take forever for him to bring the jar back, when really it had only been a couple of minutes. 'I can't believe you still have it.' She briefly glanced at the jar as she checked the heat on the cooktop and made sure they didn't have another accident.

'Didn't seem right to throw it back into the water when you weren't around, so I stashed it away and kind of forgot about it.' He set down the orange glass jar, scratched on the sides, the tinny lid tarnished on the edges.

'Have you looked inside?' She had a dulled awareness that the jar contained feelings that had long since been left behind, others that hadn't, some trivial worries, others that ran much deeper.

'Of course not.'

'You're telling me you've never looked? Not once? Not even when you were angry at me for leaving, you didn't want to laugh at me from afar,' she added good-humouredly.

'I was angry you'd left, Nina, but whatever else you think I felt back then and every day since, I can almost guarantee you that you're wrong. I've never wanted to hurt you. Not ever.'

His words lodged in her heart as though each were a broken piece of glass from the jar. 'I never wanted to hurt you either.'

He launched past her again. She'd put the rice in the gently simmering water in the pan and yet again the bubbles had reached the surface and were beginning to spill over.

She groaned at yet another cooking mistake. 'That hob is way too temperamental.'

'Sure it's not user error?'

'Careful, or no chilli, you'll have to order in.'

He put a hand against his heart as though wounded, but then looked right at her again and said seriously, 'I promise you. I haven't opened the jar, Nina.' He turned down the heat beneath the pan of rice. 'Doesn't need to be any higher than that.'

'We'll see.'

When the moment hovered between them he told her, 'We always said we would never open that jar unless we were together.'

Nina picked up the orange vessel. She never would've imagined sitting here with Leo and doing this, not in a million years. But after all this time it suddenly felt right. 'We've got fifteen minutes to wait for the rice, barring any more emergencies, how about now?'

'Let's do it.' He followed her over to the coffee table where she knelt on the stripy beach rug beneath its feet. 'Are you sure about this?'

'I'm sure.' She unscrewed the lid and pushed the jar in Leo's direction while she picked up her glass of wine.

'No, you go first,' he laughed.

She hesitated only for a moment and then put her free hand inside, not once breaking eye contact with the man she'd shared so much with, and it was as though they were those two little kids again, with nothing but adventures on the beach, ice-cream flavours and a burgeoning romance on the horizon to look forward to, no matter what their worries had ever been at the time.

Nina managed to open up the folded piece of paper one-handed. She half expected the words to have faded but they hadn't, and when she read them she laughed so hard she almost slopped her wine.

Leo rescued the glass from her hand and set it onto

the coffee table. 'We don't want to ruin your new rug. Now what's so funny? Hope the laughter isn't at my expense.'

She covered her mouth with her hand for a moment and then told him, 'This wasn't the first worry I wrote, not even the second, third or fourth, but it seems apt to pull it out now.' She showed it to him and with a squeal, shut her eyes as he read it out loud.

'My best friend is a boy.' And this time he put down his own glass. 'I assume this was me you were referring to.'

'Of course it was. But I went through a time when I thought I was weird not having a special friend who was a girl. I wanted to fit in, be normal and sometimes other girls would laugh at me for hanging out with a boy at the cabins. They'd tease me about it. Later it didn't bother me one bit, but at first it really did. I thought I was weird like they told me I was.'

'Well I suppose they were right about one thing . . .'

'Hey!' She punched him gently on the arm.

'Right, my turn. Let's see if I can do one better.' He dug in a hand, rifled around as though he was digging into a tombola to draw a winner for the grand prize.

He unfolded his selected piece of paper. 'This was one of my worries . . . a serious one . . .' He cleared his throat as if to make a grand announcement and read, 'The chippy on the pier stopped selling the big pickled onions.'

Nina's laughter burst out once again. 'Now that really is a first world problem.'

'In my defence, I was addicted to them.'

'They gave you stinky breath.' She used to refuse to kiss him after he'd eaten one even though she liked them too, with the justification that consuming one for yourself was way different from the aftertaste left lingering on someone's tongue.

She reached out and plucked another memory and they kept them coming – 'I'm not sure if this is me or you.' She passed the paper to Leo.

He looked at the writing. 'Mum and Dad keep arguing.' He pulled a face. 'That could be either of us couldn't it? I can't make out if it's my writing or yours either.'

'Given my parents divorced I'd say it's me.'

'Maybe. But mine still argued a bit over the years. Every couple does.'

Before they could dwell on relationships and all they entailed he raised his eyebrows and plunged his hand into the jar for another memory. And when he opened up the piece of paper said, 'Oh this is definitely mine . . . "I fancy Adrian's girlfriend."'

This time she had a hard job keeping the wine in her mouth before she swallowed. 'How old were you when you wrote that one?'

'No idea, which means I can't remember which girlfriend it was, and there were many.'

He was enjoying this, they both were, although she knew not every memory would bring smiles. Maybe they should stop while the going was good.

It was Nina's turn and she knew this memory was hers. 'Another first world problem . . . "Molly and Arthur ran out of doughnuts at the café on the pier,"' she read. 'I'm still woken at night thinking about that you know.'

'You and your doughnuts.' He pulled out the next memory which was one of his. He'd worried they'd never get a dog, as his mum claimed to be allergic. 'There's another worry in there somewhere from when we got the dog and I then worried I'd have to clean up vomit. You know I'm squeamish about that sort of thing.'

'How do you handle it when people are seasick?'

'Easy, don't take them on a boat,' he quipped. 'or at least hand them a bucket. Your turn,' he prompted.

She pulled out another piece of paper. 'Aw, this one is me.' She clutched it to her chest briefly before she recited, '"One day Gran and Grandad might not remember me."' With a gulp she told Leo, 'I wrote that when a girl in my class had been crying at school and her friend told me it was because her nanna had dementia and didn't remember who she was. It broke my heart.'

'I can imagine.'

'Pick another,' she urged. The wine was going down well and it was almost time to dish up the chilli.

'"Nina will never notice me,"' he read with a grin.

She felt her cheeks colour. 'My turn.' And she pulled out the next, but when she saw the words her glassy stare had him reach out to take the piece of paper from between her fingers.

He didn't read it out loud, he just folded it once he'd seen what it said and put it with the other pieces. 'Want to talk about it?'

She shook her head.

Why don't my parents love me? were the words on that piece of paper. Words that she'd asked herself over and over as her dad's job took them both away from her and her brother time and time again, the lack of contact which, when it came, felt a duty rather than anything else, then the divorce and separate houses.

Leo screwed the top back on the jar. 'Perhaps opening this up wasn't the best idea.'

'It's fine, it gave me a laugh.' At least it had until that one. That was the thing about memories, they could linger on the periphery and although deep down you knew they were there, you'd manage to push them aside. Unfortunately they still had the power to take you by surprise.

Leo checked on the rice and declared it done as she stayed put. It was as though her legs didn't want to move just yet. That worry had been the first she put into the jar, probably the whole reason the worry jar was necessary in the first place, Nina trying to make sense of her place in the world along the way. It had evolved over time, especially as Leo joined in, and as their friendship blossomed and she grew happier she'd been able to worry about things that weren't quite so soul-destroying, things like doughnuts and the fact that her best friend was a boy.

She joined Leo in the kitchen where she pulled out two big pale blue bowls as he drained the rice and divided it between them. It was a squeeze in the compact space but they danced around each other with ease, and without a word about the jar or its contents, she spooned out the chilli on top of the rice, asked if he wanted sour cream and cheese – yes please to both – and Leo suggested they head over to his cabin, put on the festoon lights and eat al fresco so they could see the water.

'Is it warm enough to eat outside?' she asked absently. The weather had definitely cooled in the last couple of days, the sun not as strong as it was a few short weeks ago.

'If we find it isn't, then I have an outdoor heater or blankets.' He picked up the wine and both glasses, now empty, expertly held between his fingers. 'I'll be back.'

And if he was giving her breathing space without making her feel he was aware she needed it, she was grateful.

His absence for a couple of minutes gave her a chance to close her eyes and take a deep breath in, focus on the sound of the waves filtering in through the open door to the cabin. Even though Leo hadn't looked in the worry jar in all this time he'd still known it was in his possession, he'd still been more mentally prepared for it than she had, especially when his worries weren't what had started it in the first place.

By the time he came back to help her with the bowls of chilli as she locked her cabin, she managed a smile as if everything was absolutely fine.

It was an evening together, they'd done it before, plenty of times.

It had just been a while.

Chapter Fourteen

Leo

They crossed from her cabin to his – thirteen stepping stones, he'd known it since he was a kid and for every day since.

The festoon lights that hung between his cabin roof above the veranda and the tree a few metres away across the other side of a minute green space swayed in a gentle evening breeze and lit up the small table as they settled down to eat. He'd thought opening the memory jar would be powerful and he'd been right. He just thanked goodness they'd had a few funny memories first, rather than the one that had put a stop to the activity.

'This is good, Nina.' Fork in his hand, he'd already eaten half of his meal before he said much at all. He wanted to give her some time after seeing those words, the words that hadn't faded over time. He wondered whether the pain had.

'You must be hungry.'

'Very.'

She nodded in the direction of the water, a forkful of chilli with the white of sour cream and the yellow of cheese on top visible in the low light. 'It's nice out here.'

'Are you warm enough?'

'I think the chilli is helping keep me warm,' she said. 'And the wine.'

He topped up both of their glasses. 'Do you see much of your mum and dad?' He thought he'd ask the question out here while they were eating and looking at the water rather than all the focus being on Nina. It might make it easier for her.

'A bit, but we're still not close. Mum is with someone else, Dad too, they have their lives and I have mine.' She waited before she added, 'Sometimes I get sad that they even had kids.'

'I get that.' He knew they'd had their own lives even when they should've been parenting. It was one thing to keep a sense of self as a mum or a dad, but quite another to do it in the way Christy and Graham had. And although he'd never say it, he and most other people who talked about her parents thought them selfish. The upside was that Nina and William had turned out all right even without their attentions, and lucky for them they'd had Walt and Elsie, two of the most doting grandparents a kid could wish for.

He had to add, 'If they hadn't had kids, you wouldn't be here. And that would be a shame, a real shame.'

After a pause she said, 'I like to think that if I ever have kids I'll want to spend time with them. I get it that parents work and they're still individuals, I think that's a good thing, but mine took it to a whole new level. Work and their social life seemed to come before everything else, me and William were way down in the pecking order.' Her fork clinked against the porcelain bowl as she set it down and picked up her wine instead. 'I was only glad how close I grew to Grandma and Grandad. I never felt like I had nobody.'

'Not the same though is it?'

'No, it's not. And that worry in the jar just brought it all back, the way I felt as a kid, the crying I did over them, the pain I felt every time I had to say goodbye.'

'I remember how upset you'd get.'

'I still felt loved in a way though. In some respects it might've been easier if they'd gone for good, but they weren't, they were there enough for me to realise I wasn't all that important. They'd hug me goodbye, they'd tell me they loved me, and in those moments I was kind of happy.'

'But they'd still leave.'

'Every time.' She set down her wine and resumed eating her dinner.

She didn't speak again until she'd finished her food. 'Me and William talked about it recently. He was as hurt as I was, but he was better able to see that his world had moved on. He's helped me start to see that mine has too, with our parents on the very edges rather than front and centre.'

'But it's hard.'

'It is. And being here made it harder. This was the place they left me . . . us. Getting away from the bay was partly because of what happened and the realisation that any of us on the boat that night could've been a victim, but it was also because I'd reached a point where I had to process.' He wasn't going to interrupt, he wanted to hear this and she'd obviously reached a point where she felt ready. Leo liked to think it had a lot to do with how they were with one another, how they were growing closer again after all this time. 'I didn't know what my parents meant to me, never mind what I meant to them. I couldn't see things clearly at all.'

She sighed. 'Most people my age are getting ready for the years when their parents will need them to help out, but for me, it's Walt who has my attention. I'm not sure what I'll do, what William will do, if Mum or Dad ever need us. I know it sounds terrible, but I'm not sure either of us would come running. We wouldn't turn our backs, but . . .' Her voice trailed off.

'That doesn't make you a terrible person. It doesn't,' he added firmly when her look suggested otherwise.

He stacked his empty bowl into hers and picked up his wine glass. They were almost next to one another at an angle, both chairs behind the table and with a view over the railing and across to the water of the bay. 'You're not a terrible person, Nina. I know Walt and Elsie always struggled to accept the way your mum and dad parented.'

'They said something?'

'No, they'd never do that. But you could see their frustration, and my parents talked about it often. You and I spent so much time together, you were one of our family for a long while.'

'I love your family. I missed them when I left.'

'They missed you too.' He held her gaze for a moment. 'My parents hated the way you and William weren't a priority for Christy and Graham but they also talked a lot about Elsie and Walt and how much of a blessing it was for you to have them around.'

'I wish I'd been able to look at it differently when I was still here.' She didn't break eye contact. 'I didn't feel I deserved to be happy either, part of me wanted that family you and I once talked about, but looking at the mess my parents had made of theirs, I didn't think I could do it to you, or to anyone else for that matter. I assumed somewhere along the line I'd mess it all up. And then when I left you and didn't say a word, I couldn't come back here, walk around the bay or town knowing what I'd done to you and to your family. You're well thought of, I couldn't bear knowing that people hated me for what I'd done.'

'Nobody hates you, Nina. I certainly don't.'

'In many ways me and William were lucky compared to some kids who may not have anyone on their side.'

He almost wanted to reach over and give her a hug, glad she was able to see the good things in her life and almost push out the bad so it didn't hold court. But he couldn't. He didn't want to scare her away when they were at last so comfortable in each other's company. He knew he was opening himself up to a whole world of hurt, hopeful for a chance with Nina again, but he couldn't help himself. He loved her.

He always had.

'I like whistling,' Jonah informed Leo the next afternoon at the boatshed. He was unpacking a box of swimwear, and while he hung them in the allotted space on the aluminium clothing rail, grouped together by style, Leo ripped the sides of the cardboard packaging to collapse it down.

'Is that so?' Leo nodded in approval.

'Yeah, but you're doing it too much. I don't mean to be rude, but could you stop.'

Leo's laughter rumbled up from his belly. 'That told me.'

The kid was right. He'd been whistling all day long, and when he wasn't whistling he was humming. It was the morning after the evening he'd spent with Nina and nothing could dampen his mood. No matter whether they did or didn't get involved again, her company made him feel better than he had in a long while.

'Hello,' came a voice from towards the entrance. And when Leo looked up he saw Maeve.

'Hi, Mum!' Jonah enthused, but kept on with the job he was doing.

Maeve came inside and gave her son a hug before announcing, 'I got off work early. Molly and Arthur are fussing over Jo.'

'Fussing over their café more like,' said Leo. 'They might be retired, but whenever they're back they love being in there. You don't mind the early finish?'

'Not at all. It's a beautiful afternoon to be out and about.'

'It most certainly is,' he added chirpily, although he refrained from whistling. He'd woken this morning to sunshine and a pleasant breeze ruffling the leaves of the tree beyond the veranda. He'd sat in the same spot to eat his breakfast as he'd sat with Nina last night, remembering, enjoying, more than a bit tempted to knock on her cabin door and wake her up to join him.

'Jonah and I were about to head down to clean a couple of the kayaks,' he told Maeve.

'I'll come down with you.'

'Great.' He knew from his brother that at the party Adrian had suggested she try familiarising herself with happy memories of the beach and the sea first before she tackled letting Jonah get closer. And it was good to see she was doing it.

Jonah's head bobbed up from the other side of the

t-shirt stand. 'You're coming down to the beach?' he asked his mum.

'Yeah, is that OK?' Maeve didn't sound nervous, she sounded determined.

Leo didn't pass comment, he just waited for Jonah to run and position the sign and then he locked up and led them all downstairs into the boatshed itself.

'You could show me around,' Maeve suggested to Jonah, who in a few years would probably tower above his mum. He was already almost up to her shoulder height.

Jonah wasted no time darting this way and that to tell Maeve where Leo kept the different water craft and all the accessories that went with them. He knew the layout almost as well as Leo. He explained to his mum how the wetsuits hanging on the rack were returns which were waiting to be properly cleaned before they were available for rehire. Leo overheard him suggesting that people might wee in them and hoped he never mentioned that in front of a customer. He showed her the paddles stacked in sections according to size, explained the various watercraft, the paddleboards and kayaks and the sizing, the bodyboards that weren't used much now the younger kids were back at school. He led her over to the surfboards and explained about the surf leashes and how they fixed around a surfer's ankle. She probably knew a lot of the stuff her son was telling her, but Maeve just let him talk in a way he'd probably wanted to talk to her ever since he'd started to come down here and help out.

'He's been learning a lot,' Maeve said as Jonah took the wetsuits from hangers and headed to the very back of the boathouse where there was an enormous plastic tub. She watched him add wetsuit cleaner to the water Leo had put in there while Jonah was leading Maeve around the shed.

'He asks a lot of questions.' Leo smiled as they watched Jonah dunk the first wetsuit to give it a good clean.

'He's always been the same way, even with schoolwork, although obviously he doesn't have quite the passion for maths and English as he does for this,' she laughed, clearly taking in how at home her son was around the water and water craft, how anxious he was to be more involved. 'Hey Jonah?'

He looked up from the tub where he'd dunked a second wetsuit. 'Yeah?'

'I'm going for a walk along by the water.'

He stood a little taller. 'You hate the water.'

She looked at Leo then back to Jonah. 'I do not hate it. I'm wary of the sea and the dangers, there's a difference.'

He didn't seem convinced, but neither could he be bothered to think too deeply about it, and he got back to his wetsuits as Leo inspected the three paddleboards due out for hire in the next hour.

When Maeve stood in position looking out to sea, the wind lifting her dark hair and allowing her facial features to soften he asked, 'You sure you're ready?'

'I've been looking this way from the café on the pier for a long time.' She inhaled the sea air. 'We all enjoyed the beach and the sea for years. It's not fair to take it away from Jonah.' She looked over at her son. 'And I need to do this for myself too.'

Leo was about to reiterate that he'd keep an eye on Jonah now when he saw someone else come down the slope at the side of the boatshed. Surprised, he told Maeve, 'Seems like you're not the only one to decide it's time.' He smiled over at his brother. 'Adrian, good to see you.' He wouldn't make a big fuss, a show, because it seemed his presence had already made Maeve's determination turn to trepidation. He could see it in the way she held her body, not relaxed like it was moments ago, but rather stiffened and ready for something bad to happen.

'You took my advice,' Adrian smiled at Maeve.

'I did.'

Adrian's attention was immediately drawn to Jonah when they all heard laughter. 'What's he doing back there?'

'Cleaning wetsuits,' Maeve smiled.

'Slave labour?' Adrian asked Leo. 'He sounds way too happy.'

'He likes it,' said Maeve, amusement in her voice.

'Adrian!' The boy had spotted tall Adrian, his opponent in Frustration at the party. 'I'm cleaning wetsuits!'

'So I heard,' he called back.

'I'm going for a walk along the beach,' Maeve reiterated, determination back. 'Might even get my feet wet.'

'Want some company?' Adrian suggested, but as soon as he asked the question a customer had Leo's attention and Jonah was yelling out that he needed help.

'I'll go,' said Adrian, pointing Jonah's way.

Maeve hesitated only briefly before she turned and made her way across the sands to the water's edge and Leo was left wondering how life had ever got so complicated for him and his family and friends.

Leo locked up the boathouse and the shop at the end of another day. The sun was setting earlier and earlier and these later finishes wouldn't be for much longer. Very soon the water would be calm some days but on plenty of others he wouldn't be letting many people out with his water craft, they'd have to wait for conditions to change.

He walked towards the cabin thinking of how happy Jonah had looked when he'd left today with Maeve. He still hadn't been in the water but having his mum there with him on the sands was a start, and Leo was almost as excited as him to see what would happen next. And as he'd promised himself, Leo hadn't made a fuss of Adrian making it down to the boathouse. His brother had helped Jonah, he'd hung around until just before Maeve returned, and then he'd waved and gone on his way. Leo hoped it wouldn't be long before he came back again.

When Leo saw Nina his heart lifted and he wondered whether she'd be as chuffed to see him as he was her, but as he got closer he saw a man in a suit emerge from her cabin. She'd been standing on her veranda with her back to him, alone he'd assumed, but now it was clear she wasn't.

He grumbled beneath his breath and walked on past before he was spotted. The man looked vaguely familiar, but he couldn't place him – all Leo knew was that he didn't want the cabin to go to a city person, someone after a weekender to escape the city when the fumes in the big smoke got too much. The guy didn't look like a family man although perhaps beneath his suit he was carefree, open to adventure, perhaps he would fit in just fine. And it wasn't up to Leo who bought it. He'd just have to put up with the new owner. But if those stepping stones linking the two cabins were going to remain, he'd have to at least like the new owners a little bit. Otherwise it wouldn't be long before he carved a different path from his cabin, around the back of the bin storage, well away from the former O'Brien cabin. There would be nothing linking them then other than proximity and he could avoid bumping into anyone on his commute, even fence off his cabin from theirs.

Leo had a quick shower before starting up the barbecue on the veranda. He cooked the fish he'd picked up from the fishmonger in town at lunchtime, his mind more on the man at the cabin with Nina than his dinner. He'd only just plonked the fish on a plate to eat with the selection of veggies he'd stir-fried alongside it in a small pan when Nina came walking across the stepping stones. Even now after all this time it still warmed him to watch her. She even hopped between each one a little, as though her stride wasn't quite long enough, when it had been for a long time.

'Hey,' she smiled coming up the steps. 'Something smells good here.'

'Sorry, I should've made you some. I owe you a dinner, although I might have to do a bit better than basic fish.'

'It smells good to me. Get stuck in – don't let it go cold on my account.' She waved her hands to motion him to start eating.

'I hope I didn't spoil the viewing for you by cooking this up.' He sliced a piece of fish and added a chunk of green pepper before popping it into his mouth.

She seemed momentarily surprised he'd known it was going on. Or maybe it was because he'd not said hello. 'He left a while ago, but I don't think it would've been a problem.'

'Did you get any interest?' Please say no. Please say they hated it.

'You could say that.'

He swallowed his mouthful. 'Don't hold out on me.' His choice of words had a spark ignite between them.

'He's very interested.'

His heart sank 'Family man?' Suddenly he wasn't quite so hungry, but he kept eating so he couldn't say too much, so he didn't let his feelings be known, so he didn't show how much he hated this.

'I don't really know, I didn't like to ask many questions, I just showed him around.' He caught a waft of lavender shampoo from the blonde hair he remembered running his fingers through more times than he could count, the locks that had settled around his body as they made love.

'Leo, he made me an offer.'

Her words had him stop chewing and set down his cutlery as though they weighed more than they actually did. 'Already?'

'Yes, and it's a good one, much more than the asking price.' She told him how much the man had offered.

He whistled. 'For a cabin?'

'That's what I thought.'

'You're accepting the offer I take it.' He still hadn't drunk from the glass of water he'd set beside his plate, but he toyed with it now, wondering how many times he could swill it around before it slopped over the edge. 'It's a good offer, Nina. And the man has good taste, I mean the location is stunning, you've done a stellar job with the décor.'

She pulled out a chair and sat down. 'It's happening so quickly.'

'That's good,' he encouraged. Much as he didn't want her family to sell their cabin to anyone at all, he knew why they were doing it, why Walt wanted and needed the money. He started to eat his fish again. She was right, he didn't want it to go cold, as it wouldn't taste very nice if it did. But having a buyer lined up this quickly might mean she'd leave the bay soon and that didn't thrill him at all.

'Yeah, I suppose so. He didn't even look around for all that long, just a quick inspection and made the offer there and then.'

'He obviously wants it badly.' But he almost choked on his mouthful of fish as he said it because all of a sudden it came to him, where he knew the man from.

'I'm getting a beer.' He didn't even ask whether she wanted one, he just brought two bottles out.

He took a big swig and as soon as he swallowed he told Nina, 'I can't believe he's back.'

'Back?' She was running her fingers up and down her bottle of beer, loosening the condensation, a habit she'd had for a long time.

'I saw him earlier and thought I recognised him. He's come here sniffing around before.' He shook his head, the nerve of him. 'Last time he was after the boathouse and my cabin and if I'd agreed he probably would've worked on Walt too. But he went away, tail between his legs, when I told him it absolutely was not an option. Not ever. Or at least, I thought he'd gone for good, but it seems not.' He looked at Nina, her shoulders had drooped, she'd got her hopes up only to have them dashed.

'So he wants the boathouse and your place too?' she asked.

'He did then and I wouldn't mind betting he saw your cabin come up for sale and jumped at the chance to make a move. He probably thinks that if he gets his hands on one cabin then he's more of a chance to get mine and the boathouse.' He harrumphed. 'He couldn't be more wrong.'

'Whatever would he do with a boathouse and two cabins?'

Leo looked at her. 'Isn't it obvious? He'll develop them – into what I've no idea, but if he gets his hands on both cabins and my business, I don't think they'll last as they are for much longer.'

Nina gulped back her beer. 'I should've known the offer was too good to be true. That money would've set Grandad up.'

'It's your decision, I can't tell you what to do.'

She attempted to see a positive side for him. 'People go mad for water craft and picturesque bays on the south coast. Imagine, if the man does rent our cabin out as an investment, you'd get pre-bookings, have a busy high season and low season even.'

'It sounds as though you have it all figured out.'

'Leo . . . don't be like that. I came here to talk to you as a friend, I thought you'd understand.'

He was doing his best.

'I just want to do the right thing.'

'I know you do.' But it still reminded him of yet more change coming his way when he'd worked so hard to move forwards and thought he'd done so, here in the bay. 'I'm taking it out on you and I shouldn't be. You've been clear all along that you're selling, but that man . . .'

'I'm sorry, Leo. I really am.'

When she refused to look at him he said, 'You can take the offer, Nina. It's up to you.' But the thought of that man renting out the O'Brien cabin filled him with dread. It meant different neighbours on a constant rotation. 'Maybe I should sell up too,' he announced.

'What? You can't do that. This place is your life, Leo.'

'Well perhaps I should've left when you all did,' he huffed. 'Changed things for myself.'

'You don't mean that surely?'

He shrugged. 'Don't I?'

She put her head in her hands. 'This is all my fault, I've ruined everything, again.'

He felt her upset as though it were his own. 'I don't want to have him badger me once you sell and I'm still here.'

'But you can't let this drive you away.'

Silence.

'Leo, I worry that if I don't take this offer another one won't come along for ages, if at all. And I know it won't be for as much.'

'Probably not, no.'

'I have to get back to my job soon and I really don't want to leave all this with Grandad. A sum like this guy is offering would see Grandad through. Even if he went downhill quickly, which doesn't bear thinking about to be honest, he'd never have to move out of his home. If he needed looking after I'd be able to employ someone to be with him every day if I had to. Do you know Walt scattered Grandma's ashes beside the oak tree they planted when they moved in? It was her favourite place to sit in the summer, in the shade, letting the heat bother everyone else but her.' She was smiling at the fond memory.

He could well imagine Elsie sitting there beneath the stunning tree. He'd never realised it was Walt and Elsie who'd planted it, he wasn't sure Nina had ever told him that.

'I can no more imagine Walt leaving his bungalow than I can you leaving this place behind, Leo.'

'It's different.'

'Is it?'

Her heart was in the right place with this. She was trying to do her best for Walt, a man who'd been there for her her whole life. But it didn't make it any easier to know not only could the cabin be exchanging hands quicker than he'd ever expected, knowing it had gone to that man filled him with dread. The bay would change yet again and this time he had a feeling it would bring with it a permanency he felt in his soul. He didn't think he'd be able to carry on the way he had until now. It wouldn't feel like home. And would the life he'd built for himself all alone really feel like it was enough?

'I'm sorry, I've ruined your supper. . .I'll leave you to it,' she said.

A part of him desperately wanted to be with her for longer, while away the evening in her company. But she'd rocked his world with the announcement that she had a buyer already.

All he wanted for now was to be left alone.

'I think I preferred the whistling,' Jonah complained at the boathouse the next day.

If Leo wasn't careful Jonah wouldn't want to spend time down at the boathouse – he was beyond miserable. So far today nothing had gone right – because of the rain, Leo had run from his cabin to the boathouse, something he'd done countless times before, but slipped at the edge of the parking area and went down with a crash. He wasn't hurt apart from a grazed elbow and injured pride, as well as a wet top that he'd changed the minute he got inside. His day hadn't got any better though. Mid-morning he'd closed the till on his fingers when a customer had the audacity to pay cash – I mean who did that nowadays? – then he'd slopped his coffee down his t-shirt and had to change a second time, he'd chased up an order for a new paddleboard for a customer only to find the order hadn't even been processed, and his afternoon kayaking session had been scuppered as the winds picked up and the girl he was teaching got too scared to stay on the water. He didn't blame her; the only reason he hadn't bailed was because handling his confusion and distress over the latest developments out on the water as the waves began to get meaner and meaner seemed easier than coping any other way.

'Did you get out of the wrong side of your bed or something?' Jonah asked.

'Sorry, mate. I've got things on my mind, that's all.'

'Don't tell me,' Jonah groaned, 'adult stuff.' He'd popped a ring pull on a can of cola, because with a quiet afternoon and no lessons lined up Leo pretty much had the whole place in order without much left to do. 'Mum always says it's adult business if I ask her what's bothering her.'

'Do yourself a favour,' Leo softened, 'make the most of being a kid, it's the best time.'

'My nan says her twenties were her favourite years, then her sixties. Sixty is way old.'

'Not that old these days.' Leo pulled open a can of fizz too and they took them over to the viewing point. Jonah took the high stool and Leo went back to the counter to grab the other one. 'It's not great out there today,' he observed as they looked out at the water.

'You ever been out in a storm?'

Leo's eyes flashed at the memory. But then he settled, he'd been out in storms before that day and a couple of times since, just never on a boat with a group of people who weren't quite as used to it as his family were. 'Of course, but I don't advise it.'

'How do you get back if you're out in a kayak?'

'Quickly,' he said. 'Weather can change just like that,' he added with a click of his fingers for emphasis, 'but most people who hire from me only utilise Stepping Stone Bay. Some of the more experienced go around to Salthaven too, but usually they've checked the weather first, they see it coming in, they have time to get back.' Not always, but there was a fine line between educating Jonah about the sea and scaring him half to death.

'Mum didn't hate her beach walk the other day,' he informed Leo. 'I think she might even let me have a kayak lesson one day.'

'Yeah? Well that is good to know. And she already told me what a great swimmer you are.'

'My teacher says I'm a natural.'

He smiled at Jonah's apparent confidence. 'Swimming is a skill for life and the stronger you are in a pool, the better you'll be out there.' He pointed to the sea that captured anyone's focus from this viewing point. The wind appeared to have died down a bit and the rain had already eased a little. 'And I get why you love it – the swimming and the sea – my entire childhood involved water, boats, water craft. It seemed the whole time Adrian and I were making plans for our next adventure.'

'What sort of adventures?'

'The sea became our playground. One of our favourite games was to take the inflatable dingy out and play pirates. I'd be in the dingy which was the pirate ship – I could imagine it with a big sail, rocking on the waves, I even had a pair of binoculars to look out to sea and back to shore.'

'What did Adrian do?'

'He was the pirate. And even though I rowed like mad to get away from him and my arms ached from pulling on the oars, Adrian always caught me up in his kayak. He'd leap on board and yell "Arr!" just like a pirate.' Jonah was laughing now. 'He was the winner, pretty much every time. He'd fix a tow rope onto the end of the kayak, secure it to the dingy and tell me he was in charge. He'd take my oars but by then I didn't care, I was so knackered. I was more than happy to lie back in the dingy and bask in the sun while my brother rowed me to shore making all the pirate sounds he liked.'

'What else did you do in the water?' Jonah asked.

'Let me see . . . snorkelling, we loved looking into the murky depths to see if we could spot any creatures. We'd use boogie boards, surf. Anything really.'

'I wish I could do those things.'

'Some day, I'm sure you will. Let your mum have some time and I bet she'll come around. And in the meantime learn as much as you can on land.'

'How is that even possible?'

'You're already doing it. You watch me when I give lessons, you listen to the way people talk and you'd be surprised how much you've already learned by osmosis.'

'Osmosis? I thought that was to do with plant cells.'

'It is, but this is a different sort of osmosis.' He finished off his drink. 'Come on, it's quiet in here, I'll run you home or to the café if that's where Mum is?'

'Café, and yes please.' He went to get his bag from behind the counter.

Leo rarely closed up early, but today he just couldn't be bothered. He loved his cabin, he loved this shop. But did he really love his life so much he couldn't leave it all behind and get away from the change coming his way?

Chapter Fifteen

Nina

When they were younger Nina and Leo had often strolled away from Salthaven and on past Stepping Stone Bay along the pavement on the main road that curved around and where impressive houses sat up higher than the road level, big glass windows looking out to the sea. They'd always wondered what it was like to live in one of those; they'd seen one with a telescope in the front window and Leo had talked about what it might be like to use that at night to see boats sailing in and out of the marina, to see further around the coast. But those days seemed a lifetime ago and seeing Leo at his cabin that he'd made his home, Nina felt the ground-level view fitted him just perfectly.

Nina had been thinking about Leo all day. More than once she'd been tempted to head over to the boat-house and talk to him. It was Walt's decision whether he wanted to accept this generous offer, but it felt as though it would affect Leo so much she wanted to keep him in the loop. Nina couldn't believe the same man had already approached him about not only his cabin but also the boathouse. His livelihood, his home. No wonder Leo was all over the place and questioning what he wanted. But hearing him talk about perhaps leaving himself pained her more than she'd ever thought it would. She'd left, Adrian had, so had Maeve, so why not Leo?

She knew why. His cabin, the boatshed, Stepping Stone Bay. It was Leo through and through. He couldn't leave, it would be like leaving behind a part of his soul, but she had no right to question whatever he decided.

Now, from her cabin Nina could see the lights on at Leo's. The rain that came and went whenever it felt like it had started up again. It took her two mugs of tea, some leftover lasagne she'd made at Grandad's, and a great deal of courage before she decided she had to head over and see him.

He didn't look overly surprised to see her when he opened the door. He had one arm in a fleece and pushed his other arm into the garment before lifting it over his head to pull down over his broad chest. 'Hey.'

'Hey.' She brightened just hearing his voice and seeing him. 'How was your day?'

'Miserable.' Oh. Maybe not the right question then. 'Everything all right? Hooks didn't fall down did they?'

'No, the hooks are there to stay. Thanks again for putting them up.'

'No worries. Want to come in?'

'I shouldn't, it's late.' She took a deep breath. 'I've come to apologise to you.' She had a raincoat on, but she pushed down the hood now as she stood on the veranda a bit closer to the door. She'd had a call from the estate agent an hour ago to reiterate the offer on the table and the only thing it had done was make her want to talk to Leo more. He felt like the only person who understood about the cabins, which was silly when you thought about it. The cabins were special to William but he had his own family and work to deal with, Walt needed the money and she couldn't make him feel guilty if he decided to go ahead. It felt as though Leo was the only one she could talk to, and yet it felt cruel. 'I probably should've kept it to myself,' she said, 'told you once Grandad made a decision.'

'I'm glad you told me.'

'I can't stop thinking about what you said.' When his eyes begged the question she added, 'That you might consider leaving this all behind.'

He looked about to say something, but instead of addressing the issue suggested she come inside. 'I just put the kettle on – stay for a cup of tea.'

'Better not, it's late and I just had a second cup as I tried to get up the nerve to come over. I'll be peeing all night if I have any more.'

He leaned against the door frame. 'You were that scared to see me?'

'Not scared, worried.' And she hated that he might think she was blasé about the sale of the cabin. She supposed she had been at first when she'd come here to do the place up, she'd thought it would be going through the motions, a matter of formalities. She hadn't foreseen quite how much she'd enjoy being here around the bay again, and more than that she hadn't thought she'd ever feel such a connection so quickly after all this time, and such distress at the thought of him giving up something he loved so much.

'Just come inside, Nina.' He didn't wait for an answer before grabbing her hand and gently coaxing her inside.

He headed over to the kitchenette while she hung up her jacket and accepted his offer of tea before choosing the armchair to sit in, the oversized squishy armchair that made her smile when she sat down because it was as if it swallowed her up a little and its edges kept her there.

When Leo brought over the tea she admitted, 'Whatever we decide, someone will be unhappy. If Grandad takes the money he's sorted for life, but he and I both know what it will do to you, whether you stay or go. And we also know we might not get another offer. So if we turn it down the worry about that continues on.'

'I can see it's a tough decision.' He held her gaze then. 'Does it feel good that soon you could draw a line under Stepping Stone Bay once and for all?'

'That's exactly the way I was looking at it before I got here.' She breathed in, always able to smell the sea even when the air was filled with so much more. 'I thought I'd come here, do the place up, sell it for Grandad, no more thinking about the bay or the cabins.'

'Or me.'

It wasn't a question and she didn't answer. Because what he'd said was true.

'How do you feel about it now, leaving the bay I mean?' he persisted.

'I see the beauty I'd forgotten about, I see the escape down here, I see how happy you are, your boathouse. It's wonderful down here, Leo. If it was practical for me I could possibly buy it myself, but as I explained it's not.'

'And would your grandad mind the lesser price if it went to someone who offered something reasonable rather than crazy?'

She smiled. 'It's a ridiculous offer isn't it? If it hadn't been, this wouldn't be an issue, I'd tell him to go away and not bother us or you ever again.' She thought about it. 'To keep it in the family I think Grandad would take the sum and be happy with it and it probably would be enough. And if I was down this way that's a whole worry off his mind. I think sometimes he feels he might have to do this all himself, no matter how much I tell him he won't. I'd be closer if I get the transfer, which I don't see as a problem at all.'

He set down his mug and sat forwards on the sofa, forearms resting on his thighs. 'I've been thinking about your cabin a lot since you told me about the buyer.'

'I know you have. You've been thinking about leaving.'

He ran a hand across his chin. 'I actually did. For the first time ever I wondered what it would be like for me to escape here, the memories, everything.' He smiled at her. 'I can't do it. You're right, this place is me. It might solve issues short term but long term I know it wouldn't, it would make an even bigger mess.'

'I'm so happy to hear you say that.' She'd never felt such relief, because the way he'd looked when he'd suggested he might leave the bay behind had told her he was serious and it also told her how much it would break her heart if he went through with it.

'I've been thinking about your cabin in a different way,' he said.

She sat forwards, intrigued.

'I took out loans for the boathouse, so financially I'm not in a great position, but I could talk to the bank, see what I can do about raising the money myself.'

'You mean you'd be interested in buying the cabin?'

'You never know until you try,' he shrugged. 'And I really don't want Walt to turn down the offer because of me and have to wait for ages for another buyer to come along. He'll have all that stress and it isn't fair.'

'I don't know what to say . . . I mean, it's an obvious solution when you think about it. If it works.'

'I can't offer the same as the other buyer but I can see the bank and try to get to the asking price.'

Nina didn't know what to say other than, 'Grandad will go for it, I know he will.'

'Even though it'll be less money?'

'Yes.'

'Well let's not get ahead of ourselves. It might not be an option, remember.'

But she was smiling. 'Except it might be. And Grandad would jump at the chance to have it go to you and nobody else. You know he thinks the world of you.'

'Then let's see what the bank says.' He'd started to smile now as well.

'Let's see what the bank says,' she repeated.

Somehow, even though it was no less real that the cabin would still be leaving the family with a sale, selling it to Leo if he could come up with the funds could leave everyone content with the outcome.

'What would you do with a second cabin?' she asked, already hopeful, because ever since he'd suggested he might leave the bay behind she realised that she'd always assumed he would be around. And thinking that he might not be was almost unbearable.

'I hadn't thought that far.'

'You could always join them together and make one big cabin,' she grinned. 'One day you might have a family.' Her smile faded as she tugged the ends of her cardigan across her lap and over her thighs. She'd thought he had one when she saw him on the beach that day with Maeve and Jonah and the memory pulled at her again, enough to realise this man had once been her world and maybe he wasn't out of it yet.

'We used to dream about "one day", you and I. Do you remember?'

Softly she said, 'Of course I do.'

'And you really think Walt would take the asking price rather than the ridiculous offer?'

'There's more to life than money.' She smiled. 'I'd better go, it's late. Let me know how you get on at the bank.

'Will do.' He got up to walk her to the door.

She turned so quickly she hadn't realised how close he'd got to her as she reached for her raincoat from the hook. Her face was almost pressed against his chest. 'I'd feel better knowing the cabin went to you rather than anyone else, Leo.' She was too close to look into his eyes, as if she did that she'd almost be tempted to kiss him. 'If you kept the cabin it wouldn't feel quite like we were erasing a part of history.'

'That'll never happen.' But he went over to the kitchen and picked up the orange jar that held so many of their memories. 'Here, you should take this. It's yours really.'

She let him place it in her hands. 'I don't know what to do with it.' It felt a bit like he was trying to let go of the memories they had, their joint history.

'That's up to you.'

It felt like he was giving her a choice, a choice about their past and their future.

And she had no idea what to do with either.

Chapter Sixteen

Leo

L eo left the bank with that sinking feeling that life was about to change in a way he couldn't bear. He hadn't managed to persuade the bank manager to loan him the amount he needed to buy the O'Brien cabin.

Leo had finished work, had the appointment and headed to the nearest card shop. He knew he was going to have to paste a smile on his face for the sake of his parents at their anniversary dinner tonight. It was a celebration, not a miserable occasion, and he wasn't going to be the one to spoil it for them.

He bought an anniversary card and as he paid and the assistant slipped it into a paper bag the card was yet another reminder he'd never come close to that kind of commitment with anyone since Nina. He'd once thought they'd be like his parents, together for many many years, celebrating anniversary after anniversary. And despite the twelve years apart, slowly, since she'd arrived he'd begun to think that perhaps they might have another chance. Maybe fate had wanted to bring them together and her coming to the bay to sell the cabin had been what it took. He'd felt even closer to Nina when they'd looked through the worry jar together, their childhood selves in the room with them as they sifted through the memories. He'd comforted her after she confided in him about her parents, even more so than she had back then, as though the years gone by had enabled her to see things from another angle. And he'd seen the delight in her eyes when he suggested he might be in a position to buy the cabin and take all her worries away. He should've kept his big mouth shut until he knew whether it was even possible.

And now? Now they'd take the high offer, she'd be leaving sooner rather than later and all he'd think when he looked over at the cabin was that it had once been a special place but had turned into nothing more than a holiday rental for a man who wanted to get his hands on a lot more of Stepping Stone Bay.

As Leo walked towards his parents' house he told himself the sooner he got the facts into his head, the better. The Nina and Leo of the past had gone, and it was too complicated to even think about trying to go back to what and who they were.

Camille answered the door and he got a decent waft of the chicken piccata Adrian was making for dinner. 'Something smells good.'

She closed the door behind him. 'It does, doesn't it. And he's doing a whisky caramel and banana pudding too.'

Leo gave his gran a hug and snatched up a pen to write the card for his parents before either of them saw him. They were at the back of the house in the kitchen with Adrian according to Camille which meant he was safe for now.

'I went to see Nina earlier, took her a casserole,' said

Camille as Leo took off his shoes. 'I mean it's no fun cooking for one is it, thought she might be surviving on pizzas and takeaways.'

'You know she's not doing that, Gran. Walt has had her over for dinner enough.'

She kept her voice low. 'She told us you were going to the bank.' He shouldn't be surprised.

'She told you?'

'I was there when she came to see Walt. She wanted to be upfront about the other offer and let him know all the options. Said she felt it only fair.' She said it in hushed tones and Leo would've almost laughed if his bad luck with the bank wasn't still lodged in his psyche. 'And Walt doesn't want to sell to that man. He's so very happy that you want to buy it.'

All Leo had to do was look at her.

She looked as deflated as he felt. 'Oh, your meeting didn't go well.'

He sealed the envelope and slumped onto the grand chair in the hallway that really was for show unless anyone sat there to put their shoes on. 'No, it did not.'

'Well at least you tried.' She sighed. 'Does Nina know?'

He shook his head. 'She'll be disappointed and she'll have to go with the higher offer I suppose.'

Camille didn't say anything at first but then looked at him tenderly, the way she'd done when he was a boy. 'Be patient with her, Leo. She's doing her best.'

'I know she is.'

'You still care about her, don't you?'

'We were together a long time.' He closed his eyes a moment. 'Perhaps both of us need to let go of the nostalgia.'

'You don't mean that.'

'She never came back for me, Gran.' Camille put a hand on his shoulder as he fought back emotion, some of it to do with his failure at the bank, most of it tangled up with Nina. 'I waited for her then, waited for her to come back to the bay or for her to get in touch and tell me what was going on. For such a long time I thought she would. And she never did.'

'I know how much it hurt you. She was hurt too and she's desperate to do the right thing now.'

'Buying the cabin would've been perfect, that's all.'

'I know, love.'

'I don't expect Walt to turn down the other offer.'

She harrumphed. 'He won't take it, not now he knows it's a businessman who plans to make changes so the rest of us no longer recognise the place.'

'But this would set him up for the rest of his days.'

'Would you take it if you were him?'

Leo shook his head. Walt loved the bay as much as he did. 'No, I wouldn't.'

'He'll wait to get the asking price.'

Now he felt worse. He'd got Nina's hopes up, Walt's, and all for nothing. And now they'd have to wait, endure the pain of trying to sell a property which could be a drawn-out process in the best of circumstances. It didn't matter that the cabin was in a top location, that it was done up as the perfect seaside escape, buyers could play games and change their minds and mess Walt about. And knowing that made Leo feel even lower.

'Walt thinks the world of you, Leo.'

'And I him.'

'When he heard you might be interested in buying

I've never seen him so happy,' she smiled. 'He always wanted to keep the cabin, he wanted to see his grand-kids in it, keep it in the family. But he's always thought of Nina and William's future too, you know how close they are. When Elsie died he retreated into himself a bit and had the family worried. Nina's mother was next to useless – no surprise there – but Nina was back and forth to his bungalow every few days or nights to be with him.'

That piqued his interest. He'd never seen her. 'I never realised she'd done that.'

'All she did was spend time with her grandad. She had a full-time job, shifts all over the place, but between that she slotted in time with Walt and was at his side whenever she could manage it. I saw her a couple of times and she asked I didn't mention it to anyone that she was around. I've honestly never seen a young girl look so drawn, so flat, so exhausted. She had dark circles beneath her eyes so large you could've curled up in them to sleep. I caught her crying one day too – Walt and I had become friends by then, he'd given me a key for emergencies, and I'd used it when she hadn't answered the door.'

His heart went out to Nina, thinking she'd gone through all of that without him.

'I nearly told you, but not after the way she'd left. I knew you didn't need to know it then. But I think you need to know it now. She burst into tears on me once. Said she couldn't go on like this. That was when Walt heard her. He realised that he needed to see he still had a life to be lived, he still had people to love and who loved him. He felt terrible for being the cause of Nina's stress and over a few days we looked after her rather than

236

the other way around. I had her tucked into bed with a hot water bottle, I cooked for her and Walt and by the time she left that time both she and Walt were a lot calmer.'

'He seems happy enough whenever I see him.'

'He is. He's content. He still has a wobble every now and then, we all do. It's hard at our age. It's scary. Knowing the end is near.'

'Don't talk like that, Gran.'

'Well it is and more so for Walt. Me, I have you and your mum and your dad, all by my side. Walt doesn't have the same. Although he has me now and I've found a friendship I treasure.'

Granny Camille was right. She did have the family by her side, but it was still nice to have someone of her own age to spend the days with. Leo couldn't imagine feeling so bereft when someone left you in this world that you didn't want to function. When Nina had left, his world had crumpled, but he'd picked himself up and carried on somehow. He couldn't imagine how Walt had felt so bad yet not reached out. He couldn't imagine how Nina had kept up caring for her grandad when she had a life away from the bay, a job to do, and no support from her mother by the sounds of it.

'Come on,' Camille urged, 'the smell of dinner is making my tummy grumble.'

He stood up, gave her a hug. 'Thanks Gran, you always know the right things to say.' Because despite the outcome at the bank, she'd told him a little bit more about Nina and it made him see past his own pain to how hard it had been for Nina too, even though she'd been the one to run off. She hadn't just pushed him aside and started over. She'd still had to deal with pain, loss, grief and family issues, and all of it had been without him.

And that made him sadder than ever.

Chapter Seventeen

Adrian

'About time,' Adrian declared when his brother finally came through to the kitchen. 'Heard you arrive ages ago.'

'I've had him chatting,' Camille apologised. 'Sorry about that.'

'I was beginning to think we'd have to give your portion to the dog,' said Adrian.

Leo greeted his brother with a manly hug – distance and slaps on the shoulder blades – 'We don't have a dog.'

'Guess you'll get to eat it then,' Adrian grinned, flicking a tea towel over his shoulder as he set down the lid he'd taken off the cook pot.

It felt good to have the whole family together tonight. It was the first time they'd had a proper meal since he'd moved back – usually at least one of them was missing – Leo was still working, Camille was with Walt or either of his parents had something else planned. But tonight they were all together.

It wasn't long before they were all gathered at the table, plates of sumptuous chicken piccata in front of them and the aroma of lemons and garlic filling the room.

Talk turned to Walt's party when his mum told them

she'd seen young Jonah at the café and he had announced he'd eaten at least a dozen chicken wings.

'Didn't get a look-in with those.' As Adrian took his seat at the table he recalled Jonah's messy fingers and declaration that he wanted to get to the chicken before Leo.

'He's such a character,' Camille laughed. 'He reminds me a lot of you boys at his age, always wanting to get involved in everything.'

'He's not bad at board games either,' Adrian laughed, explaining all about the Frustration tournament they'd had, how Jonah wanted a rematch.

'You boys used to like to play Monopoly but it always finished with a big argument and you abandoning the board.' Anne shook her head. 'I think a few of the bank notes got torn too. I think we still have the game somewhere.'

'It's good to hear of kids playing board games,' Camille said. 'They spend too much time on devices these days.'

'Maeve didn't let him bring his iPad,' Adrian told her, 'not to the party. And he talked with most people until it got to the point where he really needed something else. He's a great kid.'

Leo was looking at him with a puzzled expression. He took a sip of his wine and with one eyebrow raised the way he did when he was trying to wind Adrian up, said, 'Maeve's pretty great too.'

He knew she was. Seeing her outside the café in town after all this time had hit him harder than a sail caught in the wind whipping a boat in a different direction all of a sudden. And the way she'd looked at him he knew seeing him again after all this time was significant for her as well. Because he and Maeve had had feelings for one another since before the party on the boat that night, they'd just never had a chance to see where they were heading. Because everything had changed. He thought about the way she'd talked to him on the beach before they headed to the O'Brien cabin, every glance they exchanged during the party and the odd smile that drifted his way. She seemed cautious, but he guessed he could blame that on the passage of time. He wished he'd been able to walk her to her car, talk to her more.

And now Adrian wasn't going to let Leo get away with his comment about Maeve, not with his family looking like they suspected there was more to tell on that score. Two could play at that game.

'How *is* Nina?' Adrian asked his brother.

Leo just shook his head and laughed.

'Busy at the boathouse today?' his dad asked Leo, maybe picking up that the boys were on the cusp of winding one another up further. 'I was worried you weren't going to make dinner on time.'

'Always busy, Dad.' Their parents loved to hear about the boathouse. Adrian had hated talk of it for a long time – or perhaps hate was too strong a word. He just felt indifferent to it for years, like he wanted to move back a few paces, further and further until it wasn't a part of his life any more.

'People still want lessons?' Jimmy asked.

'They do, although it's starting to tail off now. We'll still get bookings in autumn and winter but not so many.'

'I wouldn't even dip my toes in the sea now it's no longer summer,' said Camille. 'I don't blame Molly and Arthur for spending part of their year in Spain. Oh, it would be lovely and warm, sounds ideal to me. My arthritis plays up the moment the weather forecast so much as hints at a frost.'

'You're not going to abandon us for Spain are you, Gran?' Adrian checked.

'Course not.'

'You've done us proud with this meal, Adrian,' Jimmy approved, scooping up another mouthful.

'Yep, you can seriously cook,' Leo agreed.

Pleased with the praise, Adrian nodded. 'Not my only dish either. I'm good with Caribbean food after I took a cooking class last month. Thought I'd try something different,' he added when Leo's look must've shown his acknowledgement that his brother had never once been into cooking classes. He supposed there had been a lot of changes over the years, some he'd seen or knew about, other things he didn't.

'What's Caribbean food like?' Camille pondered.

'Think colourful, lots of flavour, spices. Next time I come I'll make sancocho.'

'That sounds complicated,' said Anne.

'Meat and vegetables basically,' Adrian laughed, 'with different flavours. Or I can make curried shrimp, jerk chicken.'

'Jerk chicken sounds about right,' Leo laughed, earning himself a punch on the arm at his emphasis on the first word.

Sometimes when he and Leo were together it was as though nothing had ever changed, as though they were still those two boys who'd run out of the door every morning in the summer holidays, down to the boathouse to see their parents, into the sea the minute they could. And

242

while he knew that wasn't the case, it felt good to be back here, and tonight was grounding. It told him he was really home. And he felt something shift inside of him.

When the boys and Camille handed Anne and Jimmy the card with the booking for the hotel and the show, they were overwhelmed that so much thought had gone into their anniversary. Jimmy even opened the single malt he'd had in the cupboard since one of his customers gave it to him upon his retirement from the boathouse.

'No more for me thanks, Dad.' When Jimmy tried to offer Leo one more glass of single malt he declared he had work tomorrow. 'Always an early start for me.'

'You're a good lad.' He put an arm around each of his sons' shoulders. 'You both are.'

When Adrian and Leo left together they'd only reached the end of the path when Adrian said, 'Wonder if Dad will finish that entire bottle of single malt tonight.'

'Wouldn't put it past him.' Leo zipped up his jacket with the wind whipping around as though summer was forgotten about already. 'Although it was potent stuff.'

'I can't believe he opened it at last. I tried to get him to at Christmas if you remember?'

'Yeah, I remember.' Leo laughed. 'It's good to see him and Mum so happy after all this time.'

'He'll be even happier after another few glasses.'

They crossed over once the passing car had gone past. 'You got your name down for supply teaching yet?'

'Not yet. I'm lucky I've got savings but they'll be eaten up in no time if I don't sort something soon.' Although his heart really wasn't in it. But rather than feeling miserable and sorry for himself with no idea where to go next apart from come back here, seeing Maeve after all this time had given him a form of hope. Hope about what, he wasn't sure, but he didn't mind that.

'Maybe a permanent role might suit you better,' Leo suggested.

But Adrian shook his head. 'I can't deal with the politics. The last school I worked in would've been all right if it hadn't been for the deputy head being a complete tosser.'

'I don't suppose that'll help,' Leo laughed.

'I surprised you all when I went into teaching didn't I?'

Leo gave him a look that suggested he'd asked a pretty stupid question. 'You could say that. I'm surprised Mum and Dad didn't try to talk you out of it.'

'They knew I'd made my mind up.' He took in a breath of evening air. 'I think I broke their hearts a little bit when I didn't go into business with you.'

'They also know you've got your own life to live.' He paused and then added, 'I did get to thinking perhaps I'd sell up, move away from here myself.'

Adrian stopped in the middle of the road before Leo frowned and urged him to cross to the other side. 'Did I just hear you right?' he asked when they were safely on the pavement.

'That businessman would offer me enough money to start over somewhere else.' Over dinner Leo had filled him in on the businessman he'd told to sling his hook when he sniffed around Leo's cabin and the boathouse a while ago resurfacing and offering a substantial price for the O'Brien cabin. 'I could build another boathouse.'

Adrian swore loud enough for the man walking his dog to cross over to the other side of the street. 'Leo, you can't be serious.'

'You all left, why don't I get to do that same?'

'Leo, we all left . . . but we all bloody well came back.'

'All right, enough of the cursing,' Leo smiled. 'Changed my mind anyway.'

'Glad to hear it.'

'The bay, the sea, the boathouse, it's all me. I couldn't change that even if I wanted to. My only complaint about *my* workplace,' said Leo, 'is that I don't have my brother there to run the business with me.'

'Coming down there the other day was weird.'

'Good weird or bad weird?'

Adrian considered his reply. 'I thought it would be a bad weird but it wasn't. The night I came to Nina's party was worse. That night I went down to the beach first. I bumped into Maeve.'

'Ah, now we're getting somewhere. I thought you two looked friendly at the party. As I said, she's pretty great. Did you talk?'

'A little, not for long, enough for me to have the balls to walk into the party at least.'

'Then I owe her a thank you,' said Leo.

'You know for a long time I never went near the sea, never set foot on a beach. Which, let me tell you, is pretty difficult with a wife who longs for holidays in the Seychelles or the Maldives.'

Leo began to laugh. 'You weren't tempted?'

'I leapt at the chance for New York when she mentioned it, put it that way.' They were walking along the main road now and you could hear the sea in the distance as the waves built up and then crashed down once again. 'Sitting on the beach that day with Maeve I could only see what the sea offered, not what it took. I could see its beauty.'

'Its beauty or *her* beauty.' He held up both hands. 'Sorry, I'll stop winding you up now. I apologise.'

'I still feel responsible that someone drowned on my watch.'

'Maybe that's something every skipper feels if it happens to them, I don't know.'

'I've realised since I came back here that my avoidance of the sea, the beach, this town I grew up in, hasn't made it all go away. That sounds stupid. It sounds like I'm an idiot not to have worked that out for myself. But I can only see it now after being away for so long.'

'I think Nina is having the same experience.'

'She looked happy at the party. She did,' Adrian encouraged when Leo looked doubtful. 'And I saw her looking at you more than once.'

'We have a history.'

'And a future?'

Leo shrugged. 'Not now she's selling the cabin.'

'You don't think she'll take the businessman's offer do you?'

'I don't think she or Walt want to, no.'

'Cheeky fecker, sniffing around here when he isn't wanted.'

'It's an insane offer. It would set Walt up forever and then some.'

'Selling to him could have the potential to change the fabric of the bay.'

'The fabric of the bay? That sounds almost poetic. Must be the teacher in you.' Leo looked at his brother and explained, 'I asked Nina to give me time to talk to the bank.' Leo looked at his brother and explained, 'I was going to try to buy the O'Brien cabin myself. That's why I was so late getting to Mum and Dad's dinner tonight.'

Adrian took in what his brother was saying. 'Well . . . how did it go?'

One look gave him the answer. 'I've already had loans for the boathouse to refurbish along the way.'

'Because you've had to do it solo.'

'I'm not saying any of this to make you feel bad. It's just the way it is.'

They carried on walking, past the pier, up the hill the other side and when they reached the top of the track that would lead down to Leo's cabin Adrian suggested a nightcap at Leo's place.

'You seriously need one after all that scotch?'

'I'm thinking more of a coffee.'

'I'll be up until all hours if I add coffee to the mix.'

But Adrian was still walking with him down the track. 'Good. You'll need to be awake for this, because I've got a proposition for you.'

Chapter Eighteen

Nina

Nina had seen Adrian outside her cabin last night. She'd heard voices, and although she'd assumed it was Leo with somebody else, she'd had to check, because they were so far away from any other properties and she wanted to be sure it wasn't anyone who didn't belong down there. She'd heard them laughing too and although she'd been tempted to run out and ask Leo how he got on at the bank she hadn't. Because if it was good news he would've knocked. Instead she'd sat on the sofa sipping a hot chocolate as she heard the laughter fade into the distance as they presumably went inside Leo's cabin. She'd sat there for quite some time basking in the memories of both families coming down here day after day, season after season. Something that was past, not future.

This morning Nina had just gone outside to set off to meet Maeve and put her rubbish in the bin en route when Leo came out of his cabin to do the same. And not only that, Adrian was behind him.

'Good morning you two.' She frowned, not because they were together but because she knew that look, the Magowan boys' look they'd had when they were up to mischief as kids. They were up to something. 'Big night?'

They recounted the anniversary dinner, the scotch.

'I'd better head home for a shower,' said Adrian. 'Sleeping on a sofa was one thing in my twenties but these days it makes me feel rough.' He smiled, waved at them both and off he went.

'It's so nice he's back,' said Nina. She knew it was bad news about the bank but she didn't want to hear it out loud.

'Aren't you going to ask how I got on at the bank?'

'I assume not well or you would've told me.'

'You're right, it wasn't good.' Her spirits sank even though she'd known. 'But I've got another appointment later today so keep everything crossed.'

'You're going to try again?' He had to be doing it for her and she didn't want to put him through it because if they'd said no once, surely that was what would happen again.

'I am. Fingers crossed.' He made the gesture with his hands.

'Leo, you don't have to keep trying. We'll get a buyer. Who in their right mind wouldn't want to live down here?' She gulped when she took in the sound of her own words, the heartbreak waiting behind them when everything changed.

'Nina, I want to. Let me do this. Let me at least try.'

'OK.'

'You off somewhere nice?'

'I'm meeting Maeve.'

'Send her my best,' he smiled.

When Nina reached the top of the track she turned left to set off in the direction of the pier and the café. She did her best not to get her hopes up about the bank, but a second appointment was surely a good sign.

Maeve was working until late morning and then not again until mid-afternoon and so the girls were meeting for lunch and possibly a trip to the cinema while Jonah was at school. Nina had missed this – simple friendships, someone who knew her back then and who knew her now. She had friends at work, she had a good social life, but there was something about a person having known you for years that made the friendship that much fuller and stronger; they knew the good and the bad, there was an understanding that didn't need to be explored.

Nina had on jeans and a t-shirt, but it was cooling down fast in the days now as well as the evenings as the end of September approached and so she checked she'd put her cardigan in her bag in case she needed it. And as she carried on walking she decided no matter the outcome of Leo's meeting at the bank, she should be proud. She'd come back to the bay, she'd faced her fear of the feelings it would stir up, she'd confronted her trepidation at facing Leo after all this time and they'd settled into a friendship of sorts. She wondered whether it would ever be more again, but right now she had too much on her mind, and she knew he did too. Once the cabin was sold perhaps it would make everything clearer.

Then again it might make everything that bit more messy and who knew where that would leave them.

Nina found Maeve chatting to Jo at the café, but bag in hand she looked almost ready and so Nina perched on the window seat while she waited, looking out and down along the pier, watching passers-by, a few little kids who weren't yet ready for school tearing up and down the planks, an elderly couple hand in hand for a stroll, a surfer who'd come up from the beach and was leaning his board up against the railings of the pier.

'I'm sorry to keep you waiting,' Maeve apologised, 'And would you mind if we stayed here? Molly and Arthur are out with friends and Jo hates to ask them for more help than they already give her. We thought the café would be quieter today but I can tell Jo is worried about not being able to handle a rush if she's on her own, so I'll hang around and jump in if I need to.'

'Totally fine with me.' Nina dismissed the worry. 'You go tell her and I'll grab a table.' As Nina sat down at a table for two she watched Maeve with her new boss, glad to see how well she was settling in, as though she'd been doing this a long while, not a matter of weeks.

Maeve came back over to Nina all smiles and Jo shook her head when Maeve looked up at a bit of an influx of customers who sought comfort from the autumnal weather the second the boss was on her own.

'I just don't want to let her down.' Maeve's dark hair was swept up into a swishy ponytail and her brown eyes were alight with a happiness Nina knew had probably taken her a long time to find. Nina wondered, not for the first time, how Jonah's father could have ever let this girl go.

'She'll holler if she needs you,' said Nina.

'She will. So, what's news?'

Nina recounted her talk with Leo, his appointment at the bank. 'He's trying again today but . . .' She shook her head, filled with doubts. 'It's good of him to try, Walt would love nothing more than to sell to him.'

'What do you think he'd do with the cabin?'

'I've actually got no idea.'

'Perhaps Adrian might move in to it. I know he rents

somewhere, he told me his flat has a great view, but it's not the same as being down there. It's not been easy for him to come back, particularly down to the bay, but you can tell how much it's a part of him.'

Nina began to smile. 'Do I detect a bit of an interest in Adrian?'

Maeve seemed taken aback. 'An interest?'

'I saw you looking at him at the party, you guys seem to have talked a bit. And don't think for one minute that I missed you guys arriving together.'

'We did not arrive together, we bumped into one another outside which is different. And everyone talked at the party, I was being friendly.' Her eyes moved over to the specials board. She was probably hungry – this job had to help you work up an appetite, being surrounded by good food and on your feet all day.

'He seems to be slowly getting there, back to who he once was I mean. Just like you are.'

But Maeve was still looking at the specials board. Perhaps she needed to be fed before Nina would get much of a conversation out of her. Nina was sometimes that way herself when she was at work – with shifts, she sometimes forgot to eat regularly until it hit her and she'd feel light-headed and unable to string a sentence together properly.

When Jo had settled some new arrivals at the round table towards the centre of the room, she came to take Maeve and Nina's orders although Maeve insisted she do the drinks herself.

'Jo should take it easy in her condition,' she said to Nina when she brought back a latte and a black coffee and sat down again. 'I know how hard it is to be pregnant and on the go all day.'

'I can't imagine it, it must be tough.' Although if Nina wasn't mistaken, Maeve's readiness to go off and make the drinks probably had a lot to do with avoiding talk about Adrian. She had to like him, didn't she? And they'd be good together.

Nina had a sudden memory of her grandad telling her that Jo had introduced date nights here at the café at the end of the pier and had been responsible for a bit of matchmaking along the way. It was an idea, but for now she'd avoid the subject if it made her friend uncomfortable. She knew that if it was her she wouldn't appreciate being set up despite the best of intentions.

'How's Jonah doing?' Nina asked instead. 'Last time we spoke you said he was a bit down about the amount of school work on his plate.'

'He's still adjusting to the newness of it all I think. And he's a typical boy of eleven – he's never going to want the workload, but I just keep trying to encourage him. Mind you, it really needs someone else saying it rather than me, if I say he needs to do something, the urgency isn't always there.'

'He listens to Leo at the boathouse.'

It took Maeve a while before she said, 'The boathouse has been good for him.'

'A male influence.'

'Yeah.'

Jo brought over their lunches – tuna niçoise salad for Nina, the ham and cheese toastie which came with Molly's homemade autumn tomato chutney for Maeve.

Nina had had a couple of mouthfuls and considered her question carefully. 'Have you been in touch with Jonah's father at all?'

Maeve shook her head.

'But he gives financial support I assume. I mean, it's the least he could do if he's not interested in Jonah – which is a mistake if you ask me, he's a great kid.'

'He doesn't know.'

'Doesn't know what?' She scooped up another forkful of waxy potato with a piece of tuna.

'The father. He doesn't know about Jonah.'

Nina stopped chewing. 'Seriously?'

Maeve covered her face with her hands but didn't say a word.

Nina put down her cutlery, leant over and took Maeve's hands away from her face. 'Do you want to tell me about it?'

'You must think I'm a dreadful person. Jonah is eleven. I've kept my son from his dad for eleven years.'

Nina chose her words carefully. 'I'm not here to judge.' She gave Maeve time to gather herself and turned her focus to her lunch. Nobody wanted to feel as though they were seated in front of a one-person jury.

'At the start it was too hard, too messy. I was living in a whole different country, I was starting over.'

'Was the pregnancy a surprise?'

'You could say that. I didn't realise for a while. And then when I did . . . I tried to contact the father, but he wasn't in a great place either.'

Nina shook her head. 'I'm sure life isn't supposed to be this complicated.'

Maeve managed a smile. 'By keeping quiet I made my life this way.'

'Did you try to contact him again?'

'Not as such. I heard about him from other people,

I knew he'd met someone and was happy, and I didn't want to ruin that. I knew deep down I had to tell him, but whenever I thought about writing a letter or making another phone call or sending an email, I talked myself out of it. I can't even explain why, not fully. I was scared I suppose, scared that too much would change. I had this happy little boy, I had a good life, a job.'

'And now?' Nina ventured.

'And now I'm not sure how long I can put off telling Jonah the truth. I knew this was coming, I want this to happen, but knowing it and doing it turned out to be two very different things.'

Nina couldn't imagine what it was like to have this kind of secret hanging over her. 'Has Jonah asked for a name? Details?'

'It's more questions about how old his father is, what he does for a job, where he lives, how long I knew him for. Up until a year or so ago I just said I met his father briefly at a local haunt and he didn't ask anything more. He saw it as a bit of an adventure I think. Knowing those basics, his imagination probably has him wondering whether his father is a megastar – in his dreams he'd be the star of the latest Spider-Man movie.'

'Now we're talking,' Nina teased. 'What? The actor is seriously good-looking.'

'And way too young for us,' Maeve concluded before returning to the seriousness of the conversation. 'I always knew I would tell him. I've just not been able to work out how or the best time to do it. If I'm totally honest I'm afraid that he'll be angry. He's every right to be.'

'Yeah, I suppose he has.' She finished her salad and finally Maeve tucked in to her lunch.

When the door to the café opened and Adrian came in she didn't miss the way Maeve's demeanour changed. This girl had it bad for the eldest Magowan brother and it was all Nina could do not to smile. Because any fool could see he felt the same way. Maeve might have Jonah's paternity to deal with, but here was an added complication. Love, or the potential for it anyway. She suddenly had the urge to see Leo and tell him what she was witnessing, the way they both cast glances at each other, how Maeve hooked her hair behind her ear and Adrian stood behind a customer to wait his turn and rather than perusing the specials board or what was in the display cabinet, looked at Maeve as though she was on the menu.

'Join us,' Nina called over before she could stop herself, and she ignored the look she got from Maeve as Adrian went to order something at the counter.

'Don't you dare try to set us up,' Maeve warned.

'Would I ever do such a thing?'

She looked about to answer, but when the café door opened again Rhianne's parents came inside and Elijah asked whether it would be all right for them to join the girls.

'Of course.' Maeve shared a perplexed glance with Nina.

Nina looked over to the counter where Adrian had got to the front of the queue. She doubted he'd seen the latest arrivals at the café as they were sitting towards the back. If he'd seen them he'd very likely have left already.

'It's good to see you both looking so well.' Bridget took off her cardigan and sat down. 'How's that young boy of yours?' she asked Maeve.

Maeve told them all about Jonah's school and swimming,

his Canadian accent that had already begun to fade.

'The cabin looks wonderful,' Elijah told Nina. 'We saw the photographs in the window of the estate agents. You've done Walt proud.'

'Thank you.'

'I'm sorry we couldn't make the party the other night. Thank you for the invite, we appreciated it, but it was my brother's sixtieth. Not often we're double-booked, is it Bridget?' he chuckled.

It was then that Adrian came over holding his mug of coffee, a smile on his face, until he saw the company the girls now had.

But Elijah turned and saw him before he could sidestep them or leave. 'Adrian.' He stood up, shook Adrian's free hand. 'Good to see you home.'

Adrian found himself seated in a chair before he had a chance to do anything different.

'Oh it really is good to see you all,' said Bridget. 'We've just been to the cemetery to visit Rhianne.' She told them all about the flowers they'd put on her grave, but the words washed over Nina and she knew they'd had the same effect on the others.

Neither Maeve nor Adrian said a word, and Nina simply didn't know what to say.

When Maeve got up to go and help Jo in the kitchen even though she hadn't called over, Bridget asked Adrian how he was settling back in. 'It's good you're back. You belong here.'

He managed to mutter a 'Thank you.'

'It broke my heart every time I'd ask your mother about you,' Bridget went on. 'She said you hardly ever came home, you hadn't gone out on your boat since that night.'

Adrian's eyes filled with tears that reminded Nina of the night she'd tried in vain to comfort him over what happened.

'I wish I'd been able to save her,' Adrian said in a voice barely loud enough to hear, despite being at the same table.

'You tried,' said Elijah. 'You risked your life for our little girl. And for that we thank you.'

Bridget covered Adrian's hand with hers and gave it a squeeze and with her smile she brought one out of him too.

When Maeve came to sit back down with them Bridget spoke again. 'It's good to see all of you back here together. What happened was a lot for you all to cope with, we know that, but you're such good friends, seeing you here today makes us happy, doesn't it Elijah?'

He nodded. 'It does. This place is your home just like it's ours.'

When nobody said anything Maeve said, 'Well I hope you all like doughnuts. I've asked Jo to bring us one each, glazed, sprinkles, the works.'

It broke the tension in the atmosphere at least.

Elijah began to chuckle. 'Rhianne loved her doughnuts. Did you know that she once had a competition with her friend at school to see who could eat the most jam doughnuts one after the other?'

'She never did,' Nina laughed.

'Oh she did. And she won. She ate five!'

When Jo brought the doughnuts over they enjoyed the sweet treats, all of them concluding there was no way they could eat more than a couple at most.

'Adrian, let us know when your boat is up and running

258

again,' said Bridget as Maeve piled all their empty plates on top of one another. 'We'd love it if you could take us out on it. Rhianne loved the sea, she'd hate it if she knew any of us had turned our backs on it. I love the water,' she declared. 'Always have. Although gone are the days of me squeezing myself into a wetsuit.' The corners of her mouth twitched. 'It's OK, you can laugh, I do when I think of trying to get one on.'

'What water sports did you do?' Nina asked.

'Windsurfing mainly.'

'I could never stand up on a board very well,' Maeve confessed. 'And as for handling a sail at the same time?' She shook her head.

'I could teach you some time.' Adrian seemed to have forgotten it wasn't just the two of them, the way he was looking at Maeve. 'If I can remember myself.'

'Oh you will,' Elijah told him, 'I'll bet it's like riding a bike.'

'It might well be,' said Bridget. 'I stopped when I was pregnant and never got around to trying it again. And now of course I'm out of shape.'

'Rubbish,' Elijah winked at his wife. 'And of course none of you should forget the annual Christmas Day swim that happens here. I'm a big fan.'

'You do that?' Nina couldn't hide her surprise. 'Even the thought of swapping my PJs for a swimming costume or my sofa and a blanket for the icy cold water sends a shiver up my spine.'

'I do it every year,' Elijah told her.

Listening to them talk this way took Nina by surprise because their love of the sea hadn't seemed to wane despite what happened to Rhianne. In fact their strength and their courage through this had her ashamed that she, that Maeve, Adrian, they'd all run away from it, they were weak and it was almost disrespectful how they'd let it influence the rest of their lives when here were Elijah and Bridget carrying on each day and moving forwards in a way none of them had managed.

Bridget gave her a nudge. 'You can stand with me on Christmas Day if you like. I watch, hot chocolate in hand, scarf and hat firmly on.'

Nina smiled. 'Sounds perfect to me.'

'Well I think you're missing out,' Elijah insisted. 'Nothing like an ice cold dip to wake you up ready for a new year.'

But Nina and Bridget were laughing together, wholly unconvinced.

'What's got you all so jolly?' Jo wanted to know when she brought over coffees for each of them.

Bridget explained what they were talking about and Jo, citing her pregnant belly and the babies that would be here by the end of the year, said she had the perfect excuse not to participate.

When Jo left them to it Bridget asked Maeve whether she'd join in.

'I doubt it. I did it a couple of times as a teenager; never again.'

'I'll do it if you will,' said Adrian and when he smiled at Maeve Nina was reminded of the heady days with her and Leo, when they first got together and couldn't bear to be apart.

If Maeve couldn't see the attraction between the pair of them, she was mad! Nina had no idea why she'd hold back. He was a lovely guy, great with Jonah; both of them deserved happiness.

'Rhianne used to do the swim,' said Bridget. 'She loved it didn't she, Elijah?'

'She did. And she's the reason I started. Every year I'd watch her run into the water all smiles, laughing. She often did it in fancy dress too.'

'Actually I remember,' Nina smiled. 'Wasn't she a gingerbread one year?'

'She was. An elf one year too,' said Elijah, obviously wanting to talk about his daughter. 'She got quite creative with costumes.'

'That she did.' Bridget seemed to be content conjuring up the memories too.

'I do the swim every year in her honour,' Elijah told them all. 'And I will continue to do so until the day I die.'

His words had them fall silent until Bridget said, 'Or until the doc tells him to stop.'

As they all laughed Nina felt almost like she was in the way every time Maeve and Adrian exchanged yet another glance.

When Leo came in Elijah and Bridget decided to leave the youngsters to it.

'Did you tell her?' Leo asked his brother.

'Didn't get much of a chance.'

Nina wondered what was going on. Was it about the bank? She steepled her fingers in front of her face and put them to her lips. 'Please tell me it's good news.'

'Actually it is.' Adrian took the lead. 'Leo and I had a meeting at the bank this morning.'

'Wait, both of you?'

Leo couldn't keep the smile off his face. 'Adrian here is going to come into the business with me which means with him on board I can get the finance to buy Walt's cabin.'

Nina almost threw her arms around him. 'I don't know what to say.' Her voice shook. 'This is amazing news – Grandad will be so pleased.'

Leo held his hand out to her. 'So do we have a deal?'

She was about to point out that the final decision wasn't hers, but she knew this gesture was about more than the sale of a property and so she put her hand in his. 'Yes, one thousand times yes!' And although it felt good to have her skin on his she wished she could hug him tight and let him know how much this meant to her. 'I need to go tell Grandad, now!'

Leo reached out and put a hand on her arm. 'Stay, just for a bit.'

Her gaze held his and she nodded, completely under his spell or the magic of their history, she didn't know which.

'Do you think you'll move into the cabin?' Maeve immediately directed her question to Adrian.

'We haven't got as far as thinking about what we'll do, whether it'll belong to Leo or the both of us. The main thing was to get the funding so we can move forwards and so Walt will get a fair price. Our talks are in the very early stages.'

'So you've left teaching for good?' Nina asked him.

'Like I said, we need to iron out the particulars.'

'But you're staying in the bay?' Maeve leapt in before Nina could ask much more.

'Looks like it.' Adrian's focus solely on Maeve, it was as though he was announcing it to her and nobody else.

And when Nina looked at Leo she knew she wasn't the only one who saw the sparks flying off these two.

Adrian turned to face them all. 'It was strangely good to see Rhianne's parents today.'

'It was,' Nina agreed before recounting their conversation to Leo who'd missed it all.

'You know what this means though don't you?' Adrian went on. 'Her dad does the Christmas Day swim every year in her honour.' He shrugged.

Maeve suddenly got it. 'Oh no, are you suggesting . . .'

'We've got a few months to get our confidence in the water,' Adrian told her. 'If you're worried, we could try going in the sea together. Might make it easier.'

Nina wanted to giggle like a schoolgirl when she felt Leo push his knee against hers beneath the table. Ignoring him she said, 'The swim would be a way to honour Rhianne's memory, but I'm still not sure about it when three of us have avoided the water for so long.'

All of a sudden Maeve began to smile.

'What's that smile for?' Nina asked.

She put on a stern voice and wagged her finger as if she was telling someone off. 'Jonah, you mustn't go in the sea, it's dangerous. Stay away from the water.' She laughed. 'But don't mind me, I'm going to leap in during the winter months and risk hypothermia, the wrath of a wintry sea. That's totally different.'

'When you put it that way,' said Nina. But despite the doubts about the annual charity swim it felt good to be here, the four of them, together and ready to move forwards and she couldn't wait to tell her grandad the good news.

'You might have kept him away from the sea,' said Adrian to Maeve. 'But I think Jonah would be running in there with you if you suggest it this year.'

'You're probably right.' Maeve wasn't smiling any more, in fact she looked more serious than she had the whole time they'd been in here. And when she met Adrian's gaze she held it. It was as though she was trying to convey all her feelings in that one look.

And just like that Nina felt as though she and Leo were intruding again.

Chapter Nineteen

Leo

Leo and Adrian had been to see the solicitor about Adrian taking on a part of the business but they'd only just finished the meeting when Leo got a call regarding a paddleboard delivery that was earlier than expected.

'Would you be all right to hold the fort in the shop?' he asked Adrian as they walked from town back in the direction of the boathouse. 'I'm supposed to be taking a kayak lesson in half an hour, I can't be in two places at once.'

'Jump in at the deep end, right?' Adrian joked, but Leo could tell he was psyching himself up for this.

When they'd gone to Leo's cabin for the nightcap following the anniversary dinner with their parents Adrian had told Leo that he'd been along to the marina to see his boat, but hadn't managed to go in the front entrance. He'd admitted he'd thought about selling *The Wildflower* too, something Leo had opened his mouth to protest about until Adrian told him he'd realised he couldn't go through with it. Leo had wanted to punch the air with glee because his brother's boat was as much a part of him as this place was. He suspected his brother had always known it, he'd just needed to be reminded after what happened.

The words had been like music to Leo's ears that night.

And they'd talked into the small hours about the financial side of the business, their ideas short term and long term, the passion igniting their conversation from both sides. Leo had felt like he'd got his brother back that little bit more.

Now, as he watched as Adrian inspected the water craft on sale, those high up on the walls, some down lower, Leo allowed himself a small smile as he got the float from the till ready. Adrian was here . . . his brother was back.

Leo played messages on the answerphone and noted down a change of booking for lunchtime, another booking requesting two hours with three kayaks rather than the single hour they'd originally asked for.

'Do you think they've seen the weather forecast?' Adrian had overheard Leo's call.

'Maybe not. But they're experienced, they'll be fine.' He checked his watch, the lesson only twenty minutes away. 'I'll be out for an hour on the water.' The rain was brewing in the clouds over the bay but he was sure it would hold off a little while and there was no wind to accompany it, which was a good sign.

Leo pulled the vacuum cleaner out from the cupboard behind the till. He'd not left the shop as clean as he usually would yesterday with trying to think about the business now Adrian wanted to get involved, teeing up times for solicitor appointments and another at the bank, but the job could wait no longer.

'Let me do that,' Adrian insisted.

'Hey, not arguing there.' He handed Adrian the flex and Adrian went to push the plug into the socket.

The noise of the vacuum extinguished any potential conversation for now and Leo's lesson began earlier than anticipated thanks to a keen nineteen-year-old who had college later that morning and was doing this to surprise her boyfriend for his twenty-first. She wanted to go out together in a few weeks and he was already a keen kayaker. She took to it so easily Leo suspected she'd be keeping up with her boyfriend well enough on the special day.

When Leo went back up into the boathouse he saw the new paddleboard had arrived and his brother was at the counter taking payment for a set of paddles, engaged in a lively conversation with the customer, who was explaining that he wasn't from around here but he intended to kayak on the canals near his home.

'It's all coming back to you,' Leo said when the man went on his way. He'd overheard Adrian giving the man a couple of last-minute tips about looking after his kayak.

Adrian came round to the customer side of the counter and leaned against it. 'For such a long time I've pushed all this away. Even when I offered to come back into the business with you I wasn't totally sure I wanted to be living and breathing it all again.' He took in the boathouse shop, looked beyond the window then back again at all the paraphernalia inside, up at the boards fixed to the walls, the accessories dotted about, the colourful clothing.

'And now?'

'Now, it's early days.'

'That's all I can ask of you. Give it a go.' And they had so much to talk about, the financial injection Adrian would bring, what that would mean they could do – more equipment, more lessons, maybe boat outings even. They'd have to talk strategy as well as finance, marketing, but for now it was a case of beginning with the basics.

'Have you even been in the sea over the last few years?' Leo asked his brother now.

'Harper had her New York holidays for a while but she craved the beach. I caved in the end, went to the South of France. I mean, who goes to the South of France, stays by the beach and doesn't go into the water?' He tried to make light of it.

'Someone who had a bad experience they want to forget.'

'You seem to be all right.'

'We all cope differently. And you were in charge, I know it was harder for you. Nobody could've predicted the weather changing so suddenly that night. You know Maeve has been trying to spend more time near the beach since she came down here that day when you helped Jonah?'

'Maeve?'

'Yeah, you know, dark-haired girl, kind, nice, pretty—'

'I know who Maeve is.'

'Oh I'm sure you do.' Leo was smiling.

'What's that supposed to mean?'

'Oh come on. The sparks flying between you two are something I've not seen since . . . well I don't know when. And I'm pretty sure the feeling is mutual.'

That had his attention. 'We've both talked because we're in the same situation, avoiding this place, coming back, making an effort. And besides, I could say the same about you and Nina. What about the sparks flying off the pair of you?'

'Me and Nina? We're friends again.'

Adrian began to laugh. 'Right, you keep telling yourself that.' But he let Leo off the hook. 'Has she told Walt about the cabin purchase yet?'

'She's having lunch with him today to tell him – she wanted to rush to tell him at first, but decided she'd make it extra special.'

'Thoughtful girl,' his brother grinned.

'Friends, that's all,' Leo reiterated.

'I've been thinking,' said Adrian. 'Don't worry, not about you and Nina. More about her cabin or rather Walt's. She's done a good job with it, it feels homely.'

Leo wasn't sure what his brother was getting at but he asked, 'Are you saying you want to live there?'

'Maybe. It's an idea, something to think about.'

'Sure is.' And already he had a good feeling.

When a customer came in Leo had to turn his attentions to business, and advised about wetsuit types, brands and sizing, the customer made their selection. When he left, Leo's gaze moved over towards the window, the panorama of the sea and the ominous clouds which had now begun to release droplets that pelted the glass. One of the panes of glass rattled as Adrian brought them both a mug of coffee.

'Wouldn't want to be out in that today,' his brother said simply.

'Me neither. Don't mind the rain, but the wind and the darkness is another matter. It's still daytime.' Leo put on the lights in the shop and glanced over at his brother who had moved aross to check out the new touring kayak that had been delivered today and was waiting to be put up on a rack. Leo would have to move a few things around to be able to do so.

Leo went over to Adrian. 'See something you like?'

'This one's a beauty.' Adrian ran a hand along the vessel in lime green and black, still shiny, having never been used.

'You'll be out on the water in no time at all.'

'Hope so.'

'Don't forget *The Wildflower*. Still waiting for you.'

With a deep sigh Adrian nodded. 'Yeah, I know.'

What he didn't know was that he'd be going out on the water sooner rather than later. And that this time it would be in search of something more precious than any of them had ever realised.

Chapter Twenty

Leo

Adrian seemed to be getting into the swing of things at the boathouse and commandeered most of the sales talk to customers which had Leo not only amused, but pretty happy. If anyone had told him last week or last month that this might happen he'd have said they were dreaming. But here they both were, the Magowan brothers, running the much-loved boathouse in Stepping Stone Bay.

Leo tore open the lid of a box filled with bright green rope that had been sitting on the top of the counter waiting to be slotted onto the hooks next to the orange rope and went over to do just that as the rain hit pause but the wind continued to batter the walls and the windows. When the door opened he expected a bedraggled customer, but instead it was Nina, and despite the battle she'd obviously had with the weather she was beaming.

'How did it go?' he asked, finding a fresh towel from beneath the counter and handing it to her for her hair.

'Walt is absolutely over the moon, Leo.' She rubbed at the blonde strands until she'd got the worst off. 'Oh you should have seen his face.'

'Making him happy makes me happy.' And making her happy made him that way too. Did she feel the same?

'He's already asking about Adrian moving into the cabin, what he's going to do about teaching. You know Walt, he wanted to know everything.'

Leo didn't mind one bit. 'It's good he's interested.' Now and again he thought about how disinterested her own parents had been in the minutae of Nina's life and her brother's, but Walt more than made up for the shortfall. 'Just make sure he asks if he needs any jobs doing at the bungalow, that'll take a worry off your shoulders.'

'There is one thing.'

'Go ahead.' He leant against the counter. With Adrian taking charge of any customer brave enough to venture out this afternoon, he had time to spend with Nina.

'He won't want to be a burden, but he really could do with a handrail on the walls by the front step, they're really slippery and I've got visions of him not being able to stay upright if he ventures outside, especially in the winter.'

'Consider it done, I'll talk to him and get one put in.'

'Thank you.'

'What have you got there?' he asked when he noticed she'd taken something out of her bag wrapped in foil.

'My homemade carrot cake for you guys.' She looked over to where Adrian was laughing with a customer. 'Wow.'

'I know, right.'

'He looks happy.'

Leo took her arm, moving her over to the side of the shop out of sight of Adrian and the customer. He wanted a little bit of privacy. 'I wanted to thank you again for what you and Walt did with the cabin.'

'Thank *us*? Don't be silly, we couldn't be happier. Me and Grandad.'

He shook his head. 'You could've easily taken the higher offer, there are a lot of people who would've done, and I wouldn't have held it against you at all. It was a substantial amount of extra money on the table.'

'Neither of us wanted to do that to you. This place is in your blood, this place is you, it's Adrian.' They both began to smile when they heard Adrian and the customer talking about lessons on a river versus lessons in the sea. 'He's back.'

'Yeah.' Leo stepped closer to her, a magnetic pull making it impossible to do anything else. 'The question is, what are you going to do now the cabin has had its makeover and has a buyer? Will you relocate down this way or are you leaving again, never to return?'

'What do you want me to do?'

The magnetic pull hadn't let up in the slightest. 'I wanted you to go far far away from me when you first got back here.'

She gulped. 'And now?'

'Now . . .' He reached out and hooked her hair behind her ear, his palm caressing her cheek and staying there. His pulsed raced as the body heat between them drew them even closer, their faces inches apart as they looked deep into one another's eyes.

'I've missed you,' was all she said.

'I've missed you too.' Her mouth came tantalisingly close, but then the customer and Adrian moved over to the till. 'Almost sprung,' Leo whispered, not wanting the moment to end. But they moved over to the shop floor and he didn't miss the knowing look his brother gave him.

When the customer went on his way Adrian eyed the package wrapped in foil on the counter. 'What do we have here?'

'Carrot cake, Camille insisted I didn't leave it all there with her and Walt.'

Adrian and Leo both helped themselves to a slice. 'You made this in your cabin?' Adrian asked Nina.

'I did. Well, I made it in *your* cabin,' she said.

'That has a good ring to it.'

It sure did. Leo nudged Nina, 'Great cake.'

'Do you think there's something going on between Walt and Camille?' Adrian asked.

'What, like . . . romantically?' Nina floated. 'I did wonder but I've never asked. It feels disrespectful.'

Leo demolished the rest of his slice. 'Good on them I say. Finding love is hard, you need to grab it when you can.' And he knew Nina was probably thinking the same, given the way she looked at him now, as though they were those same two people from twelve years ago, those same kids who'd been inseparable at the cabins and the bay from one year to the next.

Leo sensed Adrian was about to say something about him and Nina and romance, when the door to the boathouse flew open, taken by the wind.

'Maeve?' Nina immediately went to her side.

This wasn't the Maeve from the café or the Maeve who'd braved being close to the sea after all this time. Her eyes were wide, her usually dark complexion paled, her hair was stuck to the sides of her face from the downpour.

And then she said the words that filled all of them with dread. 'It's Jonah . . . he's missing.'

Chapter Twenty-One

Maeve

Maeve was shivering. It wasn't that cold outside but she'd been in the wind, in the rain, and only now did she realise she'd come out without a cardigan.

Adrian took off his jumper. 'Put this on, you're freezing. Did you come straight here?'

She shook her head. 'I've been looking near the flat, the playground. He just ran off. We had a fight.'

'What about?' Nina's voice cut into her thoughts.

'Come, sit down.' Adrian ushered her over to the stool nearest the till when she couldn't say anything.

She had no idea where her son was. She'd messed up, he'd asked her again about who his father was and this time it had almost burst out of her, but she'd held back. She needed to tell the father first because he had no idea of the secret she'd been keeping. And when she wouldn't share a thing with Jonah but promised him that very soon she would, he'd accused her of being a liar and he'd run off. She'd thought he'd gone outside and would come back because of the rain but he hadn't.

Maeve had known all along, ever since she found out she was pregnant, that the right thing to do would've been to tell the father she was expecting a baby. But people didn't always do the right thing, particularly when they panicked. She was living in a country that didn't at that point feel like her own, she knew the father was married, and for all she knew, happy and with a family of his own. And so she'd become a single parent and with time it just became the norm. Perhaps things might have been very different if she'd come back to the bay sooner.

'Do you think he might have gone to a friend's house?' Nina asked her now.

'I don't know. I scoured the pier, checked the chippy too, but he isn't anywhere. I thought he might have come here.'

'I haven't seen him,' said Leo.

'Here.' Adrian had speedily made a cup of tea and now he insisted Maeve take it. He got down on his haunches. 'It's camomile, bit girlie for Leo to have in the boathouse in my opinion, but it'll warm you up, calm you down.' His kind gesture, soothing voice and attempt at a joke was well-meaning but was never going to work.

'I can't sit here drinking tea when I don't know where he is.' She began to cry and her hand wobbled so much Adrian took the tea from her before she slopped the hot liquid all over herself.

'You'll be no use to Jonah if you can't think straight,' he said, urging her to take the piece of cake Leo had brought over to her.

But she shook her head. She couldn't stomach anything.

'We'll find him.' Adrian looked into her eyes, the person he'd always been still there. 'He won't have gone far, I'm sure of it.'

She managed a nod and reluctantly took a sip of the tea when he coaxed her to try it again. Whoever said a cup of tea solved all your problems clearly had no idea what they were talking about because it had little to no effect.

Nina asked again who Jonah knew around this way, whose house he might've gone to.

'He doesn't know that many kids yet and I don't have anyone's numbers. What was I thinking? I should've made sure I had numbers, numbers of everyone he has contact with.'

'What you were thinking was that it's nice he has friends, that back in our day we didn't have phones with us,' said Nina. 'We went out to play until it was time for tea. Our parents never knew where we were and it was normal back then.'

Adrian was still crouched down beside her and now he was holding her hand, his thumb stroking softly back and forth. He was looking right at her. And rather than making her self-conscious, it made her quite the opposite. 'I thought he might come here,' she told him. 'He loves it here.'

'I know he does,' smiled Adrian. 'He bossed me about with the wetsuits remember.'

'He loved doing that.' She managed a half smile, a bit of a laugh.

'So did I.'

'How about I drive around and see if there's any sign of him?' Leo offered.

'I'll come too,' Nina jumped in. 'You can drive, Leo, I'll be able to look. I can get out and pop into the pizza shop, cafés, anywhere we think he might be.'

'Maeve, you stay here with Adrian,' Nina suggested to her.

'I really thought he might be here,' she reiterated, still

focused on Adrian. Her heart had sunk when she'd peered through the door to the boathouse and had seen Nina, Leo and his brother, yet no sign of Jonah.

'Has this fight been brewing for a while?' Adrian asked, as Leo went to get car keys and a waterproof jacket.

'You could say that . . . but it all came to a head today.'

'What's up?' Adrian asked his brother who was still hanging around the counter. 'Can't find your car keys?'

'I can, but a set of keys for the shed below is missing. I must've left them in the lock.' He shook his head. 'I'll grab them and then we'll get going.' He headed down the internal stairs.

Maeve pushed away the rest of her tea. 'I've been trying to protect him for so long.'

'You're a good mum,' Adrian assured her.

'Sometimes, other times, not so much.'

'Don't be too hard on yourself. He's a great kid – a fantastic kid in fact – and he has a good head on his shoulders. He'll cool off and come home.'

Her eyes pleaded with his that that might be true. But before she could get another word out Leo came back to them with an item she recognised. 'Where was that?'

Leo was brandishing Jonah's backpack. She'd recognise it anywhere, with its faded blue pocket on the side, the frayed shoulder strap she'd sewn up more than once.

'Down by the bottom doors, where we keep the water craft.' He looked as frightened as she was and when he spoke she realised why. 'One of the kayaks is missing.'

'How did he get your keys?' Maeve couldn't understand it, didn't want to accept it.

But Adrian dropped her hand, stood up and swore loudly. He raked a hand through his hair in despair. 'I think he came when I was cleaning the shop – vacuuming. I was keeping an ear out for the door for a paddleboard delivery and thought I heard someone come in, then just thought it was the wind and me imagining it. I didn't think much of it and carried on, but then the weirdest thing was that a load of buoyancy vests were off their hooks and on the floor.' He went over to the collection he must've put back up again. 'It must've been Jonah and I'm guessing he took a buoyancy vest along with the keys.' He swore again.

Maeve began to shake, fear pummelling her from all angles. 'Oh God, he has the kayak. He's out there,' she cried, standing up and running over to the window, looking out at weather that was atrocious for the experienced, let alone a beginner.

Leo was already picking up the phone to call the coastguard, Nina had come to her and held her tight and when she pulled away Adrian had already pulled on a waterproof top and was rifling through the drawers at the counter.

'What are you doing?' Nina asked him but he pulled out a key. 'What's that for?'

'*The Wildflower.*'

Maeve recognised the name. It was Adrian's boat and he hadn't been out on it since the night of the tragedy more than a decade ago.

'Adrian you can't go out in this. Leave it to the coastguard,' Nina urged.

Maeve felt the room begin to spin and Nina steadied her as she wailed. Jonah was a good swimmer but that was in the pool, not the sea. The pool was tame, the sea an unpredictable beast. With the rain, the wind, he could've drifted miles out, he might be in the water now, separated from his craft. She bent double, put her hands on her knees, trying to catch a breath.

'I'll go with you!' She pulled away from Nina.

'No, stay here,' Adrian said firmly. 'I'm not about to put your life at risk as well.'

Maeve's shoulders slumped at the hopelessness of it all. She called across to Leo who was on the phone, 'Tell them he's only eleven! He isn't used to the sea!'

'I'll find him, Maeve.' Adrian rushed over to her again and pulled her close, held her in his arms for the briefest of moments. It had been twelve years since he'd held her that way and yet it felt like yesterday, the way he'd breathed in the scent of her hair, the way she'd fallen for him hard and fast. 'I promise I will find him.'

And when he pulled away she did the only thing she could do in this moment.

She told Adrian the truth.

Chapter Twenty-Two

Adrian

Adrian stared at this woman he'd fallen for quicker than anyone, even more so than the woman he'd ended up marrying as he tried to escape his own life. He'd fallen for Maeve quickly one day when he'd been looking for solitude not love. He just hadn't told her or admitted it to anyone else.

But now he couldn't digest the information, he couldn't talk to her the way he wanted to because the pull right now was to find Jonah. He had to find his son.

Maeve's words, 'He's your son,' rang in his ears as he ran from the boathouse, Nina close on his heels.

'I'll drive you to the marina. Get in!' She leapt into Leo's truck and started it up.

They barely talked on the two-minute trip to the marina. Nina said something about heading back to scour the streets with Leo in case they were wrong about the kayak, but Adrian knew deep down that they weren't, and looking at Maeve back there in the boathouse, she'd known it too. 'Stay with Maeve,' he urged Nina as the car screeched to a halt.

'Adrian, be careful!' she yelled after him as he leapt out into the pouring rain and ran from the parking area along the jetty to his boat.

He didn't stop running until he reached *The Wildflower*'s mooring. This moment was something he'd pushed away from this thoughts so many times before, but right now it was second nature to him. He untied the rope from the stern, his hands soaking wet but the rope familiar against his skin as he unwound it from the cleat, then did the same from the mid-ship cleat and finally loosened the rope at the bow before climbing on board.

He started the boat's engine and began to maneouvre the vessel away from the jetty, reversing before he could go on his way and find his son. Jonah was out there in a kayak having no experience of the water craft or this kind of weather. Adrian wondered about nature versus nurture – would Jonah have some affinity with the sea like Adrian did? His mum had always told him he was born with gills he was so good in the water.

Please please let Jonah be the same.

As he headed out of the marina Adrian thought of Maeve, the panic on her face, the heartbreak, the bond as she'd told him the truth. And their boy looked so much like his beautiful mother too – all that dark hair just like Maeve's, deep velvet brown eyes. He'd looked into those eyes many years before when he'd been drawn to Maeve. Part of him wished he could take her in his arms now and tell her everything would be OK.

But he didn't know that. All he knew was that he had a son and he never wanted to lose him.

The other part of him wanted to yell at her and demand to know why she'd kept his own son from him for eleven years.

Eleven years!

Over time, Adrian had come to accept he wasn't going to be a dad. Not ever. When he'd left the bay he'd needed escape and he hadn't given too much thought as to how that escape might unfurl in the future. He'd married Harper, they'd had a good life for a while, and when she'd told him she didn't want kids he'd thought he didn't either. All he'd wanted was a new life and that was what he'd got.

Adrian had ended his relationship with Rhianne weeks before he met Maeve, and they'd remained friends but nothing more. Although she did like to flirt, and did so with him and others, including his own brother. When it didn't bother him the way it should, Adrian realised how casual their relationship had actually been all along.

But it was different with Maeve, right from the start.

Adrian and Maeve had first got talking when he'd been in the library one day. Maeve turned up and, browsing shelves near to where he'd found a comfy chair, she came over to say hello. She'd already read the book he was holding and told him the reasons she admired the author, the potential the story had, what she didn't like so much, and they'd laughed when he'd insisted he didn't want spoilers, only to keep asking her what happened to this character and that character.

That evening he'd bumped into Maeve on the pier. He'd finished the entire book and the second he saw her he'd known it hadn't just been about reading the story, it had been so he could talk to Maeve more when he next saw her. He'd bought a portion of chips he shared with Maeve who'd just bought a postcard to send a pen pal in France and they talked about the book, what they liked, what they agreed on and what they didn't. They'd ended up strolling from the start to the end of the pier talking about that book, about others, about her studies and his love of the boat business.

A day or so later Maeve wandered down to the marina. Adrian had just finished cleaning the boat and replenishing supplies in the kitchen after taking his granny Camille out for the afternoon; they'd had scones with jam and cream in the sunshine, something he'd warned her might turn her stomach if the sea was choppy, but as luck would have it it hadn't been.

'What brings you down here?' he asked Maeve, more than happy to see her.

'I'm admiring the boats of course.'

He slung his bag over his shoulder. Granny Camille had already left, his dad had collected her, and Adrian had finished giving *The Wildflower* a good clean. 'That one's a beauty.' He noticed her eyeing up a yacht moored a few berths down.

'I'd be impressed with a tiny row boat to be honest,' she admitted. 'I've been in a car, on a train, a plane, but I've never been in a boat.'

'What, never? Even though you live around here. That's almost shameful,' he teased.

'Actually, I'm lying. I've been on a barge along the canal once when I was little.'

'Not the same.' He tilted his head back to the Magowan boat. 'No time like the present.'

'Oh no, I wasn't hinting.'

'Yes you were.' He called her bluff and she didn't seem to mind one bit. 'Come on, I'm refuelled, it's clean, fridge is restocked, hop on board.'

'Are you sure?' She checked her watch.

'Do you have somewhere else to be?'

She shook her head, at the same time smiling as she took his outstretched hand.

Maeve stayed by his side as he reversed out of the berth and they left the marina behind, the wind picking up as they ventured further out onto the water, serene and beautiful just like the woman he couldn't take his eyes off. Her dark, luscious hair grazed across her bare shoulder blades peaking out of the thin-strapped top she had on; when she turned to smile her full lips excited him without even a word. And he was comfortable with the quiet, the lack of chatter, the beauty of the summer sunshine, the salty sea air and their awareness of one another.

When they were some way out he dropped the anchor and grabbed a couple of cold drinks as well as choc ices from the freezer. And when she worried she didn't have enough sun cream on, given he'd sprung this outing on her, he found the sun lotion he had with him and offered it to her.

'I'm usually prepared,' she told him, 'but I was out for a walk, the last thing I expected was to be on board a boat today.' She squinted in the sunshine as she put her sunglasses on top of her head and closed her eyes so she could apply the lotion to her face with both hands. And while her eyes were shut he took in the contours of her face, her jaw line, the way her neck gently moved as she rubbed in the cream.

He looked away when she did her shoulders and as cliché as it was, offered to rub the cream into the top of her back where she couldn't reach.

'If I didn't know better I'd think you were hitting on me.' She handed him the bottle of lotion.

'As if,' he laughed, attempting to keep the nervousness out of his voice.

'I can't believe I've lived in the bay all my life and have *never* been on a boat until now,' Maeve said when they'd been on the water for more than an hour.

'You've said that ... twice.' He laughed when she turned and poked him in the ribs. 'And I can't believe it either. You haven't lived till you've been on a boat out on the sea, the freedom, nothing around you apart from waves and sky.'

'And birds!' She burst out laughing when a gull timed it perfectly and left a deposit on the silver railing of the boat.

Adrian cursed and went to get a cloth to wipe it off.

When he was back relaxing at her side she said, 'Thank you for this.'

He leant back on his forearms, his sunglasses on just like hers were again now. He liked wearing them because it meant she didn't catch him in the act every time he looked at her for longer than was necessary.

Before he realised what he'd done he'd reached over and touched the tip of her nose. 'You got sunscreen on your face? The rays are fierce out on the water.'

And she turned to him. 'I put some on earlier. You watched me do it.'

'Yes, I did,' he answered, voice soft as hers, their eyes focused on one another, his gaze dropping to her lips more than once.

She reached out to slip her hand beneath his and it was like a bolt of electricity shot through him.

And then they both lay back, the warmth of the sunshine on their partially clad bodies on the deck, nothing around them but shimmering water, the ocean of possibilities.

He wasn't even sure who made the first move. Was it him? Her? Did it even matter?

All he knew was that in those crazy hazy days of summer, where they were carefree, a little bit reckless, they'd both lost themselves in one another down below deck, their bodies at one. But that had been the only time they were together. Because less than a week later the party happened, and their lives headed in different directions.

Now, on the water, the lapping of the waves put the fear of God into him. One night was all it had taken for him to fall in love, and not only that, father a child, a son. And an amazing son at that. He'd allow himself a smile if he wasn't so terrified right now. Because he was happy to be a dad.

He just wasn't happy he'd been lied to all this time.

No, scrap that, he was furious!

Please don't let it be too late. Too late for Jonah, too late for him to be a dad and get to know that wonderful boy who'd made him laugh and smile in his company at the boatshed. The day he'd washed the wetsuits had been the day Adrian realised he might still want that family after all. Family had always been Leo's thing more than his, but maybe that wasn't the way it had to be.

His boat could go a lot faster, but Adrian stayed slow so he could shine a big torch on the murky depths, his beam forming a crescent as he slowly scanned the area where Jonah might have drifted if he lost control of the kayak. And as he stopped the boat out in Stepping Stone Bay he kept one hand on the wheel and hollered into the distance, calling his son's name over and over.

He knew the coastguard would be out soon and they'd come from the other side of the marina, so with no sign of Jonah here he wasted no time heading on from the bay and over to Salthaven where the water was always more treacherous on days like this. They needed to cover as wide an area as possible, sooner rather than later. Every second mattered when someone was missing in the water, he didn't ever need reminding of that.

'Jonah! Jonah!' He spluttered with the wind in his throat making it next to impossible to call out. 'Jonah!' he tried again as his torch went around again, three hundred and sixty degrees out to sea, closer to the shore. But still nothing.

He drove the boat on a bit further and did the same, a bit further still. These waters were friendly, fun, in the right season and weather, but now with the skies threatening above it was terrifying, especially for a young boy lost and all alone.

'Jonah!' he yelled again as he moved the boat on. He was about to come to a stop once more when one-handed he shone the torch around and caught the posts of the pier . . . and something else.

Fear cascaded through him. His torchlight honed in on something green close to one of the posts of the pier but he couldn't get there by boat, Jonah might be in the water, it was too dangerous.

Without another thought he dropped anchor, pushed his phone into the waterproof case that was kept onboard, hooked it around his neck and jumped into the sea himself. He swam with every ounce of strength he had.

Please don't let the green be the buoyancy vest and nothing else.

As he drew closer he spotted the kayak on the crest of a wave heading towards shore, but no Jonah inside. His arms chopped through the water, his legs kicked as hard as they possibly could and when he was close enough to the green material he saw two little arms hugging the pier's post.

A shivering, frightened Jonah had clung on to the post for dear life. His dark eyelashes didn't flicker, as though he was concentrating hard on staying here, holding on, staying alive.

'Jonah!' He swam the rest of the way.

Jonah's eyes pinged open. 'Adrian!' And the second he reached the post Jonah let go and threw his arms around Adrian's neck.

A hug had never felt so good. 'I've got you mate, I've got you now. You're safe. It's all over.'

It wasn't easy, but he let Jonah hold on to him while he swam them both towards the beach. On the sands, the kayak was at the water's edge, having already been washed ashore, but the boys clung to one another.

'I fell out,' Jonah cried as they stood up in water only knee-deep for Adrian, a bit higher for Jonah. 'The sea was too strong.'

Adrian scooped him up in his arms. The boy was exhausted from the water, from the fear.

'I saw the pier, Adrian.' His little voice carried on, talking, processing. 'I swam to a post. I was at the end one, then swam to the next and then the next.'

Adrian couldn't help but let a smile form at the relief of it all. 'You did exactly what I would've done.'

'Really?'

'Really.' And he pulled Jonah against him again. This

boy had no idea he was hugging his father and that was for Maeve to deal with, but for now, for tonight, they'd got a happy outcome. 'I'd better call your mum.' He set Jonah down.

'She's gonna be mad.' His teeth chattered as Adrian took out his phone.

Adrian called the boathouse, Nina picked up straight away and he heard crying in the background as she relayed the news. 'We'll be in the café,' he told her. He could see the café from where they stood, the steps that would take them up onto the pier.

Despite his shivering, Jonah insisted he help drag the kayak further up the sands.

'Come on, let's get you warm,' said Adrian, although by now they had a welcoming committee at the top of the steps and so they had help from there. 'And your mum won't be mad. She'll be happy, I tell you that now.'

Jonah was first to go up the steps to the pier, Adrian following quickly after. Already Molly from the café had a blanket wrapped around Jonah and Arthur had one for Adrian too.

His son was safe. And it was the best feeling in the world.

Chapter Twenty-Three

Adrian

Maeve came charging down the pier towards the café and Adrian grabbed her upper arms before she reached the door. 'He's safe.'

'Let me see him.'

'Why didn't you tell me?'

'What?' She seemed almost confused at the question, her head probably all over the place. But right now it was his head he was thinking about.

'Why did you keep it from me for all this time? Who does that?'

She was crying again, trying to pull away from him and go in to her son. It felt cruel to keep her from him but that's what she'd done to Adrian for eleven years wasn't it?

'Adrian, please . . .'

'Did you think I'd deny he was mine? Think I'd walk away?'

'I didn't know!' she shrieked, mostly in frustration he knew. 'I didn't know what you'd do. I'd already left the country, we had one night together Adrian, and I'd started to make a new life. I heard you were a mess, I was as well. Then I heard you were married.'

He was about to demand more answers when she

went weak in his arms, the fight gone out of her. She was sobbing.

'I need to see Jonah. Please, Adrian. Let me see my son.'

He let go of her and as she rushed inside he said quietly, 'Our son.'

Adrian didn't go in straight away, he wasn't sure he could keep his emotions in check watching her fling her arms around Jonah, but when he did he accepted a change of t-shirt and a pair of dry shorts from Steve, changing them out back for privacy, and then took a seat near the entrance on the windowseat.

As Jonah, a towel wrapped around his bottom half and wearing a jumper so big it dwarfed his skinny frame, enjoyed the attention and made his frightening experience sound more of an adventure, with details of wind, rain, how he'd managed to swim from post to post beneath the pier, Maeve settled on the windowseat next to Adrian. Her eyes were red, raw, she looked as though she hadn't slept for days.

They each had a mug of coffee to which Arthur had insisted he add a splash of whisky for the shock.

'So he knows nothing about me,' said Adrian, unable to take his eyes off his son who every now and then looked up and met his gaze as they shared in their conspiracy of tonight.

'Adrian, I—'

'I still can't believe it.'

She bit down on her bottom lip as though scared of how he'd react to anything she said right now. 'That's what we fought about,' she admitted. 'You. His father. The not knowing, it's why he took off. '

'Didn't you think I had the right to know?' He looked

at her now, the softness of her skin, the eyes he'd looked into in the most intimate moments that had resulted in a son he never knew about.

'Like I said, I didn't find out I was pregnant until I was in Canada. I left the bay pretty quickly after what happened – I mean Mum and Dad were already in the throes of emigrating, so it wasn't too hard to jump on board. At first I honestly thought it was stress making me feel unwell. It was only when it had gone on for so long that I went to a doctor that I found out I was pregnant.'

'But it was so many years.'

'If I could take it back, Adrian, I would.'

'How could you let him spend time at the boathouse, with Leo, knowing the truth? Didn't you think he might work it out?'

'That was unintentional. I never thought Jonah would go off on his own adventure. But he did, he found Leo and the boathouse.' She managed a tiny smile, and he couldn't be angry at that, it was so beautiful, and it came from a place of love for her son. 'Coming back here I knew I was going to find you and tell you, all of you, your whole family. I'm ashamed I didn't do it before, that I was so much of a coward and protecting myself so valiantly that I couldn't see past my own needs.' Her eyes pleaded with him to hear her truth. 'When I heard you were back it was only a matter of time before I told Jonah and you everything. But as you and I saw one another more I started to get scared.'

'That I'd be angry?'

'That, yes, but also that you'd never want to be near me again. I had little doubt you'd want Jonah, but a woman who lied?' She shook her head. 'I couldn't see that happening.'

He had no idea what to say. He felt as though his emotions had finally unravelled, coming back here only to be churned up with her revelations.

'I thought Leo would pick up on him being a Magowan for sure,' said Maeve, looking over at her son. 'He might look like me, but he's got so much of you in him, Adrian.'

He felt his eyes filling with tears.

'I'm so very, very sorry it has taken me so long to tell you the truth.'

He nodded.

'I thought about you often you know. I never forgot about you. Sometimes I thought I'd built it all up in my head to be more than it was. It was one night after all, over so quickly it was impossible to know whether it meant more.'

'It did. It always did.' His fingertips almost reached out to touch hers, but he drew them back at the last minute. 'Did your parents never ask you who the father was?'

'They did. When I discovered I was pregnant I'd been seeing a guy over there – only two dates, but it was easy enough to let my parents assume that the baby was his and that he'd done a runner.' When he opened his mouth to ask the obvious question she quickly added, 'We never slept together so I knew the baby wasn't his. But my parents didn't know that. And it stopped any questions and let me deal with things in my own time. I imagined what it would be like to tell you – and yet I couldn't do it. We barely knew one another, and then . . .'

She was right on that. They hadn't known one another

well enough to trust in each other and take the painful journey of what happened together.

'Time went on and the more I thought about it the more I wanted to let you know, but I had to protect myself and Jonah. We'd begun to set up a life in Canada and I felt happy for the first time in a long while. Eventually I heard you'd got married and that made me back away from telling you even more. I knew that if you were married, you could have kids, and this woman who lived in a whole other country might destroy your happiness that you deserved so much. I wasn't thinking straight, I really wasn't. It was more about survival in the short term than anything else. That night at sea shocked me, realising that in the blink of an eye our lives could end just like that. I was anxious all the time, I was worrying about doing little things like driving to the mall in case I crashed, or going for a run on my own in case I was mugged. Everything worried me on a totally different level.'

Adrian tried to let the information soak in. 'I was more about short-term survival too. Yeah,' he nodded when her expression questioned his claim. 'I was in a bad place for a long time, and if you'd told me back then I'm not sure how I would've dealt with it.' Would it have made a difference to his life if he'd known about the baby? Could he have stepped up from the start? He felt sure he could. But he'd have hated for her to try, for him to let her down when he couldn't handle more than he already was. The thing that would've been worse than not knowing he was a father would've been failing at being a dad. Failing her, failing their son.

'I should've given you the chance.'

Adrian felt his chest rise as he took a deep breath. 'We can't change history.'

'No, we can't.'

He looked over at Jonah who was laughing with Molly. 'I fell for you that day in the library and then every other moment we had since.'

Maeve looked over at her son – their son. 'I'm glad we made him.'

That had Adrian smiling for the first time since he'd laid eyes on her outside the café. 'I'm pretty glad we did too.'

'He's obsessed by the water.'

'I know.'

'Thank goodness he also somehow got an instinct for safety. If he hadn't taken that buoyancy vest . . .'

Adrian put a hand over hers and gave it a squeeze and she looked down at the skin-to-skin contact. 'But he did. And he's here. Enjoying more brownies.'

Maeve's gaze hovered between his eyes and his lips. 'He's here.' And then she turned to face her son again, the fingers on her other hand wiping away another tear. 'We'd better be careful with those brownies, he's had so many. He might pull another stunt just to get those treats.'

'Let's hope he doesn't.'

And it felt better than good to be using 'we' in a sentence, as though they were parents, together. Which of course they were.

It was taking Adrian a while to get his head around it. A dad. A father. A son.

A family.

'I'm so sorry, Adrian.' Maeve's voice shook.

'You've said that so many times. And I know you are.'

His look told her that they had so much to talk about, but that for tonight the important focus was Jonah, the fact he was here, sitting and laughing with them all and not lost.

When Leo and Nina appeared in the café Maeve went to hug her son, leaving Leo to talk to his brother while Nina went to the counter to order drinks. Adrian grinned at the sight of Jonah squirming as his mother showered him in kisses.

'The boat is back at the marina,' said Leo.

'Cheers.' When Adrian took his eyes away from his son and Maeve he found Leo smiling at him, his eyes twinkling with disbelief.

'He's yours, Adrian. I can't quite believe it.'

'*You* can't? How do you think I'm taking it?'

'Knowing you?' He gave Adrian's shoulder a squeeze. 'Like a man.'

Adrian's smile was closely followed by a frown. 'She kept it secret for so long.'

'She did. I don't think I'll ever understand that. You must be angry.'

Adrian nodded. 'Angry, happy, sad, scared, the whole gamut since I found out.' He looked Jonah's way. 'But for now . . .'

'Yeah, for now he's safe. And that's what really matters.' Leo looked over at Jonah too. 'He's the spitting image of Maeve with dark hair, olive skin, but he's got a hint of Magowan about him. His strong jaw line.' He put a hand to his own jaw. 'Like you, me, Dad. And he's left-handed too.'

Adrian grinned. So was he. 'Then he must be a genius.' Adrian wrapped his brother in a bear hug which had Leo laughing. 'Thanks man.'

'For?' Leo asked when he wrestled himself free.

'He took the buoyancy vest, he didn't panic. Those things are probably down to you and time spent listening to you drone on and on and on.' A smile spread across his face and it was his turn to be yanked into a bear hug.

The ruckus had Maeve's attention and she tilted her head in a gesture that Adrian knew meant he should go over to their table. He wasn't sure, but Leo gave him a subtle shove in their direction.

Sitting down beside Jonah he asked, 'You all right? Warm enough now?'

Jonah nodded, mouth full of brownie.

'And I'll bet Mum wasn't mad like you thought she'd be.'

Jonah shook his head.

Maeve was back in full parent mode and quite right too. 'You do know you're grounded, don't you Jonah?'

Jonah stopped chewing and sighed. 'Figured I would be.' And then recommenced eating. 'I deserve it.'

'You had me worried sick.' Maeve looked as though the frown on her forehead would come back every time she replayed the moment he ran off, the moment they all realised he'd gone into the sea. She sat up a little straighter. 'Why did you do it?'

'We argued.'

'I know that, but why take the kayak, why steal something?'

He looked at Adrian as though he wasn't going to admit anything in front of a stranger. But then he must've changed his mind. 'I wanted to do something you'd hate.' He looked down at his now-empty plate.

'Well you were right there.' But her tone softened. 'What you did was very dangerous.'

'I know.'

'And you should always go out with a buddy if possible,' said Adrian, taking his cue that it was all right to talk from Maeve's slight nod of approval. 'Even as an adult it's a good idea.'

'They tell us that at swim lessons too. That way if we get in trouble, someone else can go for help.' He hung his head, seemingly realising what might have happened tonight, that the outcome could very easily have been a contrast to what it was now. 'I'm sorry, Mum.' And when he welled up, Maeve wrapped him in her arms and held him close.

'I'm sorry we argued,' she whispered into her son's hair.

'Me too.'

'I wanted to talk about it.'

'I've said I'm sorry.'

But she shook her head. 'I don't mean having you apologise. I mean I wanted to talk about the subject of that argument.'

'You won't tell me things,' said Jonah after a moment's pause, glancing over at the apparent stranger at their table.

'And that was very wrong of me. I shouldn't have kept something so huge from you, not when the man in question is probably the nicest person I've ever met in my entire life.'

Adrian braved a look at Maeve, who didn't seem to want to stop now she'd started. He wasn't sure whether his heart beat faster at the fear he might not be what this boy wanted, or whether it was because he just wanted the truth to be out there. He'd only found out the truth today, but in some ways it felt to him like a lifetime had passed.

'The man who is your father deserved to know about you as much as you deserved to know about him,' said Maeve with more conviction in her voice than Adrian had ever heard. She reached out to cover Adrian's hand with her own.

When Jonah's gaze clocked their hands together and he looked up at Adrian neither of them looked away. Adrian had to admit he was terrified. Of an eleven-year-old boy and the effect his reaction was about to have on him.

'You're my dad?' Jonah asked.

His mouth went dry, everything around him stilled. 'I am.'

'You're why I like the water, why I'm good at swimming?' Eyes wide, he was at last solving what was, to him, a lifelong mystery.

'I like to think so,' said Adrian.

'Well it's not from my mum,' said Jonah. 'She hates the water.'

'I do not hate the water, it's just, I'm a little afraid.'

'We could all go out on the boat together.' Jonah's eyes lit up.

'That sounds like a wonderful idea,' Adrian said.

'Can I drive it?'

Adrian laughed. 'One step at a time, eh . . . one step at a time.'

Leo came over and gave Jonah a hug, told him how worried he'd been too. 'I can't lose my helper at the boat-house can I?'

'I'm sorry I took the kayak,' said Jonah. He looked sorry too.

'The kayak is round the side of the café,' Molly told them as she breezed past with a bowl of warming soup with chunky pieces of bread on the side and delivered it to a customer. On her way back she added, 'Matt brought it up here.'

Leo put a hand on Jonah's shoulder. 'You do know what this means, don't you?'

Jonah shook his head.

'It means that when you help me at the boathouse we're going to have to do a repair job, get it looking good as new.'

'I'll do it all.' Jonah's words tumbled out. 'I'm really sorry.'

'I know you are mate. And to be honest I don't care about the kayak, it was its occupant I was concerned about.' He ruffled the top of Jonah's hair. You'd never know he'd been in the water now he was dry and warm. 'I'm glad you were wise enough to take the vest. You get a big tick of approval for that, and for not panicking and controlling the kayak in the wind and rain enough to reach the pier.'

'I was lucky.'

'You were, but I suspect you kept your head.'

Jonah nodded. 'I wasn't scared, not really.'

Adrian knew otherwise. But he'd been a little boy once, and he'd have said exactly the same. It seemed the apple really hadn't fallen too far from the tree on that score.

'Walk you home?' Leo asked Nina who'd been helping Arthur serve hot drinks. It seemed the whole town had been on high alert at Jonah's disappearance and they were all inside the café now, glad the boy was safe.

As Adrian took Jonah's empty mugs and plates up to

the counter Maeve went with him. 'I know you're still angry, Adrian.'

But he shook his head. 'We don't need to get into it now. Jonah is safe.'

'I want to tell you all about him, show you photos.' She looked down at the floor. 'We've got a lot to catch up on. If you want to spend some time with me that is. I'll understand if you don't, if you only want to see Jonah.'

Adrian leaned in, just briefly so nobody would notice, and kissed her lightly on the forehead, whispering into her hair, 'I'd like to see both of you if you wouldn't mind.'

He wanted to hold his family tight and never let them go again.

Chapter Twenty-Four

Nina

Nina was spent as she left the café at the end of the pier. Despite her layers she was still shivering at the shock of what had happened. She'd never admit it to Maeve, but sitting there in the boathouse with her, waiting for news, both knowing how brutal the sea could be, Nina had begun to think the outcome wasn't going to be a good one. Right up until they'd got the phone call from Adrian she'd been fearing the worst and the emotions from that had her exhausted, barely able to put one foot in front of the other now.

She leaned in to Leo, her head resting against him as they walked. It didn't matter that they'd not done this in years, it felt right, and Leo didn't seem to want her to do any differently as they made their way from the start of the pier, up the road that would take them away from the town and towards the turning for the cabins and Stepping Stone Bay.

'You're an uncle,' she smiled, lifting her head up and walking alone again as they left the pier behind.

His profile was more visible as they passed beneath a street lamp. 'I'm pretty happy about that.' He breathed out the emotion as they walked uphill. 'I can't believe I didn't see it. I mean I do now, it seems obvious, and thinking back, Adrian and Maeve were close, although how close I *never* realised.'

'Me neither,' she said, trying not to let her teeth chatter.

'You're cold.' He began to undo his jacket.

'No, you keep that. We'll be at the cabins soon enough. And you lost custody of your jumper to Jonah remember.'

He laughed. 'That's right, I did.'

'Bet he sleeps well tonight after his ordeal.'

'So will we,' said Leo.

She couldn't help the fizz in her tummy even though she knew he didn't mean together. 'I still can't believe Maeve kept Jonah's paternity a secret all this time.'

'It's going to take Adrian a while to get his head around it for sure.'

'It's good to see her back, Adrian too.'

'It's good to see you all back,' Leo told her. 'I hadn't realised how much I felt alone when you all left. I mean some days I did, other days I got on with it. I worried about my brother, I was angry at you. Back then,' he added, to clarify.

'Do you think Maeve and Adrian might . . .'

'Make a go of it?' He shrugged. 'Who knows, early days I'd say, but the way they were looking at one another in the café just then tells me they both want to pick up where they left off. And they're parents, that counts for a lot.' His deep exhale was most likely a release from the night, for the sheer relief at the happy ending with his new-found nephew who had already been in his life at the boathouse unbeknownst to him.

'I can't believe Adrian took the boat out just like that.' She shook her head. 'When I dropped him at the marina he didn't even hesitate.'

'I can't quite believe it either. It's what I've wanted him to do for such a long time.'

They reached the top of the track that would lead down to the cabins and Leo used the torch to navigate their way down the track. 'I should bring this torch out more often, it's far easier to see your way down here. Why did I never think of it before? Last week I went to the pub for a few drinks and almost bumped into one of the trees at the edge.'

Close beside him Nina pointed out, 'That's probably more to do with your inebriation than the lighting I'd say.'

When Leo reached the bottom of the track he wanted to go and make sure everyting in the boathouse was switched off and properly locked up. 'You head to your cabin, warm up.'

She didn't want to leave his side, but the shivering was constant by now. She was about to agree when he pulled her to him and wrapped her in a hug. Her momentary surprise gave way to her melting into the familiarity of his chest, the place that felt right. He held her firmly, didn't say a thing and she felt her eyes closing as she was lulled into a sense of peace she hadn't felt with the chaos of the day.

She felt warm enough after a minute or two and looked up at him, eyes glassy, unsure of what to say.

He took the lead. 'You go inside your cabin, I'll check on you when I'm done here.'

All she could do was nod, and avoiding the puddles that had formed in the dips leading up to her veranda, she took the few steps up and let herself inside. She wasted no time taking off her layers and her jeans. She put on a fresh t-shirt and over the top of that a chunky fawn jumper and her warmest brushed cotton pyjama bottoms. In the kitchen she took the milk out from the fridge and the container of cocoa powder from the cupboard. She pulled out one mug, but hoping Leo would come inside when he stopped by, she took out a second and made sure she poured enough milk into the pan.

She felt calmer by the time Leo knocked and was more than happy to oblige when he suggested they take the cocoa over to his cabin. 'I've got the log burner,' he added, 'and you need the extra warmth tonight.' He'd taken one mug and no matter what his cabin was like, all Nina wanted to do was lay her head against his chest, against the navy jumper he'd changed into, and stay there until she fell asleep.

'It feels like winter is on its way,' said Nina as they carried their mugs the thirteen stepping stones between their cabins.

'Won't be long.'

Leo's cabin felt so homely when they stepped inside. As he sorted the log burner she took in all the little touches that made it that way – over in the kitchen there was a barbecuing cook book on a metal stand opened at a page with a recipe for a colourful sauce to use for marinading meat. Next to the stand was a bowl for eggs, another bowl for fruit which was piled high with bananas and firm red nectarines, a couple of kiwis balancing precariously on top. There was a knife block, a rectangular trivet with a metal sailing ship in its design and even a blue-and-white striped apron hanging on the hook in the corner past the oven. She smiled when she saw the little wooden placard hanging from one of the cupboard doors which said 'What happens on the boat stays on the boat.'

She moved to where Leo was in the lounge, noting the upturned corner of the navy and cream rug when he pointed out the tripping hazard. The rug was worn enough that it made the lounge feel lived in, along with the oak coffee table with its slightly rough surface and the armchair and sofas, which both dipped in the middle from use. The log burner on the far wall was cosy when it roared into life after Leo added logs and kindling as well as a crumbled firelighter, the pictures on the walls dotted around spoke of his love for the local area and the sea, with a couple of the marina and another of the bay at sunset, a framed photograph of him and Adrian with their dad, arms around one another and their thumbs up. She spotted another photograph on the mantelpiece in a single frame, of Camille holding an enormous fish.

'Camille fishes?' She cupped her mug of cocoa in her palm as she walked around taking in the cabin she'd once been so familiar with.

'She's been a few times. Not lately, but when she did, she surprised us all with how patient she was.'

'She doesn't strike me as the patient type, she's got too much get up and go.'

'Maybe she uses fishing as a chance to recharge.' He picked up his own mug of cocoa now the log burner was independently doing what it should. 'Are you warm enough?'

'A log burner, a chunky knit in summer, and a mug of cocoa.' She smiled. 'Yes, thank you, I'm plenty warm enough. You?'

'Couldn't be better.'

She sat on one side of the sofa, although the space between them was less than she thought because of the dip that drew them together. She adjusted herself and curled her legs beneath her, leaning against the corner.

'I wonder if Jonah is tucked up in bed,' said Leo.

'I wonder if Adrian is still with them.' And when she looked at Leo she smiled. 'You love it that you have a nephew, don't you?'

'Uncle Leo. It has a good ring to it doesn't it?'

'It really does. And to have Maeve as a part of your family is a blessing, she really is lovely.'

'You've grown close.'

'We have. I mean I always liked her, but I lost touch with everyone over the years.'

'She's a good mum,' Leo approved. 'And as much as part of me can't understand how she kept this from Adrian, the other part of me gets it. Things change. Even when you least expect.' His body sagged back against the soft sofa.

Nina sipped her cocoa. 'You didn't really mean it did you? When you said you might leave the bay?'

'You know I didn't, I told you that.'

She chewed her lip for a second. 'You did, but I get it, you're the only one of us who never went away.'

'Sometimes I thought about it back then but not for long,' he admitted. 'Mum and Dad handing me the business made it even harder to even think about upping and going somewhere. I sometimes wonder if they timed it that way on purpose, because it was my saviour. If I was angry I had water craft to haul around, if I was upset I'd take a kayak out, when I was lonely I had my customers. I'm not going anywhere, Nina.'

And then his posture changed. He sat forwards on the

edge of the sofa and set down his mug before resting his arms on his thighs, palms clutched together above his knees. 'You pushed me away after what happened, you never let me help. We were best friends since we were kids, we fell in love, we planned a future together. And you left. It's almost like you were scared of being happy.'

Her eyes pricked with tears and she bit down on her bottom lip to stop any that might be in danger of escaping.

'You think that because your parents didn't know how to love you properly that you don't deserve to be loved. Is that it?' he pressed.

The words on the memory she'd pushed into the jar came back to haunt her as she remembered writing them, every letter inked with pain. *Why don't my parents love me?*

'Leo . . .' Her eyes pleaded with him, her voice shook. 'It is, isn't it?'

Her voice shook as the words tumbled out. 'I worried all the time, worried that I wasn't good enough, that something would happen to me or someone I loved. I needed to get myself sorted before I could ever let anyone else in. And then it became easier to stay away, to carry on the new life that I'd built. I pushed the bay away and it was the right thing to do at the time.

'Your parents have a lot to answer for, Nina.' His hands were clenched firmly together as though he was lost as to what to do or say. 'They should've always loved you unconditionally and I'm not saying they didn't or don't, because I think they do in their own way, but they still haven't been there for you in the way they should've been. Did you leave before I might hurt you in the same way?'

She couldn't say a word. Because he was right,

309

completely right, and she hadn't even realised that was what she'd been doing until now.

His voice even softer he unclasped his hands and turned to reach out to her, his fingers below her chin until she looked at him. 'Your parents never saw you for the person you are. But I did, I always have. And you *are* good enough. You're an amazing woman. You just need to let yourself believe it and trust in it.'

'What did I ever do wrong as a daughter, Leo?' Tears pooled in her eyes and he watched as they began to fall.

'You did nothing wrong, Nina. Please know that.'

'I must've done something!'

'Hey, your mum is, to be honest, a bit of a fuck-up.' His words shocked her but they were true. 'She cared more about herself than being a mother, she left a lot of it up to her parents and thank God you had Walt and Elsie in your life, because you turned out to be *you*. And I wouldn't change you for the world.'

Even after she'd left him, ripped apart their lives so brutally he was still willing to see the good.

'You know I hear from Mum and Dad, but I think it's out of duty more than anything. Sometimes I wonder why they bother. And don't even get me started on the way Mum is with her own father.'

'I suspect Walt thinks along the same lines as you do.' Leo put his hands on either side of her face drawing her even closer. 'I'll bet he wonders how he failed as a parent, he probably wondered how he messed up. But the answer is that neither of you did anything wrong. Christy is the woman she is and that's that. Sometimes no matter their upbringing or their friends or family, people make choices and shape their lives in a way that isn't what you'd expect.'

'She's told me more than once that she has a life to live.' Their faces were inches apart, his eyes focused on her and her only.

'And while that's true, she's doing it in a way that pushes everyone else aside.'

'She'll never change,' said Nina, knowing it was true. 'I need to accept that.'

'You, William and Walt don't deserve Christy's lack of attention and care. But what you and your brother have with Walt, now that's special, that's love. That's family. And so am I if you'll let me be.'

'Even after everything I put you through.'

'The time apart wasn't easy but I learnt a lot about myself and what I wanted out of life. And now when I question it, when I float the idea of leaving, I can see deep down that that just isn't me. I'm not that person. This bay, this life, it's me. I don't want different. But I do want you.'

She'd let her face relax against his hands, hands that held the smell of the salty sea no matter how many times he washed them, as though it were a part of his very being. She might be imagining it but it was the scent she associated with him, with belonging.

His thumb moved and brushed her bottom lip and suddenly she was hyper aware of the closeness of their bodies, the familiarity but also the passage of time that made her nervous. 'Leo, I—'

'No, no talking. Not now. Everything else can wait.' His hand around the back of her neck urged her closer to him but he stopped suddenly. 'If this is what you want?'

She nodded. 'It's a long time since we've been together,' she breathed. And for once, she was letting herself feel what she'd pushed aside for so long. With Leo she felt

311

safe, connected, where she should've been all along. She put a hand against his chest, imagining the smooth skin beneath the woollen jumper.

She looked up at him and instead of hesitation, of worry, she saw desire right before he lowered his head and their lips met. Time spiralled, the past, the present, all wrapped up into one. They'd both missed each other more than they'd ever be able to put into words and each of them realised it as he scooped her up in his arms to take her into his bedroom.

'We're checking up on you,' said Grandad the moment he arrived at her cabin the next morning. She'd propped the front door open to get the fresh air now that the sun was shining again. And she'd left Leo asleep to come back here, have breakfast and take a shower.

'Checking up on me. Why?' She felt guilty for staying out all night even though she was a grown woman and they didn't even know.

'We heard about last night of course.' Walt stepped inside along with Camille.

'You heard?' Word sure travelled fast.

But it wasn't about her and Leo even though her head was consumed with thoughts about the man she still loved, the way their bodies had behaved between the sheets after so long apart. 'That poor boy,' said Walt, 'and Maeve too, what must they have gone through. Not to mention Adrian.'

'And how are you feeling?' Nina asked Camille. 'This is your great-grandchild we're talking about.'

Camille gave a small smile. 'It's a shock to all of us.'

'How are Anne and Jimmy?'

'Trying to let the news sink in. Angry on Adrian's behalf, or at least Jimmy is. But we can all see Maeve didn't do this to hurt anyone. We need to find a way to move forwards and welcome them both into our family.'

As Walt put a hand on Camille's arm and they talked about Jonah, about Maeve and Adrian, Nina tuned out a little. The only man she could think about right now was Leo and her grandad only spotted anything out of the ordinary when Camille pointed out that she'd just thrown a tea towel into the recycling bag rather than hang it up.

'What is going on with you?' Walt was watching his granddaughter.

He wasn't wrong to question her. She was all over the place this morning. In the space of the half an hour since she'd been here at the O'Brien cabin she'd poured orange juice onto her cereal instead of milk, she'd put the box of cereal into the fridge not the cupboard, and she'd thanked the lord the sink had an overflow when she'd left the taps running ready to wash up her breakfast things and stood daydreaming about last night.

Because last night had been amazing. More than amazing, it had been a dream.

'I'm fine,' Nina insisted.

'Must be the shock,' said Camille more to Walt than her.

'I'm fine, Grandad, Camille. Please don't worry about me.'

Neither of them looked convinced. And much as Nina loved her grandad she wished she could have time to process everything that had happened since yesterday and since she'd been back in the bay. She sank down into the cushions on the sofa, the newly covered furniture that made this place the perfect beachside cabin. She had to fight the smile, the knowledge that she'd spent last night in the arms of the man she loved. The love of her life. She thought again of the way she and Leo had murmured to one another in the still of the night, how they'd woken hours after falling asleep with exhaustion and made love all over again. She thought of the way she'd looked into his eyes, they'd told one another they loved each other, he'd said he'd never stopped and she knew she hadn't either.

'Nina, let me make you a cup of tea,' Camille offered.

'Honestly, there's no need,' she insisted. 'I'm fine.'

Camille and Walt bustled over to the kitchen area, presumably to ignore her claim, and she was about to call out that she really was OK and that they shouldn't fuss when she saw Leo appear at the bottom of the outside steps.

He bounded inside. 'You left your earrings beside my bed last night,' he called out, brandishing said jewellery.

And then he stopped, when in his peripheral vision he noticed they had company. 'Gran, didn't see you there.' He beamed a smile and it met with amusement from Camille and Walt. And then to Nina he said, 'I suppose that's what you call being caught red-handed.' He came over to her and didn't hesitate to plant a smacker on her lips.

'This is beyond what we dreamed of,' they both heard Camille say as they finished their kiss and Leo's lips still hovered centimetres from Nina's.

Leo stood upright and turned to face his gran. 'What are you talking about?'

'Nothing,' she said and carried on finding mugs for tea all round.

'No, it's not nothing,' Leo persisted, taking Nina's hand

and leading them both into the kitchen area. 'What's going on? Truth time. Because I know there's something.'

Walt and Camille exchanged a look before Walt pointed to his accomplice. 'Her idea,' he said.

'He's right, it was my idea.'

'What was?' Nina asked.

And so the story came out. Walt and Camille had been talking for a long time before now. Both of them thought Nina and Leo belonged together but Walt could never get Nina close enough to the bay to realise it.

'I suggested he dangle the idea that he wanted to sell the cabin,' Camille confessed. 'With William in another country we both knew it would be you who came to help Walt do it up and prepare it for sale and that that would mean you'd have to come to the bay, be close to Leo.'

'We did it for the right reasons,' said Walt, guilt written all over his face.

'Grandad, what would you have done if Leo hadn't been able to offer to buy the cabin? Would you really have gone through with selling it to that man, the one who wants to get his hands on the boathouse too?'

Grandad shook his head. 'I knew I could keep the pretence going for a while and then pull out if I wanted to. I wasn't lying when I said I worried about my finances and my future, that was all true and so I'd sell the cabin eventually. But I like to think I've got time to think about the options.' He paused. 'Are you very annoyed with me, Nina?'

She leaned her head against Leo's chest. 'How could I be annoyed? Your plan worked, didn't it?' And she felt Leo's arms wrap around her from behind, his chin rest on top of her head.

'It could've easily backfired, Gran,' Leo said seriously. 'It wasn't easy for either of us you know.'

'I know, and I'm sorry.' She did look sorry but Nina sensed that like all of them, deep down, she wasn't at all. Because look at Nina and Leo now.

Leo

'Is this what I think it is?' Adrian walked down the side of the boathouse hand-in-hand with Maeve, Jonah following closely behind, and caught Leo kissing Nina in the October sunshine that hadn't shown itself for almost a week – a week in which Leo had been glad to have the rain because the more rain that hammered down on the cabins and the boathouse the fewer customers he had and the more he got to cosy up to Nina.

Leo pulled a slightly embarrassed Nina to him. 'Must be something in the air,' he said nodding to his brother's hand still entwined with Maeve's.

'Hi Leo, hi Nina!' Jonah reached them and didn't bother lingering, he was straight over to the shed below the boathouse ready for the double kayak he'd be taking out on the water today with Adrian.

'It's been a while,' Adrian confided in the adults. 'What if I don't remember how to do it?'

'You will,' Maeve assured him. 'You drove your boat that night without even thinking about it.'

'That was different.'

'No it's not.'

Adrian pulled her to him. 'One day I'll get you into the kayak with me.'

'OK,' she said.

Adrian pulled back. 'Yeah?'

And she laughed. 'Yeah. As long as I sit in front.'

'Bossy,' he joked before his son took his attention, impatient at the adults taking their time, wanting to get the kayak down from its rack and out on the water.

'Don't worry, Dad,' said Jonah who had got used to calling Adrian that right from the start, and Leo swore every time he said it his brother got a bit of a kick and it tugged at his heartstrings. 'We'll both be in the kayak and we'll have our vests on. If you can't remember how to do it, it doesn't matter. We can learn together.'

Leo found the appropriate paddles and Nina and Maeve took them out to the sands while Jonah and Adrian lifted the kayak out and into the sunshine. They set it down while they put on their buoyancy vests.

Leo watched Nina laughing with Maeve. Sometimes it was hard to believe all these people had been away for so long. He'd already thanked Granny Camille for meddling, he was glad she had, because if she hadn't he might not be here right now with the woman he intended to spend the rest of his life with.

Leo went to Nina's side and put an arm around her shoulders. Standing alongside Maeve they watched Adrian and his son take the kayak down to the water with the paddles and none of them uttered a word as they watched Adrian climb in first and then Jonah. Jonah had been saying he was lightest and the least scared so he'd get in last and Leo was pretty sure Adrian might have been playing up to it a little bit to make Jonah think he was helping more than was really needed. But he guessed that was what fatherhood was, it was bonding, in whatever way worked, and it was good to see Maeve, Adrian and Jonah already starting on their way to being the family they all deserved.

'They look happy,' said Nina as the kayak, on the gently bobbing water of Stepping Stone Bay began to move with their paddles turning in the air, dipping back down, their rhythm not bad considering Adrian hadn't been in the sea for such a long time.

'They're naturals,' said Leo.

'Like father like son.' Maeve's voice gave away the emotion behind her comment.

'We'll leave you to watch them both.' Leo put a hand on Maeve's shoulder. 'They'll be fine, you know that don't you?'

The look she gave him said she really did.

Epilogue

Two months later . . .

'It's freezing!' Nina said, and not for the first time since they'd got down here to the beach.

'Bloody cold,' Elijah agreed. 'Why do you think I opted for a costume with decent coverage?' He was dressed as a Santa with a big white beard that must've been keeping his face warm, never mind the comfort of the big red jacket and black trousers.

It was Christmas Day and locals crowded onto the sands at Salthaven ready for the annual swim event that raised money for charity. The proceeds would go to the local lifeboat station and although the charity changed every year, it felt poignant that this one had been elected this time round.

Nina had managed to get a transfer to the hospital thirty miles from Salthaven without much trouble at all. The new workplace wasn't really close but it was do-able. She'd rented a flat not far from her grandad until the sale of her flat was finalised and after that, she wasn't sure what the next step would be. All she knew was that she was here now and it was everything she'd thought she'd left behind and more. It was home.

'If Rhianne could see me now,' Elijah grinned, waving

across at Bridget who had a mug of something steaming in her hand.

'Couldn't persuade Bridget to join in?' Nina asked him.

'Next year, she promises me, but I couldn't do it to her today . . . she's had a cold for the best part of a fortnight and I for one don't want to be responsible for cooking a turkey later if she's out of action.'

Nina began to smile when Leo came over to her. He'd helped Camille and Walt to bring down supplies of mince pies for the ravenous swimmers following the event and now he looked ravishing in his Christmas pudding costume to match hers. They each had on brown stripey bottoms and then a brown puffy top half with white trimming to represent icing and could barely hug one another, so settled for a peck on the lips.

'Here they are,' Leo announced and Nina looked over to where Adrian, Maeve and Jonah were making their way across to them. Three penguins all in a row.

'Mummy penguin, daddy penguin and baby penguin,' Nina grinned as they reached them. Jonah was fussing with his black cap, adjusting it so the orange beak sat right in the middle. They each had identical white furry tummies with black bodies and the two huge eyes sewn to each of their caps had Nina laughing. 'You all ready for this?'

'Nope,' said Adrian.

Maeve held his hand. 'He's worried how cold we'll all be.'

'Dad told me we can play the pirates game in the summer if I get good at kayaking,' Jonah informed Leo.

'The pirates game?' His mind flashed back to his childhood. 'I'll warn you Jonah, Adrian is good at it, he'll probably win.'

But Jonah merely shrugged. 'He said that about Frustration and I beat him loads of times.'

Adrian began to smile and when Jonah saw a boy he knew from school dressed up as a Dalek and begged to go say hello all Adrian said was to make it quick, it was almost time.

'So the pirates game, eh?' Leo smiled to his brother. 'Might have to join in.'

They chatted about some more of the games they'd played as boys as the masses congregated ready to get into the water. Right now they were separated from the sea by a nice big stretch of sand but the cold made everyone anxious to get this done. Helpers hovered on the periphery with towels to wrap swimmers in as soon as they emerged, the scent of mince pies filled the air and the odd waft of coffee too.

'Happy?' Nina asked Leo who was watching his brother with Maeve, this family he hadn't been looking for but had somehow found.

'Happier than you know,' he whispered into her hair. 'But I'll be even happier once this is done and I'm out of this costume and in a nice warm shower.'

'We're doing good,' she told him, 'the event has already raised a couple of thousand pounds and donations often come in afterwards apparently.'

'Brilliant,' he agreed. And when they heard an announcement that people should get ready for the off he looked at Nina, 'Ready?'

'As I'll ever be,' she grinned.

And as the countdown reached one and the crowds surged towards the water, some fast, others waddling in cumbersome costumes, Leo and Nina shared a look that said this was it, this was what they'd been destined for as those two kids when they'd met and become firm friends, as they'd opened up their hearts to one another.

Nina and Leo.

Together today, tomorrow and for ever more.

Acknowledgements

Helen Rolfe would like to thank everyone who worked on *The Boathouse by Stepping Stone Bay* in the UK.

Credits

Helen Rolfe and Orion Fiction would like to thank everyone at Orion who worked on the publication of *The Boathouse by Stepping Stone Bay* in the UK.

Editorial
Charlotte Mursell
Sanah Ahmed

Copyeditor
Francine Brody

Proofreader
Sally Partington

Audio
Paul Stark
Jake Alderson

Contracts
Anne Goddard
Ellie Bowker

Design
Chevonne Elbourne
Joanna Ridley
Nick May

Editorial Management
Charlie Panayiotou
Jane Hughes
Bartley Shaw
Tamara Morriss

Finance
Jasdip Nandra
Sue Baker

Production
Ruth Sharvell

Marketing
Brittany Sankey

Publicity
Ellen Turner

Operations
Jo Jacobs
Sharon Willis

Sales
Jen Wilson
Esther Waters
Victoria Laws
Rachael Hum
Anna Egelstaff
Frances Doyle
Georgina Cutler

If you enjoyed *The Boathouse by Stepping Stone Bay*, you'll love Helen Rolfe's heartwarming story about family, forgiveness and second chances ...

Home is where the heart is ...

Joy has made a family for herself. She's turned her beautiful old farmhouse into a safe haven for anyone who is looking for a new beginning. She's always ready with a kind word, a nugget of advice and believes that anyone can change their life for the better, if they really want to.

Libby has exchanged her high-flying job in New York for a break in the quiet Somerset countryside. She's soon drawn into Joy's world and into her family of waifs and strays - including Drew, whom Joy once helped get back on his feet.

So when a secret from Joy's past threatens everything, can the unlikely group come together to give Joy a second chance of her own?

HELEN ROLFE

Christmas at the Village Sewing Shop

'The perfect festive read'
DEBBIE JOHNSON

Can three sisters stitch
their family back together?

Can three sisters stitch their family back together?

Loretta loves running the little village sewing shop in Butterbury. Some of her most precious memories are sitting with her three daughters Daisy, Ginny and Fern, stitching together pieces of material - and their hopes and dreams.

But this Christmas the family is coming apart at the seams: Fern feels like she's failing at motherhood and marriage, Ginny's passion for her job as a midwife is fading, Daisy is desperate to prove she's changed since her wild younger years - and most of all, Loretta seems to be hiding something . . .

As they come together to create a new festive quilt, the bond between the sisters begins to heal. But when Loretta reveals the real reason she's brought them all home, can the sisters mend the quilt, and their family, in time for Christmas?

The smallest things can make the biggest difference . . .

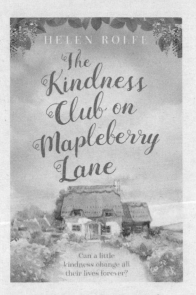

Veronica Beecham's cottage is the neatest house on Mapleberry Lane. A place for everything, and everything in its place - that's her motto. But within her wisteria-covered walls, Veronica has a secret: she's hardly left her perfect home in years.

Then her teenage granddaughter, Audrey, arrives on the doorstep, and Veronica's orderly life is turned upside down. Shy and lonely, Audrey is struggling to find her place in the world. As a bond begins to form between the two women, Audrey develops a plan to give her gran the courage to reconnect with the community - they'll form a kindness club, with one generous action a day to help someone in the village, and perhaps help each other at the same time.

As their small acts of kindness begins to ripple outwards, both Veronica and Audrey find that with each passing day, they feel a little braver. There's just one task left before the end of the year: to make Veronica's own secret wish come true . . .

Come and find love by the sea . . .

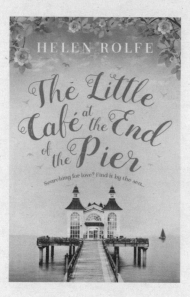

Searching for love? You'll find it at the little café at the end of the pier . . .

When Jo's beloved grandparents ask for her help in running their little café at the end of the pier in Salthaven-on-Sea, she jumps at the chance.

The café is a hub for many people: the single dad who brings his little boy in on a Saturday morning; the lady who sits alone and stares out to sea; the woman who pops in after her morning run.

Jo soon realises that each of her customers is looking for love - and she knows just the way to find it for them. She goes about setting each of them up on blind dates - each date is held in the café, with a special menu she has designed for the occasion.

But Jo has never found love herself. She always held her grandparents' marriage up as her ideal and she hasn't found anything close to that. But could it be that love is right under her nose . . . ?

Welcome to Cloverdale, the home of kindness and new beginnings . . .

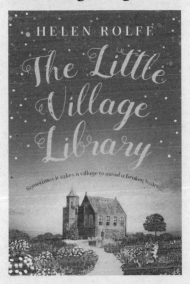

Sometimes it takes a village to mend a broken heart . . .

Cloverdale is known for its winding roads, undulating hills and colourful cottages, and now for its Library of Shared Things: a place where locals can borrow anything they might need, from badminton sets to waffle makers. A place where the community can come together.

Jennifer has devoted all her energy into launching the Library. When her sister Isla moves home, and single dad Adam agrees to run a mending workshop at the Library, new friendships start to blossom. But what is Isla hiding, and can Adam ever mind his broken past?

Then Adam's daughter makes a startling discovery, and the people at the Library of Shared Things must pull together to help one family overcome its biggest challenge of all . . .

Step into the enchanting world of Lantern Square . . .

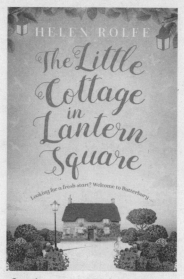

Looking for a fresh start? Welcome to Butterbury . . .

Hannah went from high-flyer in the city to small business owner and has never looked back. She's found a fresh start in the cosy Cotswold village of Butterbury, where she runs her care package company, Tied up with String.

Her hand-picked gifts are the perfect way to show someone you care, and while her brown paper packages bring a smile to customers across the miles, Hannah also makes sure to deliver a special something to the people closer to home.

But when her ex-best friend Georgia arrives back in her life, can Hannah forgive and forget? With her new business in jeopardy, Hannah needs to let the community she cares for give a little help back . . .

Meanwhile, mystery acts of kindness keep springing up around Butterbury, including a care package on Hannah's own doorstep. Who is trying to win her heart – and will she ever give it away?